Ber Carroll (also known as B.M. Carroll) was born in Blarney, Co. Cork, and is one of six children. (Yes, she has kissed the Blarney Stone many times, and talking is her favourite pastime after reading.) Ber moved to Sydney in 1995 with her boyfriend, Rob, who is now her husband of twenty years. She spent her early career working in finance but resigned when she realised that she couldn't hold down a demanding job, be mum to two young children, and write books to contractual deadlines. Ber's kids are teenagers now, and they are as distracting as ever ... but they do provide great writing material. There is also P.J., the family dog, who thinks everything revolves around him (Ber was in the 'under no circumstances are we getting a dog' camp, but now she is besotted). Despite the many distractions, Ber is the author of eleven novels. Her last four novels have been written under B.M. Carroll to reflect that her writing has become darker and more suspenseful (which is also a reflection of her state of mind!). *You Had It Coming* was shortlisted for the 2022 Ned Kelly Award for Best Crime Fiction and the 2022 Davitt Award for Best Adult Novel.

PREVIOUS BOOKS BY B.M. CARROLL

The Missing Pieces of Sophie McCarthy
Who We Were
You Had It Coming

THE OTHER SIDE OF HER

B.M. CARROLL

affirm press

First published by Affirm Press in 2023
Boon Wurrung Country
28 Thistlethwaite Street,
South Melbourne, VIC 3205
affirmpress.com.au

10 9 8 7 6 5 4 3 2 1

 A catalogue record for this
book is available from the
National Library of Australia

ISBN: 9781922848017 (paperback)

Cover design by Luke Causby/Blue Cork © Affirm Press
Typeset in Garamond Premier Pro by J&M Typesetting
Proudly printed in Australia by McPherson's Printing Group

For Harry

There's a saying in Ireland and some parts of England: 'I love your bones.' She never used the saying until she had children of her own, never really understood its true meaning. It means I love you inside and out. It means I love you to bits (the good bits and bad bits). It applies to children who grow before your eyes, the small child contained somewhere within the young adult who is suddenly taller than you: children who exasperate one minute and delight the next, whose strengths and weaknesses are as achingly apparent as your own.

A mother can see inside her kids, into the soul of them. All their talents, quirks and potential; all their flaws, insecurities and darkness.

'I love your bones': *I love every little thing that makes you who you are.*

1
Beth

Today

Her eyes fly open, her heart thudding under the weight of the doona. The room is middle-of-the-night dark. A noise woke her up. The click of a door. Dream or real? She strains to hear. Silence, except for her own panicked breathing.

She swings her legs out of bed to check on Tilly. She is used to making this journey in the dark; turning on lights would make it easier to navigate but harder to fall back asleep afterwards. Her eyes adjust, the carpet cushioning her footsteps across the landing. The house is warm after the hot March day, with heavy rain forecast for later in the week. The rain is badly needed but Beth isn't looking forward to it. There's a leak in the garage roof that strikes with the same unpredictability as her ex.

Tilly is lying on her side, the sheets kicked off, her lava lamp bathing the room with a pink hue. She's snoring softly, her hair in its usual tangle, and Beth is overcome with a rush of love. Seven years old. Enjoy this age, other mums have told her. They're fairly independent but still need you; still playing and riding their bikes, instead of being glued to their phones and social media. Beth *is* enjoying it, when she's not stressing about making ends meet, or worrying about Kane.

She backs out of Tilly's room, leaving the door ajar, which her daughter insists upon. She is almost back to her own bedroom when she stops short. Another faint sound from downstairs. The roll of a drawer being opened? Someone is down there.

Beth knows what to do, she has practised for this, but that doesn't make it any less terrifying. A four-metre walk feels like four kilometres; she waits between each step to regain her balance and listen for further sounds. The bedside table is nothing more than a black shadow. Her hand feels around its surface, cautious not to knock the glass of water or the photo frame, before closing in on the familiar shape of the alarm fob. Now, step by careful step back to Tilly's bedroom, closing the door as softly as she can, locking it from the inside.

Beth sits on the bed and takes Tilly's small hand in hers; her daughter is going to be petrified when she wakes up. Beth braces herself, steadies her own shaking hands, before pressing down hard on the red button.

The wail of the alarm splits the night apart.

~

The panic button goes straight to emergency services. Two weary-looking male officers are on Beth's doorstep in less than ten minutes.

'Nothing's been taken, as far as I can tell,' she tells them breathlessly. 'This way ... The back door was left open ... My car keys are on the floor just there.'

On the face of it, the break-in was a foiled attempt to steal her car, the thief abandoning the keys once the alarm began to scream. The fact that Beth's handbag is still on the kitchen counter, with her purse and credit cards intact, supports this theory.

Her house is known to the local police, which is why they were so quick to respond. Kane's name is suggested almost immediately. When did she last hear from her ex? Does he still live at the same address? Is there a reason he would feel entitled to the car? The answer to the last question is that Kane feels entitled to *everything*. Every item she owns. Every cent in her bank account. Every thought in her head.

The police officers have a look around, noting some damage to the lock on the sliding door that leads out to the back garden. It is a dark, cloudy night; not a lot can be done beyond sticking a head inside the shed and running a high-beam torch along the fence line.

'It looks like the intruder has gone, Ms Jenkins.' The older one, a heavy-set man in his fifties, has done most of the talking. 'Do you have somewhere else you can stay tonight, to be on the safe side?'

Beth tries to weigh it up while Tilly clenches her hand. Descending on her dad in the dead of night seems extreme, given that the threat has obviously passed.

'It's okay. I feel safe enough to stay here.' Her voice sounds feeble and unconvincing.

The police officers leave with the promise to send detectives first thing in the morning. Beth deadlocks the front door and arms the alarm system. She became complacent about setting the alarm every night. Tilly triggered it a few times sleepwalking, frightening the life out of both of them, but that's not a good enough excuse. No more complacency, no more letting her guard down. The only positive is she continued to keep the fob on her bedside table, the panic button within reach.

Tilly comes into Beth's bed with her. Poor thing. Waking up to the shriek of the alarm. The intimidating presence of the police officers. The worry that whoever it was might come back. It takes a long time to settle her down.

'But what if they are hiding somewhere, Mummy?'

'The police would have found them, pumpkin. They know all the best hiding spots.'

Tilly finally stops twitching and succumbs to sleep but Beth has never felt more alert, her muscles rigid and ready to spring into action, her thoughts going a hundred miles an hour in the darkness.

Is there a reason your ex-husband would feel entitled to the car?

There is a reason, although Beth felt too tired and mortified to go into it. Suffice it to say, the car was a sore point, for both sides.

Is this the start of another battle round with Kane? Just as she was beginning to relax a little. Just as she was beginning to hope that they had reached an understanding. Maybe he needs the car as collateral. Maybe he is out of his depth in some new venture. She'll make discreet enquiries tomorrow. See what she is up against this time.

The old saying comes to mind: *what's worse, the devil you know or the devil you don't?* Kane terrorising and stealing from his own family, or a faceless stranger creeping around her house?

Beth eventually falls into a turbulent sleep. She dreams of desperate hands rifling through drawers, cupboards and clothes. Possessions are strewn on the ground, trampled on, smashed. She experiences a paralysing sense of violation. Until she realises that she is not the victim: she is the guilty one, the thief.

2
Ryan

Six weeks ago

The drive home from work is the bones of a two-hour commute: the price of living so far outside Sydney. He and Mia made the move four years ago, swapping city for countryside, concrete for open space and clean air. Elliot was literally climbing the walls of their two-bedroom inner-city apartment; he needed space to expend his endless energy. They, too, needed space, having had enough of cramped apartment living and perpetually complaining neighbours.

Ryan has become used to the commute. He uses the time productively, breaking the journey into segments. The first forty-five minutes is spent making phone calls – checking in with either his mum or his sisters – while at the same time negotiating the bumper-to-bumper traffic on Silverwater Road. On reaching the motorway, he winds up whatever conversation he's been having and listens to a playlist from Spotify. Music with a strong beat to keep him alert. The traffic on this section is fast and heavy at this time of the evening, and prone to suddenly stopping. One small lapse in concentration could lead to a multi-car pile-up. The exit from the motorway signifies the last leg of the journey, which takes around twenty minutes. Ryan tunes into the local radio station for this part. Gets his head ready for what might be waiting at home. 'Good day or bad day?' he'll ask on arriving in the door. Mia won't need to answer: her expression will say enough.

Ryan works in a warehouse in Silverwater, a job he fell into after school and never moved on from. The money was attractive to an eighteen-year-old who wasn't academic and didn't aspire to tertiary education. He bankrolled Mia while she was at university, and she bankrolled him once she graduated and started earning double his salary. Unfortunately, nobody's bankrolling anybody at the moment. Mia has been out of the workforce for most of the last ten years, since Elliot was born. Ryan is the sole income earner, which he doesn't mind except for the fact that his income hasn't changed that much since he was eighteen. He's in his thirties now. He's a father, a husband and mortgagee, all of which come with staggering responsibilities.

The property they purchased is two hundred metres from Lake Macquarie's foreshore, eight kilometres from Morisset's town centre, and forty kilometres from Newcastle's CBD. A train is pulling into the station as he passes through Morisset, giving the illusion of a quick, efficient service. Transport network aside, the town has everything they need: a select choice of schools, supermarkets and restaurants. Should they want or need anything more, Newcastle is their next port of call. Ryan's job is the only thing lassoing him to Sydney. The commute is worth it, as is the crippling mortgage. Elliot is doing so much better. Mia was right: constraining him to a two-bedroom apartment was cruel.

Ryan passes some of the neighbouring properties: Kellie and Dino on the right-hand side, then Heather and Philip on the left. Finally, he reaches the entrance to his own property, where he stops, pulls up the handbrake, and hops out of the car to open the gate; a remote-controlled mechanism will be one of their first purchases when Mia is earning again. Once through the gates, he repeats the process, leaving the engine running as he propels the gate back into place. The driveway is about three hundred metres of compacted gravel. As he approaches the house, he sees his son jumping wildly on the trampoline. Up, down, tumble. Up, down, somersault. The trampoline was a gift from Dianne, Ryan's mum. Elliot loves it, spends hours on it every day. There's no sign of Mia, which is odd: she closely monitors what their son is up to. Ryan beeps the horn to get Elliot's attention. He fills with pleasure as he sees his son's face light up, then winces at the reckless manner at which Elliot exits the trampoline, clearing the steps with an ungainly jump that almost has him faceplanting on the grass. He corrects his balance and comes barrelling towards the car.

'Hey, mate. Take it easy coming off that trampoline, eh? And wait until the car is stopped before you run in front of it ... Now where's my hug?'

Elliot embraces him loosely, before pulling him towards the trampoline, words gushing as he explains the game he's been playing. Next he's dragging him to the side of the house, where his bike has been abandoned in what looks like a hurry. Then inside, to indicate a mound of half-built Lego in the playroom. The house is a 1980s bungalow, five bedrooms, three living areas, triple garage. A lot of space for three people, in addition to five acres of land in which Elliot can run, explore and endeavour to burn off some energy. Cyclone Elliot, they affectionately call him.

Mia appears from the direction of the kitchen. Her face is pinched, her mouth in a tight line. Must have been a tough day.

Ryan smiles at her tentatively. 'Hey, I was wondering where you were hiding.'

'We need to talk.'

His smile falls away. His wife rarely interrupts this special time with Elliot. His son usually drags him from pillar to post when he arrives home, trying to fit in every thought and game since Ryan left for work. He's more frenetic at the moment because he's on a break from medication. School holidays are a good chance to ease off the drugs and some of their worrying side-effects.

'Elliot, it's challenge time. Are you listening?'

His son jerks to attention. 'I'm listening. I'm listening.'

'Great. It's a triathlon challenge, today. Stage one: ten laps of the house on your bike. Stage two: one hundred bounces on the trampoline. Stage three: run all the way down to the gate and back. Let me know when you're ready and I'll start the timer.'

'I'm ready, I'm ready,' he shrieks.

'Go!'

Elliot flies down the hallway, yanking open the front door before crashing it shut in his wake. Mia and Ryan wear matching grimaces. The original door had glass panes. This one is Elliot-proofed.

A moment of silence. Ryan assesses his wife. She is stunningly beautiful, despite everything she has been through. The nonstop pace of day-to-day life. The broken nights with never enough sleep. The heavy burden of their financial worries. The disaster they had two years ago. Today she's wearing denim shorts, a striped t-shirt and white sneakers. Dark brown hair, a golden sheen on her skin. But her tan is not as deep or as convincing as other summers. Up close, her navy-blue eyes are jaded and wary. Her face has thinned, and her mannerisms have become more abrupt over the years – a mirror of Elliot?

'What is it?' Ryan asks, stepping closer. 'What's happened?'

'Come here,' she says, taking his hand and guiding him towards the kitchen.

This is their favourite part of the house. An enormous open area comprising kitchen, dining and living. Floor-to-ceiling glass looking out on the limestone patio, the pool and its surrounds, then lawn and garden beds, followed by paddocks and trees. Mia doesn't have time to appreciate the view. She goes to the kitchen island, picks up her phone, clicks and scrolls.

'Here.' She shoves it at him.

The news headline on the screen is in large bold font. The words punch him in the face.

Million-dollar reward for information on missing Irish backpacker.

Fifty per cent of the reward is being put up by the family, fifty per cent by NSW Police, according to the attached video-clip.

'It's two years since we saw our daughter.' Siobhan McAllen is speaking from her home in Dublin. 'We just want to know what happened.'

'You *know* what happened, for God's sake,' Mia interjects, standing tensely by the kitchen counter. 'Tara went for a swim at an unpatrolled beach. She got caught in a rip.'

'Shush,' Ryan says. 'Just let me listen.'

The journalist runs through the basic details of Tara's arrival in Australia, her short-lived job as an au pair in the Newcastle area, before she headed for the bright lights of Sydney. Drinks at one of the infamous Bondi pubs popular with backpackers. A fateful swim at dusk on the southern end of the beach.

'It doesn't add up,' Siobhan McAllen says, the camera zooming in on the framed photograph clutched in her hands: a younger version of her daughter with pouting lips and heavily applied mascara. 'Tara didn't like swimming in the ocean. And she definitely wouldn't have gone swimming in an unpatrolled area.'

'She's wrong,' Mia interrupts again. 'Tara was in our pool every chance she got. She *loved* swimming. Plus, she'd been drinking. Her decision-making was compromised.'

'Tara's body was never found,' the journalist continues in a sombre tone. 'There are no witnesses who observed someone struggling in the water.'

The segment ends with a repeat of the reward amount and a phone number to call with any information.

Ryan exhales a shaky breath. 'That's a shitload of money.'

'I know.' Mia's fists clench and unclench as they rest on the counter. 'This is the last thing we need right now.'

His wife has been updating her résumé and skills, with the aim of making another attempt at returning to work. Now this reward may derail those plans, put everything in jeopardy for the second time.

'But we're safe, aren't we?' he asks, searching her face for reassurance.

She was the one who orchestrated the plan, managing it like one of her large, complex projects. Each step outlined in detail, the risks identified and mitigated, all the while conscious of Siobhan and the family, seeking to give them closure and not leave them in a terrible state of limbo. Now here is Siobhan, bleating that 'it doesn't add up'.

Elliot comes bursting through the door before Mia can assure Ryan that they're strong enough to withstand another round of scrutiny and questions.

'Stop the timer, Daddy. I'm here, I'm here.'

Ryan stops the timer. Gives his son the attention he needs and deserves. 'Thirteen minutes, forty-nine seconds. I think that must be a record. You're Superman.'

The rest of the evening follows a strict routine. Ryan plays Lego with Elliot, fishing out the right colours and sizes while his son presses them into place. They have dinner, where Elliot is encouraged to chew his food properly and wait his turn to speak. Elliot is allowed an ice-cream for dessert, because his reward chart shows that he has been trying really hard today. Their last activity of the day is a family walk. The lake's calming influence is just a few minutes from the house. Mia links her arm through Ryan's while Elliot runs full steam ahead. The view is breathtaking. Blue melding with orange as the sun falls towards the horizon, the water rippling and reflecting the colours of the sky. The breeze lifts Mia's dark-brown hair back from her face, revealing the graceful curve of her neck. On her left upper arm, the tattoo she had done after Elliot's birth: a small yet intricate tree.

'The tree symbolises strength and growth,' she said at the time. 'Being a mum makes me feel incredibly strong. As he grows and learns, so will I.'

Not a day goes by without Ryan thinking that he's not good enough for her. Not a day goes by without her beauty stopping him in his tracks. But her eyes, the same colour as the lake on a sunny day, flash with trepidation as she turns to speak.

'That amount of money will make people stop and think.' Her fingers are digging painfully into his arm, transferring her fear. 'The cops will want to talk to us again. No matter what happens, we must keep Elliot out of it.'

3
Mia

Two years ago

The girl, Tara McAllen, is due to arrive at Morisset Station at midday. Poor thing will be exhausted. More than twenty hours on a plane, and half that again in various transit lounges and the train up from Sydney: she'll be jet-lagged, disoriented, dying for a shower and a proper meal. Mia will make sure that Tara makes a priority of phoning her mum. This is her first big venture from home – she is only nineteen! – and her mum will undoubtedly be on stand-by, regardless of the late hour in Dublin.

The train is approaching: one minute away, according to the announcement board. Mia can feel the rush of air that precedes its arrival. She and Ryan had high expectations of this service when they moved to the area, envisaging Ryan commuting by train every day. The reality is that the train takes even longer than the motorway and necessitates an additional bus ride for Ryan at the other end. As a result, her husband uses the family car for the commute, and they had to invest in a second car as a run-around for Mia. The run-around, albeit as cheap as they could get away with, is a further drain on their already stretched finances. For this reason, the train station always has an air of disappointment, of unfulfilled promise.

The train arrives with a whoosh. Announcements are made over the intercom. *Stand clear of the doors. Morisset, then all stations to Newcastle.* Half a dozen passengers alight; this is not a busy time of day. Tara is easy to spot. Dyed black hair in a perky ponytail. Leopard-print leggings and a skimpy black top. A large khaki-coloured rucksack, which must be heavy because she dumps it on the ground while she gets her bearings. Mia waves to catch her attention before hurrying down the platform.

'Hey, Tara. I'm Mia. Great that you got here okay.'

Tara seems surprised to see Mia's outstretched hand. She shakes it awkwardly. She is wearing a lot of make-up, fake eyelashes and badly applied tanning product.

'Let me take your rucksack. The car is this way.'

One positive about Morisset is that parking is never a problem: the commuter car park is not even half full. Mia is driving Ryan's SUV today: bigger boot and a newer model, lending a better first impression than the eight-year-old hatchback she usually gets around in.

'Is this all there is?' Tara asks as she surveys the paltry line of shops across the road from the station. The shopfronts are unexciting, the only pedestrians in sight are elderly, and the whole scene screams the sedateness of a hot Saturday afternoon in country New South Wales. The people in this town are friendly and caring, with strong community values. The town has everything Mia and Ryan need, and more. Of course, Tara would prefer a big shopping mall and a thriving social life. What nineteen-year-old would want any different?

'Afraid so. But Newcastle isn't too far away and it's a great little city. Even better than Sydney. Well, that's how the locals feel.'

'How far to your house from here?'

'Ten minutes or so.'

Tara's face hardens as she makes the calculations. The house is outside Morisset, which is outside Newcastle, which is outside Sydney.

All these details were in the job description, but Tara was obviously envisaging something more built-up.

'Where do you live in Dublin? Is it rural or city?' Mia asks, taking a right turn out of the car park. It's a shame that the main street is so particularly quiet today. Maybe if some of the younger population were hanging around, Tara might look less despondent. First impressions can be hard to shake.

'City,' Tara says. 'Close to everything, you know?'

Point made. Her accent is flatter than the Irish accents Mia encountered through work. Plenty of Irish accents in Sydney's technology industry. In fact, Mia favoured the Irish candidates whenever she had to hire for a new position: they were invariably hard-working, intelligent and fun. These are the reasons she gravitated towards an Irish au pair.

She decides to move the subject away from geography. 'You must be hungry. Ryan and Elliot are making lunch, a barbecue. You can have a swim in the pool if you need reviving. Try to stay awake for as long as you can. Nothing worse than getting out of sync on your first day.'

At least the weather is delivering. Perfect blue sky. Searing sun. Tara's leggings are too warm. She'll feel better once she's had a swim and changed into something more suitable.

But Tara is not ready to change the subject. 'How will I be able to go anywhere? Is there a bus?'

'Yeah, there's a bus, but it depends on the time of day. Ryan and I can give you a lift, if needed.'

Tara hasn't even arrived at the house and she's already planning her escape. More worryingly, she is yet to meet Elliot face to face. There was a FaceTime call a few weeks ago where everyone met briefly. Elliot waved and said hi before disappearing to continue whatever game he was playing. Tara's mum, Siobhan, said hello and enquired about the weather and what Tara would need in terms of clothes. Mia gave Tara and

Siobhan a tour of the house and garden, spending a long time showing off the pool, which she believed to be their strongest selling point.

Mia is only beginning to realise how inadequate that FaceTime call was. From Tara's perspective and her own.

Energetic eight-year-old, her carefully crafted job description said. The understatement of the year.

'Tara is used to kids,' Siobhan proclaimed. 'There's a brood of younger cousins.'

Tara is staring sullenly out the car window. She is not coming across as child-friendly, or any form of friendly for that matter. Mia understated Elliot's challenges, but was Siobhan just as bad, overstating her daughter's affection for children?

Mia pulls up at the gate to the property, and although it would be easier for Tara to get out to facilitate its opening and closing, she does it herself. The gate is rusted and doesn't do much for their street appeal, but the wattle trees and magnolias lining the driveway make a better impression.

Tara sits up a little straighter as the tyres crunch over the compacted gravel. The house is yet to come into view.

'Why is the driveway so long?' she asks in an accusing tone. 'Why does the house sit so far back from the road?'

These questions would come back to haunt Mia. It was like Tara had foreseen something, a premonition of what was to come.

~

Mia tries to see the house through Tara's eyes. Blond brick. One level. Five bedrooms, three bathrooms, the expansive kitchen: the heart of the home. But Tara is not of the age to get excited by stone benchtops or the bi-fold doors that connect the kitchen to the outside patio. She only has eyes for the pool.

'This is really nice,' she says, crouching down to run her hand through the water. Then she points a finger, topped with a hot-pink fake nail, to the two sunbeds positioned side by side on the limestone pavers. 'That's going to be my office.'

Mia feels a glimmer of hope that everything is going to be okay. That the promise of a suntan will make up for the poor location. That the lure of the pool will compensate for the drudgery of childminding. So far, her only interaction with Elliot was a standoffish 'howya' on her arrival. She didn't notice that the boy was clutching a toy A380, a clue that he loves everything to do with planes and airports, the subject matter offering an excellent icebreaker. Ryan received a faint smile, a nod, and a slightly more interested 'howya'. Her social skills are clearly on the underdeveloped side.

'Why don't you have a shower or a swim while I finish getting lunch ready?' Mia suggests smoothly. The meat is ready, chicken skewers and homemade burgers laid out on foil-covered trays. Elliot is occupied helping Ryan clean up the barbecue. Mia can throw a salad together while Tara freshens up.

The girl decides on a swim, retreating to her new bedroom and reappearing shortly afterwards in a skimpy black-and-white-print bikini. Her fake tan is deep brown around her midriff, and splotchy on her neck and ankles. Is she aware that tanning products usually don't offer any sun protection? Mia averts her eyes from Tara's bare flesh and offers her a bottle of sunscreen.

'Whatever you do, don't underestimate the Australian sun. We have a saying – slip, slop, slap. Slip on a long-sleeved top. Slop on sunscreen. Slap on a hat.'

Tara takes the bottle of sunscreen in a manner that suggests she has no intention of using it, or adding 'slip, slop, slap' to her vocabulary.

'Can I swim too? Can I swim too?' Elliot asks, en-route to the dishwasher, barbecue utensils in hand.

Tara looks appalled at the idea of sharing the pool with her eight-year-old charge.

Mia intervenes quickly. 'No, honey. Let's give Tara a bit of space. You can swim with her next time.'

Elliot goes rigid with disappointment. His lower lip juts out, hands clenching around the barbecue utensils, potential weapons. Mia knows that look: her son is on the precipice of a gigantic meltdown. Damn! Damn! Damn it!

Ryan comes in and reads the situation immediately. 'Hey, mate. Get your bat and stumps. Let's have a few overs before lunch.'

A few tense moments while Elliot teeters. It's only a matter of time before Tara sees a meltdown, but please not today. She is jet-lagged and obviously erring on the side of 'what the hell am I doing here?' Things are rocky enough without her seeing Elliot at his worst.

Her son, thank heavens, accepts the consolation cricket game. Mia deftly deals with the dirty utensils while Ryan produces a cricket ball. The boys are gone within moments, heading to the front garden where Ryan has levelled out a cricket strip. Tara waits until they are out of sight – she clearly doesn't want Elliot changing his mind – before scurrying towards the pool. She throws one of Mia's good bath towels on a sunbed and jumps feet first into the deep end, without – Mia can't help noticing – stopping to apply sun cream. Her head emerges, a genuine smile of happiness on her face, and Mia warms to the girl. She is young, unsophisticated and far away from home. She needs time to adjust. They all do.

Mia assembles spinach leaves, sliced tomatoes, cucumber and capsicum while Tara does a few lazy lengths of breaststroke. Some crusty bread, a jug of lemon squash, and the meal is ready. She takes the food outside and calls everyone to the table.

'So, Tara, what are your plans while you're in Australia?' Ryan asks after an awkward silence. 'Anything you specifically want to see or do?'

'Just want to soak up the sun – we get so bleedin' little of it at home. It's a bit surreal that it's summer holidays here. January in Ireland is so depressing, you know?' Her eyes dart to Elliot. 'When do the kids go back to school?'

'The end of the month,' Ryan and Mia answer at the same time. They laugh, Elliot giggles, Tara's thin lips form a grimace.

'Do you have any friends who are travelling here?' Mia can already tell that Tara is the kind of girl who gets glammed up to go out every weekend: pub hopping, drinking from over-full glasses of wine, dancing until the early hours, spending Sundays in bed recovering. Sydney would be more her scene.

'Nope. Mum said I'll meet people. I hope so.' Her grin has an edge of panic. 'Find a friend. Ha. Ha.'

'There's probably an online group you can join,' Ryan suggests. 'Other backpackers in the area. So much easier to hook-up these days.'

She snorts. 'Yeah. Or I can just go on Tinder.'

Ryan blushes, his definition of a hook-up different to Tara's. Mia can't help feeling alarmed. Tinder can be a platform for predators, liars, cheaters and old men looking for sex. What if something were to happen to Tara? She is only nineteen, technically an adult but at the same time blatantly naïve and gauche. Should Mia ask Siobhan for some guidelines on her daughter's social life and if anything is out of bounds?

'Why aren't you having salad?' Elliot blurts out, noticing the lack of greens on Tara's plate.

'Bleedin' hate vegetables,' she states, without a thought as to how this might be perceived by a child. 'Anythin' that's green or orange doesn't go in me mouth.'

Elliot's eyes widen in shock. He glances down at his own plate, his brain already formulating words of resistance.

Mia disguises her irritation and leans across the table to explain to her son. 'Kids need to eat lots of veggies so they can grow big and tall. When you're over eighteen, like Tara is, you can decide not to eat veggies because you're already all grown up. That makes sense, right?'

Elliot's small face is filled with doubt. 'But ...'

'No buts. You can have an ice-cream when your plate is empty.'

Rules, consistency and rewards. Tomorrow, Mia will endeavour to explain their parenting strategy to Tara.

The girl needs to think before she speaks.

4

Beth

Today

The storm starts around dawn, rain thrashing the tin roof of the garden shed. Beth groans and hauls herself out of bed to shut the window and mute the racket. Of course, falling back asleep is impossible.

Last night plays out in her head. The wail of the alarm intermingling with Tilly's screams. The car keys flung on the kitchen floor. The overwhelming despair that Kane could be cranking things up again. But it could be worse. She could be without a car this morning. No way of getting Tilly to school, or herself to work.

The detectives, two females in plain clothes, arrive just after eight. Tilly is in her school uniform, and Beth is dressed in black jeans and a t-shirt. If this were a normal morning, they would've already left the house.

Beth shows the detectives around with the dazed, out-of-body feeling that comes from too little sleep. She and Tilly watch as they inspect the windows and doors. The detectives gamely go outside into the driving rain, walking the perimeter of the back fence, presumably checking for traces of footprints or other clues. It's not long before they come back inside, shaking rainwater from their coats and shaking their heads: the rain has washed away anything there was to find.

The more senior detective speaks. 'Just a few further questions, if we may, Ms Jenkins.'

'Call me Beth, please. Tilly, here, take my phone. Wait in the front room.'

Tilly pauses, torn between curiosity and the desire to play her favourite game on the phone.

'Matilda Anne Jenkins,' Beth gives her daughter a little shove in the right direction, 'out of here.'

The senior detective's questions retrace the events of last night, before zoning in on Kane. 'When was the last time you had contact with your ex-husband?'

'About six months ago.'

'What was the nature of the contact?'

'It was a court appearance regarding unpaid child support.'

Beth doesn't intend to provide any more details. For a start, Tilly is in the next room and prone to eavesdropping. No little girl should be reduced to a dollar amount to be paid every month (or not paid, hence the court appearance). Tilly aside, there is the abject humiliation. Admitting to strangers how stupid she was, how long it took her to realise what was going on and to get out. The court appearance brought everything to a head. Kane was ordered to pay the outstanding amount; his response to the ultimatum was a full custody application. It was then that Beth realised the truth. He would never give up. This would go on and on unless she relented. Being in a constant state of battle was invigorating for him while devastating for her. The only way to end it was to cut her losses, no matter how unfair it was.

'And he has broken into your home before?'

'At least once.'

Over the years there were things that went missing – small amounts of cash, a pair of gold earrings, silverware that was a wedding present – but she was never able to pin it on Kane. The earrings might turn up. Had she spent the cash elsewhere? When had she last used those silver salad servers? The last time Kane paid a visit, there was no mistake. He trashed the place, breaking picture frames, lamps and crockery. He up-ended drawers, tossed clothes and shoes from cupboards and wardrobes, and helped himself to every item of jewellery that she owned. Beth invented a story about a trapped possum, to explain the breakages and mess to Tilly. Her daughter was only five at the time, easier to hoodwink. A few days later, Beth opened the book she'd been reading to see FUCK YOU scrawled on the page she had bookmarked. Up until that point there had been some doubt. Maybe it *was* a stranger, a drug addict, a petty criminal or a teenager looking for kicks. But here was Kane's calling card, waiting for her in the book, knowing the terrifying effect it would have and at the same time how hard it was to prove. Beth immediately called her property manager, seeking permission to install a back-to-base alarm system. The landlord agreed to pay half, and she paid for the balance by taking out a no-interest loan with Shepherdess Finance, a charity that lends money to vulnerable women. A frank, humiliating discussion with the local police ensured that they were abreast of her situation. Kane was questioned and avoided being charged thanks to a water-tight alibi provided by his brother. Beth was used to him getting away with things, didn't expect any different.

'My ex feels hard done by,' she adds now, as though it were a legitimate explanation. The detectives only need to look around the room to see how sparsely she lives: the second-hand sofa, the cheap prints on the wall, the rickety table and chairs. Of course, they would have seen this bare-minimum set-up before, and worse. The damage that couples inflict on each other. The extraordinary lengths taken to see the other reduced to nothing.

Before leaving, the detectives dust the doorhandles and other hard surfaces for fingerprints. Beth calls Tilly to come and watch, explaining to her daughter how everyone's fingerprints are unique. Tilly holds her hand close to her face and examines the pads of her nail-bitten fingers in fascination.

It's nine-thirty by the time the detectives are finished. Beth thanks them and sees them to the door. She sends a quick text to her boss, Debbie: *On my way*. Then she grabs her handbag and activates the house alarm, berating herself again for being slack last night. She honestly thought that she and Kane had turned a corner. If he dropped the custody application, she would sign a binding child support agreement for a payment amount of zero. The result being that she has virtually no money in the bank and survives from week to week. What more could he want from her? Her sanity? A distinct possibility.

The garage can be accessed through an internal door in the hallway, which means Beth and Tilly don't need to get wet. Beth immediately notices water dripping from the plasterboard on the garage ceiling: that frigging leak. No time to deal with it now, other than the strategic placement of a bucket to catch the water. The rent is very affordable, thanks to the owner being overseas and out of touch regarding prices in the area. The downside is that she is expected to cover any small maintenance jobs. Her dad usually helps out with that side of things.

The full ferocity of the rain is felt as soon as they've reversed out of the garage. It rolls down the windscreen, the wipers struggling to keep up. Beth pauses, assessing the blurry image of her home as she waits for the garage door to close. The house is a duplex, sharing an internal wall and driveway with the neighbours. Pippa and Ian have been a stable presence for Beth and Tilly, providing on-tap friendship and wisdom. Beth should ask them if they heard or noticed anything untoward last night or yesterday. She has rebuilt herself in this small house. She has invested everything she has – mentally, financially, physically – into meeting the rent and all the other expenses.

Maybe it's time to downsize even further. Find an apartment in another suburb. Then Kane would have no idea where to find her the next time his hatred reaches boiling point.

Rain lashes the windscreen and the barely visible road. Beth grips the steering wheel, her knuckles white and rigid. There's a traffic update on the radio: *flash flooding, expect delays*. The rain wasn't due until later in the week. For some reason it has come sooner and more violently.

~

Beth parks in an undercover car park in the CBD, reasoning that the appalling weather warrants the extra cost. The clinic is a hundred metres or so from the car park; she ducks between shop awnings, avoiding the worst of the deluge. The waiting room is empty and smells of the jasmine-and-vanilla room spray that Debbie favours. Beth places her bag and jacket in the cupboard behind reception and slips on an aqua-coloured tunic over her clothes. A quick scan of the bookings screen establishes that her first appointment cancelled: a blessing in disguise.

Beth sanitises her hands and knocks lightly on the door of her usual treatment room. She slips inside. The room is darkened, with soft piano music playing on the sound system. Debbie bends over to address the client, her voice barely more than a whisper.

'Beth is here now, Charlie. I'm going to hand over to her if that's okay with you?'

'Sure,' Charlie mumbles, face-down on the massage bed.

Charlie is one of Beth's regulars and very easy-going. Debbie hadn't quite started, so the changeover is conducted smoothly. Debbie is glad to get back to the unmanned reception desk, and Beth is keen to make it up to Charlie for the inconvenience.

'Sorry about that,' she says, removing the hot stones from the water that keeps them warm. 'I'm having one of those mornings.'

'What's been going on?' he asks, his voice muffled and curious. 'Hungover? Big party last night?'

'I wish,' she says wryly. 'We had a break-in. Detectives came around this morning.'

Charlie's shoulders become rigid with concern. 'Oh. That's not good ... Anything valuable taken?'

'Looks like they wanted my car. Lucky for me I woke in time and activated the house alarm.'

'May I ask why the alarm didn't activate itself?'

Because Beth had become complacent. Because she had been lulled into a false sense of security. Stupid. Stupid. Stupid. Charlie doesn't know many details about her private life, other than the fact that she's divorced and has a seven-year-old daughter. It's imperative that he sees Beth as a professional. Someone who is competent and steady. She doesn't want to divulge anything that would tarnish that image.

'Stop asking hard questions ... Focus on your breathing ...'

As a rule, Beth tries to keep talking to a minimum. The less talking, the more likely her client will relax and reap the full benefits of the massage. Charlie comes once a week for a back-neck-and-shoulders. His problems are caused by bad posture and long hours at his desk. He maintains that Beth's massages are the best in Newcastle and has referred her to a number of his friends and colleagues.

'I think he fancies you and there's nothing wrong whatsoever with his back,' Debbie has proposed more than once.

Maybe he does genuinely like her. Or maybe he is just the proverbial nice guy, equally pleasant to everyone. Or maybe he is acting, with some ulterior motive. Beth doesn't trust her instincts with men. Charlie *seems* solicitous, reliable and decent. He's thirty-four, two years older than her, the kind of guy she would have mocked at school for being too studious. She suspects that he would have been less than impressed with her at that age too: her impulsive streak, her abhorrence for rules and structure. Beth has learned the hard way that rules and structure are the scaffolding of life. She has learned that honesty and decency are more important than any other quality. She has also learned that it can take a long time to really know someone, and to never fully trust what you see on the surface.

Beth works particularly hard on Charlie's lower back, where the muscles are tight from too many hours of inactivity at his desk. She uses her thumbs to knead the skin and tissue, following with one of the large stones, its heat helping release the tightness.

'Take your time,' she says, before leaving the room when the massage is done. 'There's no rush.'

Charlie emerges within a couple of minutes, his face flushed. Dark-framed glasses, white business shirt, charcoal trousers: he works as a management consultant in one of the new office blocks on Hunter Street. What does a management consultant actually do? Beth has no idea. Debbie books him in for next week and Beth throws him a grateful smile before welcoming her next client.

She and Debbie don't get to speak properly until after the lunchtime rush.

'Sorry again about this morning,' Beth says, sipping the coffee that Debbie bought her from the café across the street. The skinny flat white, plus an oatmeal bar from their stash of snacks, will have to pass for today's lunch.

'Not a lot you can do about it, love. At least the rain scared off a few clients and the delays were minimal.'

Debbie works hard to keep the clinic solvent. Beth is the only full-time staff member; the other therapists are part time or casual. The central location means a hefty rent, and there is always some other business that will undercut prices. For this reason, loyalty is something they try to foster in their clients.

The door to the clinic opens with a bang. A woman fights the wind to get her umbrella down before coming inside. Beth's next client is here.

~

It's still raining solidly when she finishes work but at least the wind has eased. She navigates through the sodden streets of Newcastle, thankful for being warm and dry in her car. She could have woken this morning to an empty garage. She could have woken to the headache and financial consequences of needing to find a replacement car. Beth loves this car; it's one of the few things in her life that gives her no trouble. She bought it a year and a half ago for $10,000, facilitated by another low-interest loan from Shepherdess Finance.

'Get a Corolla,' her dad had advised. 'You won't regret it.'

She hasn't regretted it. This car is reliable: she doesn't need to worry about it not starting, or breaking down and leaving her stranded, which happened a few times with its predecessor. Just as important, this car comes without bad memories: no flashbacks of driving around on an almost empty tank, not being able to afford even a token $10 in petrol; or sleeping on the back seat, curled up with Tilly, trying to pretend they were having an adventure.

Twenty minutes later Beth pulls up outside after-school care, which is housed in one of the double classrooms on the school campus. Thanks to the weather, the kids have been cooped up all day and there is a disgruntled atmosphere when Beth walks into the classroom. She checks Tilly's schoolbag to make sure nothing is missing, zips her bright yellow raincoat up to her chin, and then it's a dash between puddles to the car.

'Mummy, will the burglars come again tonight?' Tilly asks in a grave tone, as they turn into their street.

'Definitely not. They know we have an alarm now and they'll be too scared to come back.'

'Will the policewomens catch them and put them in jail?'

'Yes. *Definitely.*'

'I don't want them to take my toys or your money, Mummy.'

'They won't, pumpkin.'

The house looks dark and threatening on pulling into the driveway. Beth deactivates the alarm before clicking the remote for the garage door. On getting out of the car, Tilly doesn't see the bucket from this morning; its contents tip all over her school shoes.

'Oops. Oh dear. It's all right, pumpkin. Just water, that's all.'

For a moment it looks like her little girl is going to burst into tears, but then she sees the funny side and a grin appears.

The awful weather has caused a prematurely dark evening. The hallway is gloomy and menacing. 'It's dark in here. Turn on the lights, Till.'

Tilly runs ahead, flicking switches, leaving wet footprints in her wake.

'Good girl. Now hang up your raincoat and get out of those poor shoes.'

Dinner is spaghetti bolognaise and garlic bread, Tilly's favourite; she still calls spaghetti 'biscetti'.

'What do burglars get for dinner, Mummy?'

'The food in jail is really yuck.' Beth elaborates, adding Tilly's least favourite foods to the menu, 'Like beetroot and mushrooms and tuna.'

They spend the rest of dinner coming up with other suggestions: slimy ham, old egg sandwiches and mushy bananas. Afterwards, it's upstairs for bath time and reading.

'Fetch your reader from your schoolbag, Till. Let's cuddle up in bed while we read.'

Tilly drags her feet, too young to realise how transparent she is being. The slow walk to her schoolbag. The drawn-out search. The pretence of not being able to find it, before being told to look harder.

Other parents gush about how much their kids love reading, how they beg for just one more page. Tilly finds it hard; for her, reading is a chore.

Finally, she is curled up next to Beth in her cute elephant pyjamas, smelling of shampoo and toothpaste.

'Oh look, this one is about the rainforest. How interesting!'

Twenty minutes later Beth has learned some genuinely thought-provoking facts about rainforests, and Tilly is more than ready to call it a night. She snuggles down with her favourite toy, a squashy hippopotamus ingeniously called Hippo.

Downstairs, Beth closes the curtains and turns on the TV to give the illusion that she is not alone. It took ages to return to normal after Kane broke in two years ago. Double- and triple-checking that the windows and doors were locked. Constantly on alert for suspicious sounds. Imagining someone creeping around outside. Broken sleep, vivid nightmares, the house alarm the only thing that offered security.

She goes to the kitchen, pours a modest-sized glass of wine, and tells herself that midweek drinking is warranted under the circumstances. Back in the front room she scrolls through the contacts on her phone. Rachel, Kane's sister, works in the emergency department of John Hunter Hospital. Her erratic work hours mean that text messaging is often the best form of contact; it also lessens the awkwardness that remains on both sides.

Hi Rachel. Had a break-in last night, someone trying to steal the car. Alarm scared them off and Tilly and I are fine. Just wondering if you could let me know the status with K. Thanks, Beth.

Rachel is her only ally in Kane's family. In everyone else's eyes, Beth is a leech who bled him dry before breaking his heart. Rachel was always more observant than the others.

'Those clothes are too small on Tilly, Beth.'

'Let's meet for a coffee. My treat.'

'Are you sure you're ready to go back to work? It's only been a month.'

Rachel guessed that Beth didn't have the cash for a coffee in her purse but assumed that her brother and his wife were working hard towards a common goal, scrimping and saving to build a financially secure future. She assumed wrong. Only one of them was financially secure.

Beth is cognisant that she should also let her dad know what happened, but that is another delicate dance. For years she covered things up from her father. At the start she was naïve, trusting, and resolute that Kane had her best interests at heart. Then she became embarrassed, ashamed and scared. When things got to the point where her dad *had* to find out – she and Tilly were homeless, sleeping in the car – he promptly fulfilled her worst fears. Storming over and barging into the house. Punching Kane in the mouth. Earning himself an AVO in the process.

Beth has the urge to talk to someone who can understand her fear and give it due consideration. Caitlin, her best friend, is a social worker and hard to rattle. Caitlin also has a jam-packed social life, with an astonishingly fast turnover in boyfriends. Chances are she is probably in a bar somewhere with the latest hunk. As expected, her friend's phone rings and rings, eventually going to voicemail. Beth decides not to leave a message.

No response from Rachel yet. She could be at work, or she could be struggling with what to say: how to hit the right note between caring aunty to Tilly and loyal sister to Kane.

Beth swallows back her loneliness with a large gulp of wine. Then she sends Debbie an unnecessary text about work tomorrow. After that, she forwards her dad a photo of Tilly in her yellow raincoat, taken under the awning at after-school care by one of the supervisors.

Both Debbie and her dad are quick to send replies. Beth tries to convince herself that she is not alone, and that she and her daughter are safe.

5
Ryan

Five weeks ago

The doorbell rings mid-Saturday morning. Mia is in the study, doing an online course to update her skills. Ryan and Elliot are engrossed in a 200-piece 3D puzzle of the Sydney Opera House, which has the dual purpose of helping his son maintain concentration as well as keeping him quiet while Mia works. Ryan assumes it's his mother at the door; Dianne is the only person who drops in ad hoc.

'Probably Grandma,' Ryan says to Elliot, as they make their way down the hall. 'Let's try not to be too noisy. Remember, Mum needs to concentrate.'

It's not Dianne. There are two visitors, a male and a female, both a little bit older than Ryan. He knows straight away, from their formal dress and expressions, that they are police detectives, but he doesn't let this knowledge show in any way. Pleasant, open expression. Friendly greeting.

'Hello. You're not Grandma!'

This earns cautious smiles. A good start.

The female speaks. 'Detective Sergeant Amy Goodwin and my

31

colleague, Detective Senior Constable Martin Stavros. Can we come in for a minute?'

The reward has been posted a week. Amazing how money makes the wheels turn faster; last time it was a couple of months before detectives came to visit.

'Of course. This way.' Ryan leads them to the kitchen, the 3D puzzle spread across the large oak table. 'If you could just wait here while I get my wife.'

Maybe they will wonder why he is going to get Mia instead of sending Elliot. Maybe they'll guess that he wants to quickly brief her. Maybe their appearance at his doorstep is more than a formality and they have a genuine lead.

Ryan knocks on the door of the study, which is really just a bedroom with a desk squashed against the wall. Mia swings around on her office chair, removing one of her earphones in order to hear him, an annoyed expression on her face.

'Sorry to interrupt, babe.' He endeavours to speak at his normal pitch; the detectives would expect to hear a conversation. Any suggestion of whispering will arouse suspicion. 'Can you come? The police are here.'

His stare says the rest. Be calm, Mia. Don't talk too much or too little. Try to appear helpful.

Mia is the ultimate professional. She introduces herself, shaking hands with each detective. She offers tea or coffee, which is declined. She dispatches Elliot to his room, with permission to play Minecraft, a game he finds highly addictive and is only allowed under strict conditions. Then they all sit around the kitchen table, the two detectives on one side, Ryan and Mia on the other. Ryan averts his gaze from the unfinished puzzle of the Sydney Opera House sitting between them. Is he the only one who finds its presence suddenly poignant? Tara's abandonment of the countryside for Sydney and its nightlife.

Detective Goodwin begins to speak. She is attractive in a starkly different way to Mia. Freckled skin. Dyed blonde hair. She explains about the reward, how it is one of the devices used by police when all other lines of enquiry reach a dead end.

Mia nods and frowns. 'I'm sorry, I thought Tara drowned. Are you saying that something else happened to her?'

Goodwin's face is blank, an expression they must teach detectives to perfect during their training. 'That's what we are trying to find out. Let's just say there are some inconsistencies. The timeline and the facts deserve re-examination.'

Ryan thinks this is a good point for him to speak. 'We'll help in any way we can. Just tell us what you want to know.'

Goodwin glances at her colleague, who has his notebook out. The two of them seem to be able to communicate without words. Ryan wonders how long they've worked together, how many other interviews they've conducted in tandem.

'Let's start by confirming dates,' Goodwin says briskly. 'The day Tara arrived, and the day she left.'

Questions they've answered before.

'She arrived on the second of January,' Mia replies. 'I picked her up from the station and I could tell straight away that she was disappointed with where we lived. It wasn't a huge surprise when she handed in her notice at the end of the month, although I'd been secretly hoping she'd warm to the place. She gave two weeks' notice, which was decent of her, I suppose. It was mid-February when she left. The fifteenth or sixteenth, I think.'

'What form of transport did she use when she left? Train, bus, car?'

'Train. Ryan drove her to the station. I stayed with Elliot, our son.'

The detective turns her gaze to Ryan. Inscrutable brown eyes assessing him. 'And what frame of mind was Tara in the last time you saw her?'

33

'Upbeat. Smiling.' He shrugs in what he hopes is a convincing manner. 'She didn't talk that much in the car, but I could read her face. She was happy to be out of here, excited to be going somewhere with more action. She refused help with her bags when we got to the station. My last sight of her was jogging up the steps to the platform. She had her hood up. It was raining.'

'Did she make friends while she was here?' the detective asks next. 'Did she go out socialising?'

Mia smiles briefly. 'You bet! She linked up with other backpackers. Met up with them in Newcastle on weekends. We'd drop her to the station most Friday and Saturday evenings. Sometimes she'd get a lift home in the early hours of the morning – God knows who from! – and sometimes she'd stay out the entire night. I worried myself sick, because I knew she'd be drunk and not making safe decisions, you know? Gave me an insight into what it's like to parent older children. I just want Elliot to stay the age he is right now.'

'Did you ever meet any of her new friends?'

'No. Although one of them drove up our driveway like a lunatic one Saturday afternoon. I took the rego number and told her I didn't feel safe with strangers being on our property. She got dropped off at the gate after that.'

Goodwin's face is as deadpan as ever. 'Do you still have that registration number you wrote down?'

Mia plays her part perfectly. Surprise. Slightly flustered. 'I didn't actually write it down, I took a photo. But I could have deleted it since. I'll have to check.'

The last lot of detectives didn't ask about Tara's friends or who was giving her lifts. Their questions centred around her mental state, trying to establish if her late-evening swim had been a suicide mission or a drunken misjudgement of the conditions.

'That would be great, thank you.' Amy Goodwin smiles for the first time since sitting down at the table, and Ryan exhales a breath he didn't realise that he was holding. 'Perhaps you can show me around the property, Ryan, while Mia checks her phone?'

Ryan's relief is short-lived. Why does she want to look around? Does she think that they still have possessions belonging to Tara? The bedroom has nothing of hers; they were scrupulous about clearing it out.

The detective must sense his reluctance. 'I'm a visual person. It helps me picture how Tara lived when she first got here. But you're within your rights to say no.'

He might be within his rights but it's crucially important to give the impression of being willing to help.

'Of course,' he says, careful not to look at Mia, who has begun to scroll through the photos on her phone. 'I suppose we should start with Tara's bedroom.'

Tara's old bedroom is situated on the right-hand side of the house, next to the one that Mia uses as a study. Ryan opens the door, standing aside to allow the two detectives to proceed before him. Double bed with crisp white linen. Curtains in grey-and-white chevron. Some black-and-white prints on the white walls. A casual chair and a shag rug complete the modern look.

'Tara shut herself away in here when she wasn't needed to supervise Elliot. She'd only emerge for meals or to sunbathe. Or to go out at night.'

Detective Goodwin scans the room. There's no denying it: this is a nice bright space. Her eyes come to rest on the bed.

'Is this the same linen from when Tara was here?'

'God, no. Tara had an obsession with fake tan. It ruined the bedclothes. Mia had to throw everything out.'

'Has anyone else slept here since Tara left?'

'My mum, Dianne. Sometimes she stays over to babysit. And we've had a few other guests. Just friends. We're a bit out of the way. Visitors find it easier to stay the night.'

Ryan casually points out the family bathroom – where Tara cracked one of the floor tiles when she dropped her hair straightener – before leading the detectives back to the kitchen. Mia is no longer there; probably gone to coax Elliot away from Minecraft. Their son's bedroom and the master suite are on the opposite side of the house.

Operating on instinct, he leads the detectives outside. He crouches down next to the pool, to remove a palm frond from the water, before mentioning again how much Tara liked to sunbathe and swim.

Stavros, the male detective, takes the bait. 'So, from your observations, Tara was confident in the water?'

'Yeah.' Ryan keeps his voice level and slow. 'She knew how to dive, float and swim under water. She always did twenty or so lengths in freestyle or breaststroke. It really surprised us when her mum said that she wasn't confident in the ocean. We didn't see any evidence of that.'

The next question is exactly as Ryan anticipated. 'Did she go to the ocean while she was staying here?'

'Yeah, at least a few times. Caves Beach is about thirty minutes away. My son loves exploring the caves and rocks when the tide is out. Tara would swim, catch some sun, take selfies to taunt her friends back in Dublin. The beach was the only place she was happy to go with us on weekends.'

Stavros asks to look inside the garden shed and the garage. It's obvious that there has been a transition of roles between him and Goodwin. Is this something they do to put people on the back foot? Ryan has been meeting Amy's eyes, smiling and grimacing and trying to forge a rapport. He has all but ignored her pale-skinned, ginger-haired colleague. Was that a mistake?

Just the lawnmower, garden tools and a few bags of fertiliser in the shed. The triple garage contains Mia's car, plus their bikes, fishing rods and camping gear. Ryan's car is parked outside.

'How long have you had this car?' Stavros asks, sizing up Mia's Ford Focus.

'About a year. It's just a runabout. At weekends we mostly use my car.'

'And how long have you had *your* car?'

'Almost six years.'

'Did Tara drive while she was here?'

He shakes his head. 'She didn't have a licence. In hindsight, things would have been better if she knew how to drive. Some independence for her as well as more flexibility on places she and Elliot could go together. Would've made things a hell of a lot easier when Elliot was back at school.'

Ryan takes a steadying breath; he is aware that he has been talking slightly too quickly. He doesn't want the detectives here, of all places. He doesn't want to discuss the cars or risk them noticing details like the rectangular shape on the back wall where the bricks are lighter in colour. He's so nervous that his right hand is starting to tremble – a tic that used to affect him at school, whenever he was required to do public speaking or read aloud in class.

Stavros shares an indecipherable glance with his colleague.

They step back into the hall just as Mia and Elliot are coming out of Elliot's bedroom further down.

'Just convincing this young man that he's had enough Minecraft for one day,' Mia says breathlessly. 'Oh, and I've found that photo of the rego – I didn't delete it.'

Stavros confers with Mia, recording the rego number in his notebook.

Amy Goodwin looks at Elliot thoughtfully, before turning to Ryan. 'Do you mind if I speak to him?'

What does she mean *speak* to him? Grill the kid with questions? Try to trick him into incriminating his parents? Elliot can incriminate you even when you've done nothing wrong; you are never quite sure what's going to come out of his mouth next.

Mia is distracted with Stavros; it's up to Ryan to answer. He lowers his voice. 'Okay, but he knows nothing about what happened after Tara left here and we'd like to keep it that way. We don't want him upset.'

The detective nods and approaches Elliot. She bends over a little, so she and the child are eye to eye. 'So, young man, you're a Minecraft fan, are you?'

Elliot nods enthusiastically. 'It's my favourite game.'

'I like it, too. I like building worlds and machines that can do *anything*. It's so fun ... Did Tara like Minecraft?'

Elliot shakes his head. 'No. But she let me play it more than Mummy does.'

'Is there anything else you remember about Tara?'

The detective is good with kids. Getting down to their level, talking about games before zoning in on what she really wants to know.

'Tara didn't like vegetables,' Elliot says, as though that is the worst crime in the world.

Amy Goodwin laughs and seems happy to leave things at that.

Ryan is lightheaded with relief.

~

'What inconsistencies?' Mia wails as soon as the detectives' car is out of sight. 'What do they mean?'

Ryan puts his arm around his wife's shoulders and hugs her close. 'They can't tell us details – it would show their hand. All I can think of is that thing about Tara not liking the ocean.'

'They're *wrong*. Tara *loved* the ocean. She swam when we were at Caves Beach ... didn't she?'

For all the emphasis in Mia's voice, there also exists a trace of uncertainty, detectable only because he knows her so well. Siobhan seemed adamant in that video-clip: her daughter did not like to swim in the ocean. Had there been a bad experience in her childhood? Getting wiped out by a wave, or being carried out on a rip? Something Mia couldn't have possibly known about, despite her meticulous planning.

Ryan casts his mind back. 'I remember her standing in the shallows. I just assumed she went further out, but I can't recall specifically – I would have been focused on Elliot. Maybe it's not that at all. They did seem interested in our cars. How long we've had them. Whether Tara could drive. Fuck, I hope nothing showed on my face.'

Ryan has never been a good liar. As a child, his mother would only have to glance at his face to determine if he was being truthful; a hard smack inevitably followed. Mia can also see right through him, although he rarely has occasion to lie to his wife. He can only pray he was not as transparent to the detectives.

Mia shrugs his arm from her shoulders. 'Damn Siobhan for putting all that money on the table, thinking that a million dollars will change the outcome. I know she's heartbroken, but can't she see that this is making things worse? It's obvious that Tara is not alive. Surely drowning is better than some of the other alternatives?'

A few moments of silence where their thoughts contemplate those sinister alternatives. At least now the detectives know about Tara's less than cautious attitude to her personal safety. The drinking. The partying. Getting lifts with people she didn't know. The owner of that rego plate is going to get a nasty shock.

'And I am *furious* that female detective spoke to Elliot.' Mia's cheeks are flushed, a combination of anger and distress. 'He's a kid. His memory is hardly reliable. It was inappropriate, unethical.'

'At least he didn't say anything incriminating,' Ryan says with a half-smile. 'He defused things. It was okay.'

'It's *not* okay.' She is close to tears. 'We need to make sure it doesn't happen again.'

How much does Elliot really remember about his former nanny? What is he liable to say on closer questioning? Like other kids, he sees, hears and repeats things he is not supposed to. The only saving grace is that he is so distractible.

Ryan takes Mia by the arm, its thinness a measure of her frailty. He steers her back to the kitchen, sits her on a chair, puts on the kettle. Mia was strong when it happened, leading the way, making all the hard decisions. It was afterwards she collapsed. She said that Tara's face was invading her sleep and every waking hour. She worried about her abandoned career, their dismal finances and all the other repercussions. Then it was Ryan's turn to be strong, to lead. They've always made a good team in that way. One of them propping up the other as needed.

Mia has her tea black, no sugar. Ryan hands her the cup, kisses her forehead, and goes to check on Elliot, who is being suspiciously quiet.

6
Mia

Two years ago

Her new job is with a technology company that specialises in customised software. Mia's role is to project manage the software rollouts, liaising between the customer and the software engineers. This job has been years in the making. Waiting for the right role to match her qualifications and experience. Waiting for the right – family-friendly – company not too far from home. Deciding on the most appropriate childcare plan. The latter was always going to be the trickiest part.

Tara is bleary-eyed this morning and only half-listening to Mia's instructions.

'Just keep to the timetable as closely as you can. It's all there – mealtimes, playtime, structured activities. Sorry, I know it seems over the top, but Elliot responds so well to routine. Make sure he doesn't sneak any bad food – the last thing he needs is a sugar rush. As for Minecraft, only if you need to distract him, and only as a last resort. If he's feeling overwhelmed, suggest that he has a time-out to relax and get control of himself. He'll go willingly if you suggest it early enough ...'

Tara has witnessed a few of the meltdowns during her week-long settling-in period. Her expression said more than words could as she observed the wailing, the thrashing and the cyclone of emotions. Mia would probably have worn the same expression at Tara's age. Given her own self-discipline, she would have found it hard to understand how a child of Elliot's age could have such poor self-control. Now that she's a mother, it's fundamentally different. She understands all the different factors that can contribute to a meltdown; her daily mission is to ensure that those factors are mitigated as much as possible with the right routine, the right food, the right activities and the right amount of love and understanding.

Now she is entrusting Tara with that mission. Tara, who is unable to contain her yawns or disguise her lack of enthusiasm for the day ahead. Mia is overcome with the desire to call it off. Is there another solution, one that doesn't involve leaving Elliot? She has asked herself this question a hundred times before, especially over the last week as her doubts about Tara have multiplied. Every time she arrives at the same conclusion: returning to work is not just necessary, it's vital. The bank has issued an ultimatum: their mortgage repayments, which have been interest-only for the last few years, will revert to the full amount in February. Elliot's best interests include keeping the home he loves. Mia shudders at the thought of how much he'd regress if he were confined to an apartment again.

'Okay, Mummy has to go to work. Give me a big hug. Wish me luck.'

Elliot flies into her arms – he never needs to be asked twice for a hug. In one of his hands is a piece of Lego, which presses into her neck. She ignores the pain while she kisses his face, ruffles his hair.

'Be good for Tara,' she instructs, before meeting the slitted eyes of their au pair. 'I won't be able to check my phone that much. I'll try to call at lunchtime.'

Mia starts the engine and gives Elliot one last wave before reversing and turning the car. Her cheeks ache as she drives down the driveway, gravel crunching definitively under the tyres.

Don't cry. He'll be okay. Tara is capable enough.

She brings the car to a stop once she reaches the gate at the main road. Instead of getting out, she takes a few moments to compose herself.

Elliot will be okay. You'll be okay, too. You can do this.

She has the urge to phone Ryan but her husband is already at work; he leaves before 6am to beat the worst of the Sydney-bound traffic. She visualises him driving the forklift at the warehouse, wearing his high-vis shirt and earmuffs. The forklift is noisy, monotonous work; Ryan doesn't enjoy it.

We're all doing the best we can, she tells herself.

Then she finally gets out of the car to open the gate.

~

Her first day comes with a few hiccups. Her work laptop hasn't been set up – somewhat ironic, considering Citiware is a technology company – and so she can't perform any independent work. The occupant of the desk next to hers – a grumpy-looking man in his fifties – has expanded his files to her workstation and is obviously disgruntled about the need to retract his stuff into his own area. But her boss, Geoff, is really nice and she knows instantly that they're going to become friends. Geoff is mortified about the laptop and helps clear the overflow of files from her desk. He takes her around the office, introducing her to various people, and accompanies her to all her meetings, providing background information and context whenever the subject matter goes beyond the superficial. At lunchtime, Geoff suggests a nearby Thai restaurant, which is obviously popular with Citiware people because he nods and says hello to several of the patrons. He asks about Ryan and Elliot while they eat from the set menu. Geoff has twin girls – eleven going on sixteen, he says with a roll of his eyes – and his family life sounds familiarly chaotic.

43

He smiles benignly. 'No reason why you can't work from home every now and then once you get settled in. All the systems are in place for it. Of course, depends on the particular projects you're working on and their needs.'

Mia says a silent prayer of gratitude. The prospect of working from home – even on a limited basis – eases some of the anxiety that has been bubbling under the surface all morning. How are Tara and Elliot getting along? Have they kept to the routine? Has Elliot been able to behave?

She's had no opportunity to phone Tara, with Geoff constantly by her side. Before leaving the restaurant, she excuses herself to use the bathroom. She sends Tara a rushed text from the cubicle. *How is everything going?*

The response is instantaneous: *Grand.*

Tara must have been holding her phone when the text arrived. Hopefully, Elliot is engaged in a safe activity and she is just snatching a few moments to herself. Mia desperately wants to ask more questions – Have you been for a walk? Did Elliot eat his lunch? – but there is no time.

Sorry I haven't been able to call. Glad it's going well. Talk later.

She uses the toilet, applies a fresh layer of lipstick, and unties and reties her ponytail. Her phone beeps again. Tara has sent some photos. The water dragon who suns himself every day next to the pool. A flock of cockatoos visiting the back paddock. A close-up shot of a yellow bottlebrush tree.

Exploring the backyard.

Mia could cry with relief. They're having a good time. Everything is okay.

She assesses her reflection, her fingers touching her brand-new ID card, which is attached to a lanyard around her neck. *Mia Anderson – Senior Project Manager.* She is part of the workforce again. If she puts all her worries about Elliot to one side, it feels validating to be back in the game.

The afternoon goes pleasantly fast, and her new laptop is delivered to her workstation by an apologetic technician just before she leaves for the day. Mia beams her gratitude; at least tomorrow she'll be able to bury herself in the online files and get up to date with the projects she's been assigned to.

On the drive home, she turns up the music and speeds towards her son. Geoff dedicated his whole day to her, which was extremely solicitous but at the same time extremely exhausting. Trying to impress him without showing off. Trying to pretend he wasn't assessing everything she said and did. But despite the strain, it was a definite success.

You're back. You're doing this. The money will make such a difference.

She uses Bluetooth to phone Ryan, who is also on his way home, although his commute is significantly longer than hers. Jubilantly, she gives him the highlights. Jubilantly, he congratulates her. She can see his grin. She can feel his relief.

Newcastle is behind her now. The road home is a straight run, this section fringed with fields and farms. Brown cattle and horses with shiny coats chew grass in the evening sun. At this time of day, she is usually at her lowest, counting down the minutes until Ryan walks in the door. This is a different kind of exhaustion – mental more than physical, mellow rather than cranky – and she is ready to devote whatever time is left in the day to her son. She is ready to give him her best, which is not always the case when they've had the full day together.

She is expecting to see Elliot on the driveway with his bike, or playing on the trampoline, his usual activities while waiting for an imminent arrival. But the driveway is empty, as is the trampoline.

'Hello?' Mia calls, on opening the front door. 'I'm home.'

Elliot doesn't come running. In the distance, she hears a distinctive sound: tapping against a background of music. Minecraft.

Mia is conflicted. Go straight to Elliot's room, which will mean an instant battle: not the homecoming she imagined. Or seek out Tara for a briefing. She decides on the latter; better to find out in advance what went wrong – Tara was explicitly told that Minecraft was the last resort.

Mia proceeds to the kitchen, assuming that Tara is making a start on dinner – the last item on the list of instructions, but only if Elliot is being well-behaved. She gasps on seeing the benchtop, littered with cereal boxes, dirty cutlery, and a container of milk that hasn't been returned to the fridge.

'Tara?' she calls, emerging into the hallway and projecting her voice towards the girl's bedroom and bathroom. No answer.

Mia doubles back and opens the French doors. She steps outside, squinting her eyes against the low-down sun. The sun loungers are empty. One of them holds a balled-up beach towel that hasn't been hung to dry.

'Tara?' she calls, going back into the house. There's only one place left to check. She flings open the bedroom door and there they are: Elliot playing Minecraft; Tara sitting on his bed, doing something on her phone.

'Oh, howya. We didn't hear you come in. Look, Elliot. Your mam is home.'

It's not surprising they didn't hear her calling: the volume of the game is deafening. Elliot glances over his shoulder with a distracted smile; nobody can compete with the lure of Minecraft.

Mia takes a deep breath, makes a snap decision. She will not chide Tara about allowing Elliot to play the game, or even about the state of the kitchen. Neither will she grill her about the minutiae of the day, despite her strong desire to know every last detail. If Tara feels anything like Mia does, she'll be glad she got through it; the last thing she'll want is a full-blown analysis. At least she is here with Elliot, supervising him. In a fashion.

Mia approaches her son from behind, wraps her arms around him, breathes in his boy scent. 'I missed you, buddy,' she says. 'Did you have fun today?'

No answer. His eyes are trained on the screen.

'Okay, buddy. Ten more minutes of the game. Then no tantrums.'

She turns to give Tara a complicit smile, but the girl has disappeared. Obviously not keen on having a detailed handover. Or even a superficial chat.

This has been a first day for everyone in the family. They all need time to adjust.

7
Beth

Today

The evening is overcast, the ground soggy from yesterday's deluge. A mosquito buzzes in front of her face as she presses the doorbell. The sound resonates loudly inside the house. Pippa and Ian are well into their eighties and very hard of hearing.

Tilly hops from foot to foot impatiently, always excited at the prospect of a visit next door. Pippa keeps a cupboard full of lollies and chocolate, one way of guaranteeing the everlasting love of a seven-year-old. Another attraction is Fuzzy, the cat, whose haughtiness makes Tilly all the more determined to win him over.

'Are they home, Mummy?'

'I think so, pumpkin. Just give them time.'

Pippa comes to the door. She is a tall woman, holds herself well, white hair cut in a chic style that enhances her prominent cheekbones. Pippa used to be a GP and didn't retire until her mid-seventies. She is also the mother of four middle-aged children, and grandmother of fifteen. Despite her own extensive family, she always has time for Beth and Tilly, treats them like part of her own brood.

'Well, look who it is. Come in, come in. Ian is out playing bridge. That man is addicted.'

Being in Pippa's house always reminds Beth of her grandmother. The smell of potpourri and furniture polish. Beth's grandmother died when she was eighteen, shortly after her parents' divorce. Her grandfather passed away the following year. When her mother relocated to London a few months after that, it felt like the cornerstones of her family had crumbled, leaving Beth untethered during her late teens and early twenties. Her dad tried his best, but he couldn't replace what had been lost and had his own struggles to contend with. Looking back, she can see why Kane was so attractive. Nine years older with his own house: the allure of a fully mature, financially secure man. She fell head over heels for the stability he offered; it took years before she realised the extent of her mistake.

Pippa opens the infamous cupboard, takes out an array of treats for Tilly to choose from.

'Just one,' Beth says, watching carefully.

Lollipop stuck firmly in her mouth, Tilly goes to seek out Fuzzy, who has so far declined to make an appearance.

Pippa retrieves two cups from another cupboard, without checking if Beth wants tea. This is part of their ritual: there is no need to ask because the answer is always yes. If Beth doesn't have time for tea, she doesn't come past the front door.

'I had the police come by today,' Pippa says. 'They said you had an unwelcome visitor the other night.'

It's reassuring to know that the police are checking in with the neighbours. Pippa and Ian are home more than Beth is, thus more likely to spot someone scoping the house or acting suspiciously. If the police have been here, it means they've also spoken to Kane or will do so very soon. Beth can imagine his vehement denial, the veins on his temples bulging with indignation and fury. She shivers.

Pippa's expression is sympathetic. 'Sorry, neither of us noticed anything out of the ordinary. But maybe one of the other neighbours has information.'

Maybe. Everyone on the street is good in that way. Watchful. Caring. Looking out for others, not just themselves.

'Sorry if my alarm gave you a scare.'

'Didn't hear a thing.' The old woman gestures to her hearing aid. 'I take this out most nights, to let my ears breathe. Ian's the same, although that man could sleep through an earthquake even when his ears were perfectly good. Never heard the children crying or thunderstorms or whatever ... So, what actually happened? Was anything taken?'

'Nothing taken. Car keys flung on the floor, so it would appear that's what they were after.'

Pippa stares at the kettle thoughtfully. 'You know, Gabby was talking about an increase in burglaries only the other day.'

Gabby, Pippa's second eldest, is a crime analyst at the police district office in Waratah. She would have statistics to support her concerns.

'Gabby thinks we should get a security camera as an additional precaution. I said we would think about it.'

Pippa installed a house alarm at the same time as Beth, but she is also lax about setting it at night, due to Fuzzy's nocturnal activities.

How much would a security camera cost? Would its presence be a deterrent or an after-the-fact asset? Has Gabby seen something in the crime statistics to make her especially concerned about this area?

'I'll see about organising a quote,' Pippa says, dispensing milk and sugar. 'Shall I ask for you as well?'

Given that the houses are joined together, it saves on installation and repair costs to have things done at the same time.

Beth briefly thinks about her paltry bank balance, and the not-so-paltry amount she owes to Shepherdess Finance. Does she really need a security camera on top of the house alarm? Depends on who she is protecting herself from. Depends on whether this was an opportunistic crime or a targeted one, a one-off or the start of another onslaught.

'Yes. Definitely. But I might not go ahead. Things are tight at the moment.'

The best thing about Pippa is that Beth feels she can be honest with her. There is the strong sense that her neighbour has seen and heard everything before, both through her career as a GP and being the matriarch of a large, boisterous family.

'Okay, dear. No pressure. Hopefully a random incident that won't happen again.'

Beth sips from her mug of tea and tries very hard to convince herself that Pippa is right.

~

Friday brings another hectic day at work. Beth is due to meet Caitlin for a drink on King Street at 6pm. She is not really in the mood for going out, but her dad has been booked in for babysitting and it's been weeks since she's done anything social. In the clinic's tiny bathroom, she swaps her black t-shirt for a patterned green top. She scrunches her auburn curls with hair product and puts in dangly earrings that complement the top's colour. Some lip-gloss and mascara and she's ready to go.

'Have fun,' Debbie sings, waving her off.

Beth tries to take her advice, tries to quell the sense of foreboding churning in her stomach. Newcastle has its usual Friday-evening buzz. Office workers, university students and young families swarm the pedestrian areas and restaurants. Caitlin has already secured a table and two glasses of white wine. As usual, she looks utterly gorgeous: her smile lights up her face and everyone around her.

'So tell me more about this break-in,' she says, launching straight in.

Caitlin was amazing throughout the protracted divorce from Kane, providing emotional support as well as practical advice about police procedures and Beth's legal rights. Not once did she say 'I told you so'. One of the reasons why she is such an excellent social worker as well as friend.

Beth gives another, more detailed, rundown of the events on Tuesday night.

'So the car keys were on the floor?' Caitlin checks, siphoning for clues of Kane's potential involvement.

'Yep.'

'Nothing else taken?'

'Nope.'

'Your car is a pretty ordinary car, hon. Much better pickings in the other houses.'

'I know.'

'Does Kane have a girlfriend at the moment?'

'I'm trying to find out from Rachel. She hasn't answered yet.'

Kane has had several relationships since the break-up of their marriage. Girls barely in their twenties, easy to impress, easy to fool. When they were still sharing custody, he would make sure the girls answered the door to Beth. Some of them gushed over Tilly, others were awkward with her. Despite being alarmed by their youth, Beth didn't mind their presence: at least it meant that Kane was on his best behaviour.

Caitlin takes a long sip of wine before delivering her assessment. 'I'm sorry, hon, but this sounds like something he would do. Lulling you into a false sense of security. Knowing just how much you crave normality, a quiet life. I see this with other women – it's amazing how quick their defences come down. They so badly want to believe it's over, that the worst is behind them, and it's devastating when the abuse starts up again. Twice as powerful and debilitating ... So, this is what I think – you need to assume it was Kane until proven otherwise.'

52

Beth nods with gratitude and resignation. 'Yeah. You're right.'

They finish their drinks. Caitlin orders another glass of wine for herself and a soda and lime for Beth, who has to drive home. The bar, which was only half full thirty minutes ago, is jammed with people. Caitlin is attracting attention but she is oblivious to her effect. Long honey-coloured hair, clothes in of-the-moment fashion, that megawatt smile. She pays for the drinks, being both pleasant and businesslike with the bartender, thwarting his attempts to flirt.

For the duration of their next drink, Caitlin talks about her new boyfriend. Beth doesn't pay much attention to the details: her friend's boyfriends never last long. For the drink after that, the subject matter is mostly Tilly. Caitlin is her godmother and her devotion to the little girl is absolute. One day Caitlin will make an excellent mum, if she ever decides to keep a boyfriend for longer than five minutes. In the meantime, Tilly gets her undivided love and attention. She calls Caitlin the 'Fun Godmother' because she is always up for playing games and knows exactly how the mind of a seven-year-old girl works.

By 8pm, Beth is ready to call it a night. Her back and feet ache: professional hazards. Her head is beginning to throb from the music, which has gone up in volume since they got here, and the lack of air from too many bodies squashed into what is not a very big space.

She gives Caitlin a long hug. 'Let's not leave it so long between drinks next time.'

The lapse has been more her fault than Caitlin's. Going for drinks or a meal involves money and babysitting logistics. Caitlin, to her credit, puts on a show of enthusiasm for pizza-and-movie nights at home, but Beth knows her friend of old: a night on the town is the distraction she craves after the mental exhaustion and grind of social work. Besides, Caitlin has a wide circle of friends and invests a great deal of effort into keeping in touch with everyone, hence her hectic social life. Beth is cognisant of the fact that she is but one of Caitlin's many close friends whereas Caitlin is her only close friend.

Caitlin herself pointed this out.

'I'm worried that your social circle is too small.'

She also pointed out other worrying facts.

'He is a fair bit older than you, hon. Are you sure that you want the same things?'

Over the years, she kept asking the right questions.

'Are you okay, hon? ... Are you happy? ... Do you need help with anything?'

Beth rebutted all of Caitlin's concerns. Convinced herself that Kane had her best interests at heart. Nevertheless, Caitlin kept that lifeline open. Kept asking the questions that needed to be asked. Never once judged or tutted or got impatient with Beth's sluggishness to accept her reality.

Outside, dusk has draped over the city, giving everything a tint of beige. The evening is humid, flashes of lightning in the distance. This time of year, storms are sometimes a nightly occurrence, a short eruption at the end of a hot day. Beth walks briskly; it takes less than ten minutes to get from the bar to the high-rise car park. She has parked here twice this week: on Wednesday, due to the torrential rain, and tonight, for the convenience – the extra cost another dent in her budget. Then there's the cost of tonight's drinks and Tilly's Surf Safety excursion that's coming up at school. The truth is that money is as much of a problem now as it was when she was married, the only important difference being control. She can decide to have a drink with Caitlin in exchange for beans on toast for dinner. And she can offer to do a couple of hours' overtime to cover school excursions. Every dollar spent needs to be tracked and totted up. Her head often feels like a cash register, clocking up numbers, spitting out totals, identifying shortfalls. But at least she's in control and can use her discretion.

It's fully dark by the time she reaches the car park. She uses the machine on the ground floor to pay for her ticket, and rides the lift to the fourth floor, where she left her car this morning before work. She is the only person at the ticket machine, and the only person in the small airless lift. Her hand tightens around her car keys, her whole body infused with a sudden sense of danger.

She emerges on to the fourth floor to see that there are plenty of cars left in the bays, but not a soul in sight. Someone's car alarm is wailing, echoing against the pillars and the claustrophobically low ceiling. Her rubber-soled shoes squeak on the smooth concrete as she hurries to the far side of the car park, the wailing getting progressively louder.

The Corolla finally comes into sight. A sigh of relief: the flashing lights and ear-splitting noise are coming from another car, a Land Rover on the same row.

Nevertheless, her heart is racing as she gets into the car and locks the doors. She drives a little too quickly down the ramps, tyres screeching on the tight turns. Her nerves are jangling. Not just because of the deserted car park and the screeching alarm. Because of Kane.

The cops will have been to his house by now, questioned him about the break-in.

Guilty or not, he'll be raging. Guilty or not, he'll make her pay. And it's naïve to think that a young new girlfriend would lessen his rage.

8
Ryan

Four weeks ago

He is starting his lunchbreak when he notices a missed call on his phone.
A voicemail has been left: Detective Sergeant Amy Goodwin requesting
him to give her a call. Her voice is authoritative, slightly harsh: this call
has been made for a specific purpose, not just to relay information. He
senses that something is going to be asked of him, something unwelcome.
A cold sweat materialises on his skin. The homemade sandwich he was
about to bite into suddenly makes his stomach want to heave. He abruptly
leaves the kitchen area, located at the rear of the warehouse, and goes
outside to the parking lot. The day is sunny, the sky cloudless, yet it feels
like there is a filter between him and the real world. Who should he ring
first? Mia or Detective Goodwin? No point in panicking his wife until
he knows the exact reason for the call. No point in panicking himself.
Yet he feels like throwing up, a purely physical reaction that no amount
of rationalising can abate.

Deep breath. Steady voice. 'Detective Goodwin. Sorry for the delay
responding. I don't carry my phone with me while I'm on the job ...
How can I help you?'

'Thank you for calling back, Ryan. I appreciate that you're at work so I'll make this brief. I wanted to ask if you and your wife would consent to a DNA sample.'

The ground shifts beneath his feet. He puts a hand on the bonnet of a nearby car, in an effort to steady himself. He realises that he has already hesitated too long in his reply.

'Can I ask why?' Hopefully, a reasonable question to ask.

'Of course. We would expect to find your DNA on some of Tara's belongings so we would use the samples for elimination purposes.'

So they're taking DNA profiles from Tara's stuff. Presumably her rucksack and clothes. Fuck, fuck, fuck!

'You and your wife are not suspects so this is purely voluntary,' the detective adds in a matter-of-fact tone. 'You are within your rights to refuse.'

She is using the same tactics she used on the weekend, when she asked for a tour of the house, informing him that he wasn't legally obligated and at the same time her demeanour implying there was no good reason to refuse.

'What does it involve?' Is he asking too many questions?

'It's completely painless and self-administered. You scrape the inside of your mouth with the swab, which is a bit like a cotton bud. Then you hand it to the police officer, who presses it onto a specially treated paper. The paper is sent off to the laboratory for analysis and you get to keep the swab because there is a legal requirement that the sample is shared with the person providing the forensic material. And that's pretty much it.'

There is no way out of this. They're going to have to say yes and come up with a compelling list of reasons for why Mia's DNA is so heavily evident in Tara's things.

'Sounds pretty straightforward,' Ryan says, unable to control the waver in his voice. 'I'll call Mia now and let her know.'

'No need,' the detective says briskly. 'I've already spoken to her. Obviously, we needed to obtain her consent directly.'

Ryan hangs up the phone, looks around for somewhere to sit; he feels too shaky to go inside, to eat his lunch, to pass the scrutiny of his workmates. He walks slowly across the car park, to the low brick wall on the perimeter. The wall isn't exactly clean but neither are his work pants; the warehouse's concrete floors and high roofline provide a haven for dust and loose dirt. He sits down, inhales a few gulps of air, and tries to order his thoughts.

Detective Goodwin has already spoken to Mia. Why didn't she say this at the outset? Is she trying to play them against each other?

Fuck! It's happening: a full-blown investigation with DNA samples and God knows what else. From now on he and Mia will need to censor their phone calls, messages and online activity. They were fully prepared for this two years ago. Will their responses be as solid given the lapse of time? Will their reflexes be as faultless as they need to be? They can't afford the tiniest slip-up; Ryan feels as unprepared and panicked as he would for a surprise exam at school.

Thank fuck he has Mia to lean on, to guide him. His wife didn't text or call to forewarn him about the samples. Smart girl. She's already playing the game.

~

Their DNA samples are collected at the local police station by one of the on-duty sergeants. As Detective Goodwin promised, it's a straightforward and painless procedure: a swab scraped inside the mouth, self-administered, less than fifteen minutes from start to finish.

Afterwards, Ryan and Mia go for dinner at one of the restaurants on the lake. Ryan's mum is minding Elliot; using the opportunity to go on a 'date' seems like something a normal, guiltless couple might do.

Mia orders steak and salad. Ryan – unable to focus on the menu – decides to have the same.

'I just want to know what these *inconsistencies* are,' Mia says, after the waiter departs. Their table is outside, on the jetty. Only one other couple, thankfully not within earshot. Nevertheless, Ryan feels uncomfortable having this discussion in such a public place.

'Shush. Not here.'

'This is safer than our house, or the car,' she bristles. 'We have to assume they've got listening devices.'

Ryan takes a deep breath, dragging air into his lungs. All day his chest has felt tight, his breathing too shallow. This is what it was like last time. The feeling that he was running out of oxygen. Every muscle tensed, measuring each word and action. Paranoid about using his phone or other technology, leaving a digital footprint. Trying to guess and second-guess. Flying blind a lot of the time.

The waiter arrives with their pre-dinner drinks: a beer for Ryan and a glass of sparkling wine for Mia. Ryan downs half his beer in one gulp. Mia has the same instinct, her champagne flute close to empty when she puts it down. They both manage a smile.

Mia leans across the table, laces her fingers through his. 'We can do this, darling. We just need a refresher course. Remember, the internet is our enemy. Don't use our phones or laptops if we need to research something that could be deemed as remotely suspicious. Public libraries are our only resource. Phone and text each other as per normal. "Running late for dinner." "Need anything at the shops?" Business as usual on the domestic front.'

'I need to concentrate, pay attention to every little thing,' he adds, because concentration has never been a strong point.

'Yes, you do.' She nods emphatically. 'Going back to the "inconsistencies" they've supposedly found, it's crucial we know what direction they're heading in ... If the detectives won't tell us, maybe the family will?'

Ryan's breath catches in his throat. 'Are you suggesting that we phone Siobhan?'

'Isn't that what concerned parties would do?' Mia counters. 'Check in with the family?'

Yeah. Maybe. It's impossible to think objectively. He and Mia fall into a profound silence, their hands remaining interlocked, eyes gazing into each other's souls. He loves his wife with his whole being. The things he has done because of this love. The things he has done to protect her and their son and their precious family life.

I did what I had to do. I did what I had to do.

This mantra sustained him through those awful few weeks and months when a knock on the door and the game being up seemed imminent.

I did what I had to do. I did what I had to do. I did what I had to do.

No matter how much he tries to convince himself otherwise, he knows that not many husbands would have done what he did. And not many husbands could live with themselves afterwards, waking up each morning, guilt pumping through their veins in place of blood.

His fingers tighten around Mia's. Their hardships over the last few years have proved the endurance of their love. And also its ruthlessness.

~

Dianne is playing Snakes and Ladders with Elliot when they get home, shortly after eight. She lands on a snake just as they are coming through the door.

'Oops, Grandma is going whoosh all the way down. Oh well, just have to try to make my way back up again.'

Dianne is a no-nonsense grandma. Practical, bossy, as likely to dispense a scolding as much as a hug. With her dyed brown hair, leathered skin, and fondness for kaftans, she is both familiar to her grandson and not too familiar, predictable while at the same time being unpredictable. Her frequent visits offer Elliot the opportunity to test his resilience and social skills.

'No, no, no,' Elliot cries. Ryan glances at the game again; his son has also had the misfortune of landing on a snake. His small face scrunches up, bottom lip wobbling.

Dianne is philosophical. 'Not you too! Well, there are lots of ladders coming up. Only a matter of time before one of us gets lucky, Elliot.'

Dianne hasn't always been so adept at dealing with her grandson. When he was little, she held the 'that child needs more discipline' view – in fact, the very same view she held about Ryan when he was a kid. But Dianne has come to admire their parenting strategies and can see the improvement for herself. When she stays the night, usually one weekend a month, she experiences the full gambit of ADHD highs and lows. Elliot being bright, inquisitive and affectionate. Elliot hissing, grunting and lashing out. Elliot needing to be asked ten times to brush his teeth or tie his shoelaces. Dianne sitting next to Elliot in the back seat of the car with a ringside view of her grandson's fidgeting, frustration, tantrums and tears. Nothing like a car trip to change the mind of ADHD naysayers.

Now Elliot traces his token down the length of the snake with a scowl. Dianne praises him, and reassures him again that there are plenty of ladders coming up. Board games are wonderful for teaching kids that success can follow failure, and that disappointment is often short-lived.

The game ends about ten minutes later, and Elliot is told – the first of many times – to go and get ready for bed.

Once he is safely out of earshot, Dianne asks how it went at the police station.

'Pretty straightforward,' Ryan replies. 'Just a swab. We went for a quick dinner afterwards. Hope you don't mind.'

'Of course I don't mind,' she tuts and pushes her seat back from the table. 'If anyone deserves a nice meal, it's you two. What about this reward, though? What an odd approach to take. Bribing people to come forward, dollar signs in their eyes. How can you trust what they have to say?'

Nobody like his mum for calling a spade a spade.

They walk her to the door; she lives an hour's drive away, in Gosford, and isn't overly fond of driving at night. Ryan's dad died seven years ago after a short battle with stomach cancer. During the week, Dianne splits her time between her daughters, who still live in the area and have two children apiece. On weekends she drives to Morisset to see Ryan and his family. Ryan's relationship with his mum is much improved from when he was a teenager. He was a restless kid, and Dianne was a harsh disciplinarian; there were fights, punishments and friction. Mia's influence improved the relationship, put it back on track. In fact, Dianne and Mia get on so well there's a family in-joke that Mia is Dianne's favourite 'child'. Jokes aside, their relationship is important to Mia, seeing as her own parents and brother are estranged. Mia cannot tolerate her family's deep-rooted conservatism, their outdated views on everything from religion to contraception to the roles of women in society. There was a large disparity in the financial support Mia received at university compared to her brother. Then an ignorant comment about birth defects caused by the contraceptive pill, implying that Elliot's disorder was somehow due to Mia's choice of contraception in the years before conceiving. Dianne is far from perfect but she has staunchly approved of Mia since the day they met.

'You sure you don't want to stay the night, Mum?' Ryan asks.

'No, no, I've got an appointment in the morning. Best get home.'

Elliot hurtles down the hallway and into his grandma's midriff for a goodbye hug. Ryan and Mia exchange resigned smiles; he's still not in pyjamas but it's impossible to chastise him when he is being so affectionate.

'Thank you for watching him, Dianne,' Mia says, a catch in her voice. 'You're so good with him.'

Dianne kisses Elliot's dark hair, hugging him closer to her bosom.

'Nobody is as good with that child as you are,' she says to her daughter-in-law, before turning to leave.

~

Ryan and Mia go to bed straight after Elliot. By 9pm, the house is in darkness. The turmoil and anxiety of the last few days has led to exhaustion, which eventually, after an hour of tossing and turning, leads to sleep. Ryan dreams that he and his mother are driving in the red station wagon they had for most of his childhood. They're on the freeway, Dianne is behind the wheel, and she is angry with him for some reason. She's berating him, her fury building with each kilometre travelled. Up ahead, an articulated truck blocks the road. It's on fire, toxic black smoke pluming into the blue sky.

'Slow down, Mum,' he yells.

There's a loud bang, which sends the fire and smoke rushing towards them.

'Slow down. You need to *stop*.'

Dianne turns to look at him, disappointment flashing in her eyes, before putting her foot to the pedal.

Ryan wakes with a shout. Mia reaches out an arm to calm him.

'Shush. It's all right. It's just a dream. You're safe.'

It's not all right. It's not just a dream. He's not safe. None of them are.

9
Mia

Two years ago

Her first day has transitioned into her first week. She did it. Tara did it. Elliot did it. And as a result of all their efforts, Mia is more than $2000 richer. Money that will be in her bank account by the end of the month. Money that will change everything. Two months and they'll have enough to pay the arrears on the mortgage. Four months and they'll be able to repay Ryan's mum what they owe her. Six months: maybe a family holiday in Queensland?

Mia stops off at one of the shopping centres on her way home on Friday. She picks up a salmon quiche, a chocolate mud cake and a nice bottle of wine. Tonight is a celebration. A step into the future.

Fifteen minutes later, she turns into the driveway and jumps out to unlatch the gate. On the other side, she gets out again, to close it. Ryan is about half an hour away, but you can't be too careful with children. She is looking forward to seeing her husband, celebrating with that bottle of wine, perhaps even the abandon of Friday-night sex. She feels triumphant and edgy, a wilder version of herself.

Tara and Elliot are standing at the front of the house, waiting. Mia smiles at the sight of them. It's only when she gets closer that she notices Elliot's stance is not a happy one. She knows this child inside out. The hang of his head. The downward droop of his shoulders. Even his hands are a closed-fisted clue that all is not well.

It's okay, she tells herself, as she brings the car to a stop. *Whatever it is, we can handle it. First week. Plenty of time to finesse things.*

They start speaking together. Babysitter and child competing to tell their side of the story.

'He hit me.'

'I didn't mean it. I didn't mean it.'

'You *did* mean it. Stop telling lies.'

'You wouldn't let me finish my game. I was *in the middle* of building something.'

'I gave you a five-minute warning.'

'Mum always gives me ten minutes.'

'You got *two* five-minute warnings, Elliot,' Tara hisses. 'Five and five makes ten.'

'I only heard one,' he claims, which is probably true.

Tara's lips roll back in a sneer. 'More bleedin' lies!'

Mia has heard enough. Tara is forgetting that she is the adult and Elliot is getting more and more upset; there is no reasoning with him in this state.

'Elliot, buddy, go and have some time out.'

'I—'

'Off you go,' Mia says, her voice a practised blend of authoritative and loving.

Elliot's designated time-out space is in one of the spare bedrooms. Mia has set up a corner of the room with a beanbag, a CD player and some books. Elliot can listen to music, or read, or simply sit still until he regains control of his emotions. The calming-down process can take as little as five minutes or as long as thirty, however long it takes to transform Cyclone Elliot to Calm Elliot.

Her son stomps away, his small face set in a big scowl. Mia and Tara are left alone, regarding each other warily.

'I'm sorry he hit you,' Mia says, because the last thing Tara signed up for was physical abuse.

The girl points to an angry red mark on her arm. 'He's bleedin' strong. I'll have a massive bruise.'

'Sorry,' Mia says again. The strain of the week comes hurtling out of nowhere, making a mockery of her earlier positivity. She was insane to think they could pull this off. To believe that anyone could manage Elliot but her. Especially without the calming effects of his medication. 'Video games are addictive for most children but kids with ADHD tend to become hyper-focused and have difficulty transitioning away. That isn't an excuse. This kind of behaviour is completely unacceptable. I'll ban Minecraft for the next few weeks as punishment.'

Tara looks aghast. 'That's the last thing I want. The only time I have a break is when he's playing that bleedin' game. The rest of the day it's "Tara play with me", or "Tara come here with me", or "Tara I'm hungry". Tara, Tara, Tara ... I'm sick of hearing me own name!'

Mia has no words. What can she possibly say? How can she redeem the situation? It's obvious that Tara hates this job. It's obvious that she and Elliot are incompatible. It's obvious that this is more serious than first-week teething problems.

'I've got chocolate cake and a bottle of wine,' she offers, dangerously close to tears. 'Let's go out the back and sit down.'

~

Mia wakes up the following morning with a thumping headache and a queasy feeling in her stomach. She can't remember when she last had a hangover. She and Tara polished off the bottle of wine, and another bottle for good measure. A lot of cake was consumed and not much dinner. Ryan came home and took charge of Elliot, getting him ready for bed, coaxing out an apology to Tara and even a conciliatory hug.

Mia is struggling to remember what she and Tara talked about while they sat outside on the patio, dusk falling, then night. Plans that Tara had for the coming weekend. Boys she was hoping to meet around the pubs and clubs of Newcastle. Aussie boys: no Irish or English backpackers, thank you very much.

'I want tall, tanned, sexy ... like Chris or Liam Hemsworth.'

Mia snorted. 'I think we'd all like a Chris or Liam ... Are you homesick, Tara?'

'I miss me mam and me friends. I've called Mam every day since I got here – it's pathetic how much I miss her. But it's miserable cold there at the moment, so I don't miss the weather, ha, ha.'

Mia found it surprising, and rather sweet, that Tara had spoken to her mother every day. She couldn't help wondering, though, what the girl had relayed about her first couple of weeks in Australia. Had she put a positive spin on things, or been honest? How had she described Mia and Ryan? Mia couldn't bear to contemplate what words were used to describe Elliot. Phrases she'd heard school parents use. *Spoilt rotten. Does it on purpose. Needs a good smack.*

Once Elliot was in bed, Ryan came and joined them with a beer. Tara's energy changed noticeably. She smiled more, played with her hair, laughed girlishly. Did Tara find her husband attractive? Sometimes Mia forgot to look at him objectively. His dark good looks and muscular body, the piercing blue eyes that crinkled at the sides when he smiled. When Tara said that she wanted an Aussie bloke, did she really mean the unattainable Hemsworth-like models, or a more everyday version, like Ryan?

Mia groans and hauls herself into an upright position in bed. Voices can be heard outside in the front garden: Ryan and Elliot playing together. She is astonished when she checks the time: 9am. Her last sleep-in was as long ago as her last hangover. A reviving shower and a strong coffee are in order.

Twenty minutes later she is sitting outside in the shade of the patio, sipping her coffee. A slice of wholemeal toast and two Nurofen tablets line her stomach; she is waiting for the vice-grip headache and the nausea to recede. Tara hasn't made an appearance yet. Is she hungover, too? Probably not: she is young and seems to have infinite capacity to sleep it off.

Everything seems both duller and sharper this morning. The mix of shade and sunlight on the patio. Mia's body movements as she lifts the coffee mug to her lips. The sequence of thoughts going through her head. Did she do enough damage control last night? She wanted to show Tara that she could be fun, good company, a potential friend. She wanted to make her feel part of the family, with the usual ups and downs that happen when people live together. She wanted to forge a connection, a degree of loyalty that would make Tara think twice before abandoning them. Did she succeed?

God, she hopes so. It's a disaster if Tara decides this job is not for her, if she ups and leaves without giving them a proper chance. Mia has so much riding on her own new job. The money. The security. Not to mention the importance of reclaiming some of her old self. *Tara needs to stay*. Finding someone else could take weeks, months even.

'There you are.' Ryan comes through the French doors. Blue t-shirt, board shorts, bare feet. Tanned from being outdoors most weekends. Strong from the physical work at the warehouse. He's grinning at her: white teeth, crinkled eyes. 'How's your head this morning?'

When Mia looks at her husband, she sees the caring, devoted father to Elliot; she sees her partner, her best friend. She hasn't assessed his physical attributes in what feels like a long time. His attractiveness this morning is strangely disconcerting.

Mia ignores his question about the state of her hangover. The headache has lost some of its ferociousness.

'I think Tara fancies you,' she says with a half-smile, half-grimace.

10
Beth

Today

The text comes through on the drive home from the pub. She hears her phone ping and she knows in her gut that it's from Kane. There's a strong temptation to pull over and read it but she waits until she's home, easing the car into the garage, cutting the engine.

PARANOID BITCH. STOP BLAMING ME EVERY TIME SOMETHING GOES WRONG IN YOUR LIFE.

So the cops *have* paid him a visit and if he wasn't already out to get her, he definitely is now.

She says nothing to her dad when she gets in. He was rattled enough when she told him about the break-in. No point in agitating him further. She needs to mull this over, decide whether or not to answer the text. The last thing she needs is her dad jumping into the fray and escalating the situation.

'Have a nice night?' he asks, standing up from the sofa with a yawn.

'Yeah. It was great to see Caitlin.' She gives him a grateful hug. 'Thanks, Dad. Dinner tomorrow?'

Joe is always happy to receive an invitation to dinner. He lives on his own and has been single since his divorce. He has a lonely, minimalist existence: shopping for one, meals for one, laundry for one. A depressing two-bedroom flat with a skinny balcony in place of the three-bedroom, large-garden family home he used to live in. Like many men of his era, he relied on his wife for organising social activities and holidays. Fifteen years later, he still hasn't got the hang of doing it for himself. One or two nights a week, he'll venture to the local RSL club for a drink. Beth suspects he drinks alone, a sad, crumpled man in the corner with his schooner of beer.

'You need a hobby, Dad. Bowling or hiking or even cooking classes. Somewhere you can meet new people.'

But despite her encouragement to be more adventurous, Joe continues to plod through life: working nine to five in a tax consultant's office, relying on Beth and Tilly for his social stimulation. He visits at least twice a week, lavishing attention on Tilly and lending a hand around the house. Her dad is intelligent, good company, generous with his time and affection. In some ways it's incomprehensible that he is still single.

Beth's mum is the opposite: she flourished after the divorce. Linda met someone new within months, married again within a couple of years, then moved to London when her new husband was offered a lucrative role as vice president of European something or other. Being clinical about it, Linda was fortunate to meet someone she loved so quickly; otherwise, she too would be struggling on a single income.

'Divorce is for rich people,' Joe often says, lamenting his meagre accommodation and bank balance.

Beth hates acknowledging the truth in this. Household bills being paid by one person instead of two, not to mention the legal and court fees, particularly expensive in her case because Kane contested everything. So much cheaper to continue living under the same roof. So much cheaper, and soul-destroying.

'Why are you doing this to us?' Kane exploded during an attempt at mediation. 'This is going to financially ruin us.'

It was all about the money for him. It always had been, right from the moment she was foolish enough to move in with him.

You're not getting my car, she thinks, lying wide awake in bed. *I paid for it; the loan is in my name. That other piece of shit was worth nothing.*

The car she was driving at the time of the split was a twelve-year-old Jeep, notoriously unreliable and requiring frequent repairs. True that it had originally belonged to Kane – before he upgraded to something more in keeping with a successful real-estate agent. Beth had long since sold her original car, the money disappearing into their joint finances, so what belonged to who was a moot point, or so she thought. Besides, she needed transport to leave him, and somewhere to sleep while she weighed up her options. Losing the car upset Kane more than losing his daughter did.

'*That's my fucking car. You have no right. Bring it back.*'

Of course, Beth didn't return the Jeep. That heap-of-shit car was all she had to show for eight years of married life. But Kane couldn't or wouldn't see the inequity. He was driving a luxury car and was impeccably turned out in expensive suits and shoes. Generous with himself while being miserably tight with his wife and daughter, who he saw as a drain on his resources.

The longer Beth stays awake, the more certain she becomes that Kane is trying to cash in on what he believes he is owed. Who else would have interest in a ten-year-old Corolla? Anyone looking for a joy ride or a getaway car would be gravely disappointed with its low-spec engine.

Rachel, Kane's sister, still hasn't answered. Maybe she hasn't seen Kane in a while and needs to do some fact-checking first. Does Kane have someone new in his life? Is he being his best self, striving to impress some guileless young woman? Or is he alone, bitterly cataloguing and obsessing over all the perceived losses from his former marriage.

Once Beth knows his relationship status, she'll be able to determine where she stands and how best to protect herself and Tilly.

~

Beth has a fitful night, drifting in and out of sleep, her sense of danger never quite easing. At 7am she swings her legs out of bed, uses the bathroom, and disarms the house alarm before padding downstairs. Feeling sheepish, she opens the internal door to the garage to confirm that the car is still there and hasn't mysteriously disappeared overnight. There's the shine of its dark-grey body. Safe. Solid.

She spends the morning cleaning, doing chores and re-reading Kane's text. Does he have a point? Is she guilty of blaming him every time something goes wrong in her life? In the afternoon, Tilly goes for a play date, and Beth uses the opportunity to run out and get some groceries. At the check-out, she exceeds the limit on her credit card and endures the embarrassment of having people wait while she puts a reduced amount on the card and makes up the difference with cash and coins.

Joe arrives at five-thirty, carrying store-bought chocolate brownies and a rainbow-coloured golf umbrella. Raindrops speckle his bald head and bushy eyebrows. Another summer storm has darkened the evening sky to indigo.

'Where's my favourite girl?' he booms.

Tilly comes flying down the stairs for a hug, launching herself into his arms in the manner of someone who hasn't seen their loved one for a very long time. Beth watches with an ache in her heart: Joe is grandfather and father wrapped into one.

Tilly gives Grandpa an update on everything that has occurred since he babysat last night. A game of hide-and-seek with Fuzzy, next door's cat. Her play date with Amelia, a friend who lives a few doors down. The banana and strawberry smoothie she and Mummy made for afternoon tea.

Joe listens intently. Then he jerks his head towards the internal access to the garage. 'Now's a good time to investigate what's happening with that leak.'

The garage leak has been an on-and-off problem since Beth took over the lease: it seems to depend on which direction the rain is coming from. The handyman from the real-estate agency can't investigate while it's wet – too slippery and dangerous – and as soon as it's dry it's impossible to see the trajectory of the water. Both the handyman and Joe have examined the roof numerous times, failing to find the usual culprits: cracked tiles or loose flashing.

'Don't worry about it, Dad. We'll take a look next time.'

The leak is too elusive for Beth's frame of mind. She wants to eat dinner, have a glass of wine and some easy conversation. Her body feels heavy, deeply exhausted, which often happens in the aftermath of an incident with Kane.

Joe ignores her protests. He opens the access door and skirts his way around the parked car.

'Turn on the light, Beth. Thanks, love.'

Beth sighs and flicks the switch. Her father raises his eyes to study the water pooling on the plasterboard before it plops into the repositioned bucket.

'That's quite a lot of water.' He moves towards the stepladder, which is propped against the far wall of the garage. 'I'll just take a look inside the ceiling hatch.'

'Honestly, Dad, leave it for another day.'

'Just a look, that's all.'

One minute later, Beth is holding the ladder steady while Joe shines his phone torch into the roof cavity. Meanwhile, in the kitchen, the dinner is overcooking. She loves her dad but he can be exasperating at times. It's hard to deny him because this is when he is at his happiest: here with Tilly and her, doing something handy around the house.

'You have a loose tile, Beth. Not sure how I didn't see it the other times. Must be going blind.'

A loose tile? That *is* odd. Must be something relatively recent.

Joe comes down the ladder carefully. 'I'll go up again during the week and sort it out. So much easier now I know what I'm looking for.'

'Thanks, Dad.'

Fifteen minutes later they sit down to eat: mashed potato, meat pies and green beans. The potatoes are mushy due to being overboiled, and the pies are on the verge of burnt, but it's a wholesome, warming meal while thunder continues to rumble outside. They are a few bites in when Tilly brings up the burglars again.

'Do burglars do burgling in the rain?'

Joe takes her question seriously. 'I think they work in all weather, love.'

'But running away would be harder. They could slip and fall.'

'Very true. Then the police would catch them and put them in jail.'

'What do burglars look like, Grandpa?' she asks, chewing anxiously on a green bean.

He suppresses a smile. 'I suppose they look normal. They can be young or old, girls or boys. But one thing they have in common is that they aren't very clever. Because stealing things will get you into big trouble.'

Tilly's small face still looks perturbed. The questions about burglars have been coming steadily all week. Do burglars have kids? Do burglars prefer toys or money? Do burglars ever get burgled by other burglars? Tilly's trust in people has suffered another dent. Beth already worries about how her child's early life will affect her as an adult. The absence of her father and his side of the family. The fear and worry that her mother tries to mask, yet carries with her every day. Fear that Kane will resume his vendetta. Worry that some unforeseen cost will materialise, and this hand-to-mouth life will come crashing down.

Beth, just like Tilly, is anxious about who broke into their house and what they want. Somewhere in the middle of her daughter's questions about burglars, Beth thinks about the loose roof tile and her blood runs cold.

She allows Tilly thirty minutes of television after dinner, so that she and Joe can talk. Tilly scoots into the front room and the sound of the TV can be heard within moments.

'Glass of red, Dad?'

'Thanks, love. Just the one.'

Beth clears the dishes before pouring two glasses of Shiraz. She sits down opposite her father, steadies herself. So much for the easy conversation that she craved.

'Dad, could the slipped roof tile be caused by someone trying to get into the house?'

Joe blinks in surprise. 'I guess so. But more likely to be due to strong winds or corroded nails, I'd say ...'

'Okay. Good. By the way, the cops have spoken to the neighbours about the break-in ... and they've spoken to Kane too. As expected, he's pretty mad ...'

Beth kept things from Joe the first time around, and his shock at learning the full story led to that violent interaction with Kane and the resultant AVO, which expired only a couple of months ago. If there is trouble ahead, she wants to give her dad as much warning as possible. No more shocks.

Joe's face has drained of colour. Suddenly his wrinkles are more prominent, and he looks both older and more vulnerable.

'Kane had better not be getting up to his old tricks. He'd better not be ... or I'll ... I ...'

Her dad is struggling for words. What is there to say that hasn't already been said? What is there to say that could actually change things? Surviving Kane is about distancing yourself. Trying not to think in too much detail. Taking each day as it comes, not looking too far back or too far forward. Trusting that you are in the right, despite how good he is at making you think you are selfish, greedy, lazy and paranoid.

'I'm making some enquiries, Dad. Seeing what's going on in his life. I don't want to make accusations unless I'm sure.'

Surviving Kane is having your evidence lined up before pointing the finger.

Joe's expression is as thunderous as the weather outside. 'Do you think he sent someone here, told them you were on your own in the house? Maybe he's in debt and thought the car would square things off?'

The thought has crossed her mind. Kane is prone to overextending himself. Numerous investment properties. An impossibly tight cashflow to service multiple mortgages. Excited by big capital expenditure, while resentful of the everyday costs of living.

'Drink your wine, Dad. I just wanted to keep you in the loop. Let's not give him any more airspace till we know more.'

Joe lifts his glass to his lips, his hazel eyes, the same colour as her own, full of angst.

She was only twenty-two when he walked her down the aisle.

'I know what I want,' she told him, and everyone else who suggested she wait a few years.

She wanted unconditional love, a solid home and family life. All the things she lost when her parents separated.

In her quest for stability, she failed to see the warning signs, the junctures at which she should have stepped back and asked: who is this man? Is he right for me? Is that ambition glinting in his eyes or pure greed?

Is his love capable of transforming into a hate so powerful that destroying me will become his mission in life?

11
Ryan

Four weeks ago

'What time is everyone coming around?' he murmurs. It's early Saturday morning and they're still in bed.

Mia's eyes are closed as she answers. 'I told them 3pm but who the hell knows? You know what they're like.'

Their neighbours, Kellie and Dino and Heather and Philip, are invited around for a barbecue. Time has a strange insignificance for both couples. Kellie and Dino once arrived two hours late, with no apology. They seem to have the motto 'We'll get there when we can'. Sometimes it's late, and sometimes it's early. Very rarely on time.

Mia's dark hair is splayed across her bare shoulders. Ryan reaches out a tentative hand to stroke the strands of hair and the soft skin beneath. Saturday-morning sex is part of their routine, but this has been no ordinary week. Mia is tense and barely sleeping. He has been worried about her, about the results of the DNA tests, about the sheer power of a million-dollar reward. Sex is not top of mind but still that tantalising shoulder evokes a response in him. A desire all the more intense because it offers a reprieve from the worries that have been plaguing him all week.

He bends his head, places his lips on her shoulder, still tentative, half expecting to be pushed away. She's tolerating the small chaste kisses and, encouraged, he uses his tongue to taste her warm musky skin. He stops, to check her expression. Her eyes are open, fierce in her wan-looking face. She takes his head in her hands, forces his lips onto hers. A few moments of hard kissing, then her hand is at his waistband, pushing down the cotton shorts he sleeps in. Her hand is pulling him, up and down, up and down, and he gasps. Then she is on top of him and he is inside her, and they are having violent sex: all their fears and tension poured into the act, their union. The intensity of feeling is equivalent to the first time they had sex, back when they were in high school and barely of age. That same illicit feeling now. That same feeling of them against the world. That same wondrous climax.

Ryan collapses against his wife.

'We're in this together,' she breathes against his neck, as if he didn't already know that.

~

Kellie and Dino rock up at 2pm, and Ryan and Mia share an amused glance. Elliot is overjoyed to see their kids, Kayla and Jed, who are overjoyed to have the opportunity to swim: they don't have a pool at home. Beers all round and some cheese and crackers to nibble on while they wait for Heather and Philip. The adults sit outside on the patio and chat, while keeping an eye on the children as they shriek and dive-bomb into the water.

Soon the conversation at the table splits in two. Mia and Kellie start to discuss this month's read for book club. Dino points out that one of the trees could do with pruning and offers the use of his cherry picker. Ryan's conversations with Dino are usually of this ilk: the offering of assistance, either machinery or labour, and the specifics of a job that needs doing. Dino and Kellie are of similar age to him and Mia, but they feel like older, wiser friends. Maybe because they come from farming stock and understand life, nature and interdependency in a deeper context than others. Whatever it is, Ryan likes these plain-speaking, kind people, and values their advice and friendship. He wasn't looking forward to today – his head is elsewhere and so is Mia's – but as his wife keeps reminding him, they need to live life as normal. Work, home, social activities: normal, normal, normal. Besides, it wouldn't have felt right to cancel today's get-together. Nobody around here cancels. They arrive late or early; one way or another, they make it work. Cancelling would be bad form, even a little suspicious.

Heather and Philip arrive just after three, holding a bowl of salad and a bottle of Chardonnay. Their kids are older, in their teens, and don't attend these gatherings. Heather smiles at the antics going on in the pool – now a game of Marco Polo – and looks wistful. Philip dives into the crackers and cheese; he's clearly hungry. Mia nods at Ryan: time to get the barbecue fired up.

They have their barbecue routine down pat. Early in the day, he marinates the meat and she makes the salads. When the guests arrive, he does the cooking while she keeps the conversation and the drinks flowing. Afterwards, she clears the plates and stacks the dishwasher while he does the conversation thing. Good food, good conversation: that's the aim. They make a great team.

'Can you get an ice bucket for the Chardonnay?' Mia asks. Another nod towards the bottle Heather abandoned in the middle of the table.

Ryan takes the bottle inside with him, holding it by the neck. He locates the ice bucket – lead crystal, a wedding present – and opens the freezer to get some ice. A weakening sensation in his knees. The truth is, he can't open the door of this small, over-full freezer without thinking about the full-sized one they used to keep in the garage.

He collects himself. A small bag of ice is jammed behind stacked

80

containers of frozen dinners. Ryan extracts the bag and dumps its entire contents into the ice bucket.

Before going back outside, he pours himself a large glass of water and downs three of his magic pills. Grasping the ice bucket and pinning a smile to his face, his façade as the impeccable host is restored.

~

On Sunday morning, Mia decides that she is going to call Siobhan, brazen it out.

'Eight pm in Dublin. She'll be winding down after the week. Maybe having a Saturday-night glass of wine, if we're lucky.'

It's a bold move, making the call from the landline, but Mia is adamant that it's well within the realm of 'normal' behaviour. Tara worked for them; of course they're interested if her death is no longer being deemed accidental.

'Let's do this,' Mia says, checking her watch. 'We don't want it to get too late over there.'

Elliot, much to his delight, is allowed to play Minecraft, a sure-fire way of ensuring no interruptions. Mia makes the phone call from her study, and Ryan listens in using the handset in their bedroom.

The phone rings four or five times, the ring-tone ominous in Ryan's ear. He can hear himself breathing over the trills; he moves the handset away from his mouth. Maybe Siobhan is out. At some point after losing a child, normal life resumes: enjoying a night at a restaurant or pub, listening to live music or theatre, or laughing at the latest rom-com in the cinemas.

'Hello.' The voice that answers is female. Brusque, with an inflection that instantly reminds him of Tara's accent.

'Hello. Is that Siobhan? This is Mia ... Mia Anderson ... from Australia.'

Mia has hit the perfect tone, conveying warmth and openness, underpinned with an unspoken apology for calling out of the blue.

'Hello, Mia.' Now Siobhan sounds wary, but maybe Ryan is reading too much into her voice.

'I hope you don't mind me getting in touch, Siobhan. There has been some media coverage here, to coincide with the anniversary, and I had the urge to call and see how you are.'

'We're optimistic,' Siobhan responds, after an extended silence. 'The money will prompt people to come forward. We'll finally get some answers.'

Another pause, before Mia goes completely off script. 'There's not a day goes by when I don't think about Tara.'

Ryan grimaces into the handset. Risky. Siobhan could find this admission either comforting or suspicious.

Another, heavier, silence emanating from Dublin.

'I wish she'd been happier with us,' Mia forges on. 'I wish she'd stayed here a little longer. Found her feet before heading to Sydney.'

'No amount of wishing will bring her back,' Siobhan finally retorts. 'God knows, I've tried.'

As Ryan listens, he realises that the abruptness and silences are a mask for the Irish woman's sorrow. Her daughter died far away from home; no body to bury, not even the comfort of a proper funeral. Is it any surprise that she can't move on? Is it any surprise that she is still yearning for answers? A pile of clothes folded on the sand will never be enough.

Mia acknowledges Siobhan's grief through yet another silence. She resumes with an especially gentle tone. 'The police have asked us for DNA swabs, for elimination purposes. Naturally, we didn't object. We want to help in any way we can. They said there were inconsistencies.'

Siobhan doesn't take the hint.

'How is your little boy?' she asks instead.

'Elliot?' Mia can't disguise her surprise at the sudden change in subject. 'He's good. Had his tenth birthday in December. Growing up, I guess.'

'Does he still have behavioural issues?'

Ryan inhales sharply. He can only imagine Mia's shocked expression in the other room. Protectiveness of Elliot wrangling with special allowances for this anguished mother.

'He'll have ADHD for life,' his wife says, rebounding quickly. 'But every day he's getting better at managing his emotions and his impulses. I'm very proud of his progress.'

Yet another silence. Ryan's chest tightens; he instinctively knows that something unpleasant is coming.

'A mother knows her child inside out,' Siobhan states, each word enunciated. 'All the small little things that make them who they are. All their strange inconsistencies.'

Inconsistencies: it's no accident that Siobhan used that specific word. She is well aware that Mia is fishing for information, and she has no intention of providing it.

Siobhan McAllen doesn't have a Saturday-night glass of wine close at hand. She is stone-cold sober, and suspicious as hell.

12
Mia

Two years ago

Her new job is going well, superbly well. On Wednesday she had a client meeting where she impressed everyone with her proposed solution for one of the project's roadblocks.

'Wow,' Geoff said afterwards. 'The client loves you already. Of course, I took all the credit for hiring you.'

There's the pleasure of putting on smart clothes each morning, the delicious time to herself commuting in the car, and the light-hearted chats with Geoff and the rest of the team; this is a group of people who could potentially become good friends. Yes, work is going as well as can be expected two weeks into a brand-new job. Home is another matter. Elliot is disengaged and short-tempered due to too much time on Minecraft. Tara is struggling with Elliot's behaviour and the long, boring days. Ryan is brimming with positivity and irritating platitudes. *We're doing great. We're all in this together.*

They're not all in this together. Tara is not on board. She hates the job, hates the location. Can't Ryan see that?

On Friday evening there is no opportunity to soften the week with a bottle of wine or chocolate cake. Tara is all glammed up when Mia gets home from work. Fake lashes, glossy lips. Skimpy skirt and top. Teetering heels, chunky jewellery and overpowering perfume.

'Oh, you look nice,' Mia says, striving to sound genuine. Tara would look a hundred times nicer if she toned down the make-up and put on more clothes. There's an attractive girl in there; she just needs to learn the power of understatement.

'Can I get a lift to the station?'

No 'please' in the question. Is she too old to be admonished for bad manners?

'Of course,' Mia replies, masking her exhaustion. Getting back in the car is the last thing she wants to do: a twenty-minute round trip after a long day, and an even longer week. 'Ready now?'

The journey to the station is punctuated with Mia's concerned questions and Tara's reluctant answers. All is quiet from the back seat. None of Elliot's usual prattle of observations and questions.

'Where are you off to tonight?'

'A few pubs in the city.'

Probably no point in grilling her on specific names. How many pubs in Newcastle in total? Ten? Fifteen? Certainly not enough for Tara to get lost.

'Who are you meeting?' Mia asks instead.

'That backpacker group I joined on Facebook.'

A group of strangers in a strange city. Is Tara street-smart? Does she know how to protect herself? Not to go anywhere alone with someone she doesn't know? What is she like after a few drinks? Probably like everyone else: less inhibited, more likely to take risks.

Mia wants to warn her to be careful, not to drink too much, but Tara's expression suggests that such advice would not be well received.

'Here we are. There's a train home around eleven-thirty. I'll ask Ryan to pick you up.'

This time Tara manages some gratitude. 'Ta.'

Restricted by her tight skirt, she carefully manoeuvres herself out of the car, and totters away.

~

'So, how is the job going? And the au pair?' Kellie asks, setting down two cups of tea and a plate of biscuits and fruit. It's Saturday afternoon and they're sitting on Kellie's veranda, watching the kids play on the swings and slide. Six-year-old Kayla and five-year-old Jed are Elliot's best friends. He finds it easier to get along with younger kids: they're less judgemental, closer to his maturity level. The children in his class are more difficult to impress. To them, Elliot is the kid who loses his temper, causes disruption in class, and sometimes hits and bites (which happened only once that Mia knows about, but everyone acts like it's an ongoing threat). The kids can't see beyond his behaviour to the quirky, affectionate, intelligent boy underneath. The school parents are the same: disapproving of Elliot's outbursts, harsh in their assessment of his character, committed to excluding him from social activities as a result.

'The job's going well. I like it. I think they like *me*.' Mia sips from her tea and considers whether to have one of the biscuits. Her stomach feels unsettled. Nausea that has been simmering away all week. Probably anxiety. 'I don't even mind the drive. The bliss of being in the car on my own. Playing music as loud as I want to. Not having to talk to anyone. It's worth it for the commute alone!'

Kellie laughs. 'The only commute I get is driving the tractor to the top paddock. Maybe I should get some music on. Might startle the animals, though.'

Kellie and Dino's farm requires an enormous amount of work on both their parts, although she rarely complains. Her face always looks slightly sunburned, her clothes are of the practical variety, and her hands – rough skin and broken nails – are beyond redemption. In the city, Mia's friends were the antithesis of Kellie: impeccably dressed and groomed, polite and polished to the extreme. Mia finds Kellie's scruffiness refreshing. No point in fancy clothes or nice hair on a working farm. More than anything, she loves that Kellie is always herself: what you see is what you get. Maybe it's the effect of working on the farm, tending to animals who are nothing if not authentic. When Mia and Ryan moved to the area, they assumed they would form a friendship group with the parents at school. Instead, it was their neighbours who provided the initial welcome and the ongoing network.

'And the au pair? Tara?'

When she is with Kellie, Mia is incapable of putting a positive spin on something that is not very positive. When she is with Kellie, Mia is compelled to be honest. More so than with her own husband.

'Tara is not going so well. She doesn't like that we're so remote. And I suspect that she doesn't even like kids.'

'Oh dear,' Kellie murmurs, reaching for the biscuits. 'That is a problem.'

The children intuit that there is food on offer and come galloping onto the veranda, putting a temporary pause on the discussion.

'Wash your hands,' Kellie instructs them cheerfully, and they obediently change direction, galloping inside the house, towards the bathroom. A scuffle can be heard, probably who gets to wash their hands first, but is resolved without the need for parental intervention. Kellie's children are as unpretentious, accepting and genuine as their mother. Kayla has a lovely warm nature and Jed adores Elliot, in the touching way that younger boys look up to older ones. Mia tries to catch up with the family at least once a week so that Elliot can enjoy this feeling of belonging, of being genuinely liked and deemed worthy to play with.

The kids return from the bathroom, hastily washed fingers grabbing for the biscuits.

'No more than two,' Kellie says, stern and jovial in equal measure. 'Have some watermelon and apple, too.'

The afternoon sun streams onto the veranda. Mia temporarily closes her eyes, the chatter of the children fading to white noise. She is tired enough to fall asleep, right here, right now. Ryan picked up Tara from the station last night and it was well past midnight when they got home, Tara's giggles infiltrating the silent house and Mia's sleep. It was another hour before Ryan came to bed. Maybe he'd been talking to Tara. Or maybe he decided to read or watch something on Netflix. Either way, Mia was still restless when he finally slid in next to her. Then the ultimate frustration: he fell asleep instantly while she tossed and turned next to him, her stomach churning with foreboding.

Mia opens her eyes. The kids, their quota of food consumed, have migrated back to the base of the slide, where some sort of headquarters has been established.

Mia turns her sleepy gaze to Kellie. 'I think Tara fancies Ryan,' she says. 'Maybe that's enough to make her stay.'

Kellie splutters on her tea. 'You shouldn't joke about stuff like that.'

Mia smiles sheepishly. 'I know. Bad taste. Sorry ... Change of subject. Can you remind me what book we're doing for book club?'

Kellie and Mia are part of a neighbourhood book club that meets once a month, each member taking turns to host. The evening always involves good food, spirited conversation and far too much wine. Once the book is discussed, the conversation can go anywhere and everywhere, but sometimes – on the best nights – it meanders its way back to the novel, and everyone is more mellow and honest and in tune with one another.

Kellie reaches for another biscuit. '*Little Fires Everywhere*, Celeste Ng. You can have my copy, if you like. I stayed up late last night to finish it.'

A half-hour later, Mia says goodbye, the book tucked under her arm, blissfully unaware that the next book club night will mark a line in her life, dividing a *before* and an *after*.

13
Beth

Today

'You're booked solid this morning. The phone hasn't stopped ringing.'

Debbie is sipping from a cup of coffee as she frowns at the booking screen; the working week has started with a bang. Beth stows her bag in the cupboard behind reception and slips on her tunic. Her client is already waiting. A woman in her early sixties, with grey-brown hair and sun-weathered skin: Mary. This is Mary's first time at the clinic; she has filled in the new-patient questionnaire with handwriting that's hard to decipher. According to the form, she has been suffering from tension headaches and is hoping a massage will help.

'Come through. I'm Beth, your therapist today. Just take off your top and lie face-down on the table.'

Beth warms her hands and rests them below Mary's shoulders, the muscles taut beneath her fingers.

'I'll go gentle to start with. If anything feels uncomfortable, just let me know.'

Mary's shoulders are rigid with tension, her breathing ragged. According to the form, this is not only her first time at the clinic but also her first time having a massage of any description, so her discomfort is understandable.

'Try to relax those muscles. Imagine yourself disappearing into the table.'

Despite her instructions, Mary becomes even more tense. Some people just don't enjoy being massaged. It can be a dislike of being touched by a stranger or lying face-down in a vulnerable position. They can be shy or have body-image issues. Sometimes it's the stubborn inability to relax and switch off.

Her new client lifts her head to speak. 'Can you stop, please? I feel lightheaded.'

'Of course. Here, let me help you sit up.'

Beth helps the older woman into a sitting position. Her face is flushed. She shakily refastens her bra.

'Can I get you a drink of water? Or maybe a cup of tea?'

'Water, please. I'm so sorry. This is very strange. I felt fine this morning.'

Beth is about to step away to get a glass of water when Mary suddenly slumps to one side. Caught off guard, Beth just about manages to prevent her client from tumbling to the floor. There is a panic button on the wall, just within reach. She supports Mary with one hand, and uses the other to press the button. The sound reverberates on the other side of the closed door and moments later Debbie is rushing into the treatment room.

'What happened?' she asks breathlessly, her eyes taking in the scene.

'She seems to have fainted. Can you help me lift her fully onto the bed?'

Between the two of them, they manoeuvre Mary so she is lying on her back.

'Her breathing seems fine,' Debbie says. 'We just need to raise her legs to heart level. Get some pillows ... Thanks, that's good ... Mary?

91

Mary, can you hear me?'

Both Beth and Debbie are trained in first aid, although fainting episodes are rare. The protocol is to allow one minute for the person to regain consciousness. Surely a minute has passed by now? Beth is beginning to contemplate calling an ambulance when Mary finally comes around, her cornflower-blue eyes flickering open.

'Mary, this is Beth. You were having a massage and didn't feel well. We lost you for a minute or two.'

'Oh dear. Oh dear. What exactly happened?'

'You fainted. Has that ever happened to you before?'

'No. Never. But the doctor changed my blood-pressure medication last week and he might have said this could be a side-effect. I never listen properly to the side-effects, never expect them to happen to *me*. I suppose I should have listened.'

The woman is sounding lucid and her colouring has improved.

'Mary, can we phone anyone to come and get you?' Beth asks.

'Oh no. That won't be necessary. I just need a few minutes. I'm feeling so much better already.'

'Don't rush getting up,' Debbie says firmly. 'We're not in any hurry. How about a cup of tea or a glass of water?'

Mary smiles sheepishly. 'Any chance I could get the water and the tea? Or is that being too demanding?'

Debbie laughs. 'Not at all. If you want a shot of whiskey, I can do that, too.'

~

The rest of the day is uneventful but as busy as promised. Beth is feeling the effects by the time her last appointment comes around. Her lower back aches, and her head is threatening to ache, too: a slight tightening behind her forehead. Charlie looks tired – another person whose week started with a bang? Because he is one of her regulars, and almost a friend, she can afford to relax her professional façade. A comfortable silence descends as she performs her job, the soft music and Charlie's breathing filling the scented air. Beth's thoughts flit to Tilly, and the tasks ahead: pick up her daughter from after-school care, make dinner, followed by bath and reading time. At least another three to four hours before she can get off her feet. Being a single parent is exhausting at times. Nobody to share the load with. Nobody on hand with a sympathetic ear or a 'You relax, darling, I'll do bath time tonight'.

If Charlie notices that she is quieter than usual, he doesn't say. What she would give to trade places with him, to be the one lying on the table, another pair of hands working her stress away.

'That's you done,' she says quietly, forty minutes later. 'Take your time getting dressed.'

Out in reception, Debbie is balancing the books for the day. 'Don't worry about wiping down the room,' she says when she sees Beth's tired face. 'If you go now, you should beat the worst of the traffic.'

Beth smiles her gratitude. Debbie knows all too well how physically gruelling a busy day can be. All the kneading and leaning over takes a physical toll.

'Thanks, Deb.' Beth opens the cupboard door to get her belongings. 'Oh. Did you move my bag?'

Debbie swings around on her seat. 'Not me. Sure you didn't put it somewhere else?'

Beth closes her eyes, tries to remember back to this morning, a lifetime ago. 'Pretty certain. Where else could it be?'

Charlie has emerged from the treatment room, shirtsleeves rolled up, jacket over his arm. He hands his credit and health fund cards to Debbie without being asked: he comes often enough to know the drill. While Debbie is processing the payment, Beth checks the other cupboards, under the reception desk and the treatment room that

Charlie has just vacated.

'It's gone,' she declares, circling back to reception, her voice trembling. 'My purse, my car keys ... Gone.'

'It can't be,' Debbie insists, beginning a half-hearted search of her own, lifting a few files from the desk, as though the bag could be mysteriously hidden beneath. 'I've been here all day.'

'Not all day,' Beth corrects her boss. 'That woman this morning – Mary. The reception was unmanned while we were helping her. Someone must have seen the opportunity and taken it.'

Debbie freezes. The two women stare at each other, disappointment and dismay mirrored on their faces.

Charlie clears his throat, reminding them of his presence. 'One of your other clients?' he suggests.

Beth shakes her head instinctively. 'All it would take is someone passing by to realise that reception was empty,' she says, glancing at the glass-panelled door. 'I don't believe this. How am I going to get home? What about Tilly? After-school care closes in half an hour.'

Two of the treatment rooms are still occupied with therapists and clients; closing time is forty minutes away, which rules out Debbie. Their eyes automatically turn to Charlie.

'Let me help,' he says. 'Tell me where you need to go.'

~

'Who is *he*?' Tilly enquires, pointing her finger at the man accompanying her mother.

'This is Charlie, Mummy's friend. He is giving us a lift because Mummy can't find her keys.'

'Hello, Tilly,' Charlie says solemnly.

'Hello,' she responds, after a short, suspicious pause.

Charlie offers to carry her backpack, the little girl proceeding to dump it on his shoes. Then she slips her hand into Beth's, in a proprietary manner. They walk to the car in silence, Beth and Charlie exchanging a smile over Tilly's head.

'What kind of car is this?' she asks, her eyes narrowing as she assesses the black Volkswagen parked next to the kerb.

'This is Charlie's car,' Beth says, because her daughter is not really asking about the make or the model; she is merely trying to understand what is happening, this change to routine.

On being ushered into the back seat, Tilly has something else to say. 'There's no car seat, Mummy. That's *illegal*.'

Charlie snorts to hide his laughter. Nobody as righteous as a seven-year-old. Everything in life is black and white, good or bad, allowed or not allowed.

'This is a bit of an emergency, pumpkin. We had to come get you before the centre closed, and Charlie doesn't have a special seat. The police will understand if we get stopped.'

Will the police understand? What if they *do* get pulled over? What if she or Charlie cops a fine? That would top off a really bad day. Beth has mentally divided up the steps that need to be taken before this nightmare is over. Retrieve spare house keys from Pippa next door. Get spare car keys from drawer upstairs. Charlie to provide a lift back to the city, to where her car is parked. Then one final journey home. She can't think about the enormous favour she owes Charlie for driving her back and forth. She can't think about all the stuff that was in her handbag: at least $30 in cash, her credit cards, her driver's licence. She certainly can't think about the transgression of driving a child without a proper restraint. It's just a short journey home. Probably best that Tilly stays with Pippa while Charlie drives Beth back to the city. One illegal car journey is quite enough.

'Do you have kids?' Tilly blurts out, just as Charlie is easing into the traffic.

He smiles at her in the rear-view mirror. 'No. But my niece is about your age. She's eight. Her name is Hannah.'

'I have two Hannahs in my class. Hannah B and Hannah T.'

'What's your teacher's name?'

'Mrs Simmons.'

'When I was in primary school, I had a teacher called Mrs Higginbottom.'

Beth looks over her shoulder to catch Tilly's giggle. Charlie continues to ask questions about school – what subjects she likes, what sports she plays – and throws in some anecdotes about poor Mrs Higginbottom, who made the grave mistake of admitting to a class of Year Five boys that she didn't like insects.

Tilly forgets all about the illegal seating arrangement and is in fact very reluctant to say goodbye when they arrive at Pippa's.

'I want to stay with Charlie,' she says, bracing her back against the seat, resisting Beth's attempt to help her out of the vehicle.

'Matilda Anne Jenkins. This is not very nice behaviour. I can see Fuzzy on the windowsill, watching.'

Pippa's cat is indeed watching, his back arched as he surveys the outside world. Tilly's small face registers uncertainty. The newness of Charlie versus Fuzzy's familiarity.

She licks her lips and Beth suspects that her daughter is now contemplating Pippa's treat cupboard.

'Bye, Charlie,' she says in a mature voice totally at odds with the petulant child of moments ago. 'Thank you for giving me a lift.'

Beth hands her young daughter over to Pippa, and Pippa hands her the spare house keys in return. It's a quick exchange; Beth called ahead to alert her to what was going on. She crosses the driveway, unlocks the front door, runs upstairs to retrieve the spare car keys, and is back in Charlie's passenger seat in less than five minutes.

'Thank you for doing this,' she says breathlessly, not for the first time.

'It's really very kind of you. I hope I'm not keeping you from anything.'

'You're not,' he says simply, throwing her a smile before checking over his shoulder as he begins to reverse out of the driveway.

Does that mean there's no girlfriend or partner waiting at home? Out on the main road, Beth assesses him with fresh eyes. Shirtsleeves rolled up, tanned forearms with fine blond hairs. Her eyes veer upwards, to his profile. Strong jawline. Slightly crooked nose. His eyes are fixed on the road and she tries to remember their colour. Blue? Green?

He slows down, to allow the car in front to change lanes, and she is sharply reminded of Kane, who made it his personal mission to prevent cars from slipping in ahead of him. Kane, who would point-blank refuse to drive an acquaintance back and forth around the city, no matter what fix they'd found themselves in. Kane, whose time was meted out as carefully as his money, who saw kindness as weakness.

'Where did you leave your car?' Charlie asks, after a pleasing run of green lights into the city.

'The Sportsground.'

A few minutes later, Charlie turns into the car park.

Beth directs him where to go. 'Straight ahead. Keep going. Turn right here.'

She scans each car, searching for her dark-grey Corolla. Becoming confused, she asks him to turn down the next row. Then she asks him to stop. Getting out of the car, she presses the key fob, to see if any headlights light up in response. Turning in circles, checking the bays to her left, to her right, behind her. Nothing is lighting up. The car isn't here.

Now Charlie is out of the car too, staring at her from across the bonnet. 'Maybe you parked it somewhere else?'

Beth thinks hard as she retraces her movements this morning. The car park was only half full; she had her choice of spots. She left a book she was returning to Debbie on the back seat; she was almost at the exit when she remembered and turned back to get it.

'I left my car *here*,' she states with conviction. 'I left it *right here*. Someone has stolen it.'

How many cars are there in this car park? How many faster, bigger, newer cars? How many with *full comprehensive insurance*? If one of those other cars had been stolen, it would be an inconvenience for their owners but not a disaster. Beth stares at Charlie, a tide of despair and anger rising inside her. The anger wins and she lets out a scream of rage. It fills up her ears, and the car park, and possibly the whole of Newcastle.

14
Mia

Two years ago

Tara is only just out of bed when Mia and Elliot get home from Kellie's at 2pm. Clumps of old mascara on her eyelashes. Hair sticking out with yesterday's hairspray. Summer pyjamas revealing blotchy tan around her neck and ankles. Elliot can't take his eyes off her as she sashays into the kitchen, mid-yawn.

'Oh, hello,' Mia says lightly. 'Good night last night?'

'Yeah, me head is killing me, though.'

Mia smiles with genuine sympathy. 'How about a cold Coke and some toast?'

Tara nods but once again fails to say thank you. She perches on one of the kitchen stools, plugging her phone into the nearby charger. 'Dead as my granny's granny,' she pronounces.

Elliot is loitering, absorbing this different version of Tara. His mouth is open, a thousand questions forming.

'It's rude to stare, you know,' she informs him, from her lofty position on the stool.

Mia agrees. 'Elliot, stop being a stickybeak. Go get Tara a Coke from the fridge.'

'Can I—'

'Nope,' Mia intercepts, anticipating the question before it is asked. 'Coke is only for adults.'

Mia cuts two thick slices from a loaf of white bread. She places the slices in the grill, and while they're toasting she fills a glass with ice for Tara's Coke. Having tried the 'friend' approach last week, maybe she'll have more success mothering her.

'Want to try some Vegemite?' she asks. 'The vitamin B and salt will help.'

'Looks disgusting,' Tara says, dubiously eyeing the jar. 'Black goo.'

'Try a small bit. Ryan swears by it for hangovers.'

The mention of Ryan's name decides it for her, and she nods. Mia applies a thin layer of Vegemite, waits for the verdict.

'It's actually not that bad.'

Mia laughs. 'Told you. We'll make an Aussie of you yet.'

Tara's phone beeps as it comes back to life. She presses the home button but the touch ID doesn't work, probably due to the residue of food on her fingers. Mia happens to be looking directly down at the phone's screen when Tara types in her passcode: 527527.

Mia has always had an excellent memory for numbers. The passcode automatically files itself away in her brain.

~

It's just after 5pm when a turbo-charged engine can be heard roaring up the driveway. Mia puts down her book, which has kept her engrossed for the last half-hour, and rushes to the bedroom window. A strange car comes skidding into view, gravel spraying everywhere. Black paintwork, modified grille and tyres, a fair-haired young man at the wheel. Wrong address? As she watches, she hears the sound of the front door slamming and Tara appears. A very different Tara from a few hours ago. Make-up and fake tan reapplied, high heels reinstated. She gets into the passenger seat and exchanges a brief kiss with the driver. After a jerky three-point turn, the black car speeds back down the driveway.

Mia reluctantly abandons her book and goes to seek out Ryan. Her husband is preparing dinner in the kitchen, deftly chopping vegetables. Elliot is occupied with his Lego on the large oak table, murmuring to himself about which pieces go where. It's a scene of domestic harmony that she would take at least a moment to appreciate under normal circumstances.

'Did Tara tell you who she was going out with?' she asks, popping a piece of carrot in her mouth. She hasn't had very much to eat today; still that roller-coaster feeling in her stomach.

'Some guy she met last night,' Ryan says, without taking his eyes off the knife.

'He came flying up the driveway just now. Lucky Elliot wasn't out on his bike. Bet they haven't bothered to close the gate either.'

'I'll check after dinner,' Ryan says, this time looking up to give her a placating smile.

'I don't like strangers arriving at our house like that,' Mia perseveres. 'She only met this boy last night. He could be *anyone*.'

'I know, babe. But we need some give and take, yeah? It's not a crime to have a date with a guy she met in the pub, and it's not unreasonable that he comes around to pick her up. She's young, entitled to have fun. And there's practically no public transport out here.'

Mia gets it, but that doesn't ease her sense of disquiet. She doesn't want that guy, with his souped-up car and zero consideration for the safety of kids or others, knowing where they live. She doesn't want any other randoms, whom Tara might pick up in the future, assessing their house and how it can't be seen from the road. It makes her feel vulnerable, violated, on edge. She wants to say something along these lines to Tara when she gets home, although Ryan will get angry if she goes against his advice.

'How long till dinner?' she asks instead.

'About twenty minutes.'

'I'll walk down to check the gate. Need to clear my head.'

Ryan's smile doesn't quite reach his eyes. 'I've got wine chilling for when you get back.'

The walk is ten minutes return. Mia's sneakers crunch on the gravel. She inhales deep breaths of the warm evening air, telling herself that Ryan is right: leniency is required, give and take. Tara needs to feel at home, not like a guest. Tara is young, free, single, and incapable of thinking like a married, battle-weary, slightly paranoid mother.

Mia changes her mind abruptly when the gate comes into view. It's wide open. As if to prove a point, a car whizzes past on the road, driving well above the speed limit. Irritation rises in her throat. How utterly irresponsible. Elliot could have ridden his bike right out the gate, onto the road. Tara knows, more than anyone, that Elliot can't be trusted as much as other kids his age.

And it is becoming increasingly evident that Tara can't be trusted either.

15
Beth

Today

She is sitting in Pippa's kitchen, eating leftover lasagne. Pippa insisted that she come inside for a debrief. Then Pippa insisted that she have some dinner.

In between forkfuls of meaty lasagne, the older woman coaxes out the details.

'So let me get this straight,' she says in her calm doctor's voice. 'Someone stole your handbag at work, then used your keys to steal your car. How did they know where the car was parked?'

Beth shrugged. 'Either they already had that info through knowing me. Or they went around the main car parks trying out the keys until they got lucky.'

As she's speaking, she's dismissing the idea of the lucky thief. Kane *knows* she parks at the Sportsground. He knows that it's the cheapest all-day parking within walking distance of the clinic.

'How about your house keys? They've got those too?'

'Yeah,' Beth replies flatly. 'And my address is on my licence – if they didn't already know where I live. They can let themselves in, take whatever they want. Not that there's much to take!'

Beth had called the Police Assistance Line from the car park, who took her registration number, and details of her handbag and its contents. When asked about the time of the theft, all Beth could offer was an educated guess. The morning seemed most likely, which probably meant that the trail was as good as dead.

'So what happens now?' she asked once she'd relayed all the details.

'Now your registration number is in our system. If it comes within view of any of our highway patrol cars, an alert will go off and the officer will pull the driver over. Alternatively, if it's found abandoned or burnt out, we'll contact you to recover it.'

Abandoned she can live with. Burnt out would be a disaster.

Pippa is stuck on the problem of the house keys. 'Phone the property manager first thing in the morning and arrange to have the locks changed.'

Yes, of course. Another thing to add to her list, top of which is cancelling her credit and bank cards, which she'll do as soon as she gets home.

'Now, back to the car.' Pippa is nothing if not methodical. Beth can imagine her as a GP, ticking off the patient's symptoms, delivering her diagnosis clearly. 'You're telling me you don't even have basic third-party fire and theft insurance?'

'Just CTP,' Beth whispers. 'I drive really, really carefully.'

Her policy renewal arrived the same week Tilly's dentist declared that she had an underbite and needed an orthodontic plate. Fixing the underbite would save complications and costs in the future. As fate would have it, the plate cost the exact same amount as the insurance. So Beth had not renewed her comprehensive policy, and took a gamble that she could get by with compulsory third party: the legal minimum. She'd lost the gamble.

'Oh dear. Well, it is what it is. Hopefully, the car will turn up undamaged.'

Pippa's watery eyes are full of sympathy; she has already guessed that the lack of insurance wasn't an oversight or irresponsibleness or naïvety. There simply wasn't enough money.

Beth has to be realistic. 'Something tells me I'll never see the car again. Exactly a week after the break-in, too. What are the chances?'

Either she is the unluckiest person in the world or she has a target on her back.

She is just stunned that Kane would have the balls to do this straight after a visit from police.

~

Tilly is late going to bed and reading time is forfeited, which makes Beth feel guilty because her daughter desperately needs the one-on-one practice. But reading is excruciating when Tilly is overtired; better to do extra tomorrow than force the matter now.

Once Tilly is in bed, Beth phones her credit-card company and reports her card as stolen. At least some good news there: the last transaction was the parking fee this morning. Next is her bank, where she gets transferred to an after-hours call centre. Again, no suspicious transactions, something to be thankful for. Her next task is finding out what needs to be done to replace her licence, the irony being she'll only need a licence if she has an actual car to drive!

I just want it back, she whispers to the universe. *Doesn't have to be perfect. Just driveable.*

If it's Kane, he has gone to considerable trouble and risk, and chances are the car is gone for good. If the thief is someone else, there's hope.

She can get over the thought of hooligans taking it for a joy ride, or thieves using it as a getaway car, their grimy hands touching the steering wheel and radio controls. She can get over a dented bumper, a few new scratches, even a broken windscreen. She just can't afford to lose the car altogether.

She phones her dad, and relays the whole sorry story to him, asking if he can take Tilly to and from school tomorrow. Then she checks what buses she will need to catch in the morning, and texts Debbie to warn her that she's at the mercy of public transport and might be a little late.

Take the day off, hon, is Debbie's reply. *I'll ask Miranda to cover.*

Miranda is one of the casuals who is hungry for more hours.

Debbie is right: Beth needs time to sort herself out, to dust herself off.

She texts back to confirm that she'll take a day's leave. Then she puts her head in her hands and finally allows herself the luxury of weeping.

~

Sleep is impossible. Her thoughts keep skittering from one thing to the next. The practicalities of getting around, even for the short term, without a car. All the things on her to-do list tomorrow. Charlie's exceptional kindness and how she can possibly repay him. He always seems to be there exactly when she needs him. He was her first appointment the morning after the break-in, and her last appointment today, on hand and willing to help. It's no wonder she feels a lot closer to him now.

She reaches across to the bedside table to check the time on her phone. It's nearly midnight. Are she and Tilly safe? The house alarm is on, which is no consolation because the stolen keys have a fob attached and the alarm can be deactivated with the click of a button. How much will it cost to get the alarm reprogrammed?

For the last two years, Beth has scrimped and saved, barely managing to stay afloat. If she doesn't get the car back, she is going to sink, down, down, down to the bottom.

A few minutes later, she gives herself a lecture on staying positive.

The police might find the car undamaged. I could get a call in the morning and crisis over.

This goes on for a while, vacillating between the thief being a stranger, or Kane; vacillating between the best-case scenario and the worst-case scenario. It's exhausting, but Beth still can't sleep. The next time she checks her phone, it's 1.50am. Then she hears something. A loud creak. She strains her ears, heart thudding. Is there someone downstairs?

She sits up in bed, listens again, hears nothing beyond her own rapid breathing.

The alarm is on. There is no need to worry.

But they can deactivate the alarm.

It beeps when it's deactivated. I'm wide awake, I would have heard.

But what if I had one of those micro-sleeps and missed the beep?

This silent debate continues for a tense few minutes, until Beth finally reaches a conclusion. The creak is just the house settling. There is no one downstairs because they already got what they wanted: the car. Whoever stole it went to a lot of trouble. They wanted her little Corolla; no other car would do. And something tells her they're not stupid enough to be caught by highway patrol.

If her reasoning is correct, the thief should have no reason to return. She and Tilly are safe.

Beth finally falls asleep, defeat weighing her down in the bed.

16
Ryan

Three weeks ago

True to his word, Dino brings around the cherry picker the following weekend, the machine mounted on the back of his trailer. He stays to help while Ryan takes a chainsaw to the problem branches in the backyard. Once the branches have been felled and cut up for firewood, they drive the cherry picker around the front to prune the wattle trees and magnolias on the driveway. Ryan allows Elliot to come for a ride and his son is ecstatic, pointing and exclaiming at the view.

'I can see Dino's horses ... I can see some of the lake ... I can see ...'

Dino's easy friendship, Elliot's unbridled joy, the satisfaction of a hard day's work: it's a good day. Ryan barely thinks about the million-dollar reward or the 'inconsistencies' that Siobhan McAllen is so fixated on.

Monday is a crash down to reality. An unusually quiet day in the warehouse with far too much time to think about things. A car accident further ahead on the drive home, which causes a forty-minute delay and a sick feeling in the pit of his stomach on seeing the mangled cars, black tarp covering one of the windscreens. Pulling into the driveway, a flare of pleasure on passing the freshly pruned trees, soon after extinguished on noticing the squad car parked outside the house.

Ryan wants to turn back around and find somewhere to hide until the detectives are gone. Obviously, that's not an option. He pulls up next to the squad car, turns off the ignition, and takes a moment to coach himself.

Don't say too much or too little. Be calm. Appear to be cooperative.

Mia and the detectives are sitting at the kitchen table, everyone in the same positions as last time.

'Darling,' she says, her voice a notch higher than its usual pitch, 'you remember Detectives Goodwin and Stavros?'

It's not as if he could forget them. The double act. What questions have they divvied up between them today?

'Of course.' Ryan offers his hand to each detective before addressing his wife. 'Where's Elliot?'

She grimaces. 'Minecraft. It was the only way ...' She glances at the detectives, drawing them into their parenting world. 'Our child is obsessed with that game.'

Goodwin's smile has traces of impatience, her colleague is blank faced; these two are not so easy to divert today.

Ryan pulls out a seat and sits down, the chair at an angle, slightly away from the table. He wants to convey a little of his own impatience, of how much a fucking imposition this is after a long day at work and the commute from hell.

'We were just talking about Mia's job,' Goodwin says. 'At Citiware.'

Ryan nods in what he hopes is a non-committal fashion. Citiware is a safe, albeit unexpected, topic. Mia didn't last long enough to forge any friendships, or for anyone to get to know her beyond a superficial level. Her old colleagues have probably forgotten her name. Where are the detectives going with this?

'We've spoken to Geoff Hilton, your old boss. He said your departure from Citiware was very sudden.'

Ryan observes the rigidity in his wife's jaw, her hand on her lap – luckily not visible to the detectives sitting opposite – clenching. Mia's short-lived job is a sore point at the best of times. It had been going so well. He suspects that she still grieves the lost opportunity.

Mia's shrug is matter-of-fact, giving nothing away. 'Well, there seemed little point in staying once Tara resigned. I knew I wouldn't be able to find replacement childcare with just two weeks' notice. I was at that delicate stage of learning the ropes – I thought it best to retreat before they came to rely on me for anything. Geoff, who had hired me, was understandably disappointed. I felt awful – leaving an employer in the lurch is not my style – but a clean break seemed best ... On top of that, Elliot was back at school, which complicated things further. The idea was that Tara would accompany him on the bus, but the weather was awful that first week and they were sodden even before they got to the end of the driveway. I hadn't properly thought through the logistics of the school run when I accepted the job with Citiware. Totally my fault.'

Amy Goodwin looks vaguely sympathetic. Does she have children, or nieces and nephews? Can she appreciate the logistical difficulties with two working parents and school-going children? The detective turns her eyes to Ryan. 'And I believe you also took leave from work around this time?'

Fuck! They've been talking to his workplace, too. Ryan scrambles for a believable explanation. If Mia was at home with Elliot, why did he need to take time off as well? Think. Think.

'A couple of weeks later, if I recall correctly ... Mia came down with a bad flu and someone needed to mind Elliot, take him to and from school.'

Ryan sees Mia's face soften. His wife is pleased with his explanation. Still, it's deeply concerning that the detectives have spoken to both their employers. It suggests thoroughness. It suggests that he and Mia are central to this reopened investigation.

Stavros clears his throat, heralding his participation in the interview. 'We've had some results back from your DNA swabs.'

Already? That was quick. Did they ask for the tests to be rushed through?

The male detective's pale eyes fix on Mia. 'Mrs Anderson, your DNA is very heavily present in Tara's clothing and other belongings.'

At last, a question they had planned for. Mia doesn't rush in. She appears as though she is casting her mind back. 'That must be because I helped Tara pack. She couldn't zip up her bag and I took everything out, showed her how to roll the clothes so they would take up less space.'

'Even the toiletries?' he presses in a dubious tone.

'I would have touched the toiletries thousands of times while cleaning the bathroom. You have no idea how messy Tara was. She left things *everywhere.*'

A long pause, before Amy Goodwin speaks again. 'Well, that's all we need for now. Thank you for talking to us again. We'll be in touch if there's anything else.'

She tucks her notebook away in her pocket and Ryan has a premonition of the next time he'll speak to these detectives. An interview room with recording equipment. His rights being read to him.

He walks them to the door while Mia goes to convince Elliot that it's time to leave his computer-generated world for the real one.

Ryan stays at the doorway, watching the squad car until it's out of sight. Then he exhales a long, ragged breath. They're gone. For now.

A sulky-faced Elliot appears as he shuts the door; his son is never happy at being booted off his favourite computer game. Ryan opens his arms and Elliot, after a moment's hesitation, barrels into the embrace. His boy feels bigger in his arms. He's having a growth spurt, on his way to becoming a young man.

It's all for you. Ryan kisses the top of his son's head. *Everything we've done, and will do, is for you.*

17
Beth

Today

She wakes on Tuesday morning to the sound of a ringing phone. She reaches out one hand, feeling around the bedside table, before her grip closes around her iPhone's smooth rectangular shape. Groggily, she establishes two things: that the caller is her mum, and that she has slept in; it's gone 7.30am.

'Hi, Mum. Is everything okay?'

'Your dad messaged me about the car. Thought I might catch you on the way to work.'

'I took the day off ... Look, can I call you back in a minute?'

Beth jumps out of bed and hurries across the landing to check on Tilly. She finds her daughter still asleep, curled up on her side, Hippo encircled with both arms. She's dead to the world, and Beth decides that her girl would benefit from a day off, too. This is nature's way of rectifying the stress and anxiety of the last week.

Beth returns to her own room, slides back under the covers, propping an extra pillow behind her back. She calls her dad first, telling him there has been a change of plan and his taxi services won't be needed today after all. Then she calls the school office, leaving a voice message that Tilly won't be attending. Finally, she calls her mother back.

'Sorry about that, Mum. Just needed to check on Tilly. Can't believe we both slept so late.'

'I'm devastated for you about the car, darling. I know how much you rely on it.'

'Yeah. I'm trying not to assume the worst. It's hard, though.'

'Joe seems to think Kane might be behind it?'

'I don't know, Mum. I don't know what to think.'

'Men like him specialise in making you feel like that. Confused. Paranoid. Helpless.'

True, but Beth is weary from talking about Kane, and thinking about Kane. She's done little else all week. 'What's the weather like in London?' she asks, in a blatant attempt to move the conversation elsewhere.

'Miserable. My goodness, we're having the coldest, wettest March on record.'

Her mum sounds more British with every passing year. She still maintains that she and Tony will return to Australia to live, but her complete immersion in life over there implies differently. Linda and Tony moved to the UK when Beth was nineteen, shortly after their marriage. Tony received a job offer he 'couldn't turn down' and Beth point-blank refused to entertain the idea of joining them once she finished her training. She was too angry with her mum to see the opportunity for what it was. *Furious* with her for ditching Dad, for meeting someone new, for following that someone to another country, for having the gall to flourish after the divorce. Now that Beth is older, she can appreciate the dilemma that Linda found herself in. Romantic love versus parental love. Adventure versus the stalemate of a resentful child and a broken marriage. Her departure ultimately had a positive effect, forcing mother and daughter onto a different playing field. The long distance blurred their differences as well as any lingering blame.

113

Of course, Beth realises now that living in another country would have been a wonderful, exciting experience, which might have prevented her from manufacturing excitement in other more inappropriate ways here at home. Plus, being in London would have put her far beyond Kane's reach; she met him at the tender age of twenty and married him just two years later.

'So young,' Linda had commented when she returned for the wedding. 'What's the big hurry?'

No point in following that train of thought because as much as Beth regrets marrying Kane, she will never regret Tilly.

Beth cradles the phone to her ear while her mum talks about the weather, the latest gossip in her office, and Tony's obsession with buying a motorbike.

'Total midlife crisis,' her mum says, laughing. 'If he thinks for one minute that I'm getting on the back in my leathers ...'

Beth starts laughing, too. Talking to her mum always cheers her up, offering a glimpse of her whirlwind, carefree life, all the more precious because of the unhappy years she went through to reach this stage.

This could be me. I just need to put my head down, get through these tough years, and who knows what's waiting in the future?

Beth hangs up a few minutes later, shutting down further attempts by Linda to talk about the car and Kane. The fact is, her mum can't offer any practical help from the other side of the world. Keeping the conversation light is a salve for the clamour inside Beth's head.

~

Tilly wakes up just before nine; the last time she slept so late was when she was sick with bronchitis. Once again, she has a thousand questions about who took the car, will they go to jail, and how will she get to school tomorrow.

114

'Grandpa will take you to school, pumpkin ... Are you going to finish your cereal?'

Tilly shakes her head. 'I'm not hungry, Mummy.'

They have a quiet morning pottering around the house and Tilly bounces back a little. Beth is glad she kept her at home, dedicating time to reassure her, make her feel safe, rather than packing her off to school full of anxiety.

In the afternoon they go for a bike ride, from their house to the local soccer fields where there is a popular bicycle track and playground. Beth, in her endeavours to slow down to her daughter's speed, wobbles along and Tilly pumps her feet furiously. The sky is blue and cloudless; Beth inhales deep breaths which help contain her own anxiety bubbling beneath the surface.

Once they reach the fields, Beth sits down on a bench to watch her daughter do laps around the track, her helmet a blur of purple in the distance. Beth unzips their backpack and drinks from her water bottle before checking her phone. One new message. From Rachel, Kane's sister.

Hi B. Sorry for the delay getting back. Working nights and sleeping days, time just gets away from me. Kane has been seeing someone the last few months. Georgia is really nice and they seem happy together. Mum said he sold one of his investment properties, so cashflow is improved. I really don't think my brother tried to steal your car. I know he hasn't behaved well in the past but I think he has genuinely turned a corner. What more can I say? Lots of love to Tilly. R

Beth is overcome with a rush of complex feelings. In theory, she should be happy: Kane is always at his best when there is a woman on the scene. She should also be happy that he finally saw sense and sold one of the investment properties; Beth learned to hate those properties and what they signified in their marriage: that money and assets meant more than happiness and wellbeing. *Lots of love to Tilly*, Rachel signed off. She has made an art of sitting on the fence, balancing a careful relationship with her brother and niece, sacrificing Beth in the process. All their interactions are civil yet lacking in full-fledged support because that would mean taking sides.

Beth slides her phone into the front pocket of her backpack, pulling the zip on Rachel's text message. Tilly has abandoned her bike at the edge of the playground in favour of the climbing wall. There she is, still wearing her purple helmet, using all her tenacity to grab onto the climbing holds and hoist herself upwards. Kane has no idea what he is missing out on; no amount of money in the world can substitute for a child's love and presence in your life. Tilly barely asks about him. Just the odd remark or question in the six months since the change in custody arrangements. Beth expects that Tilly will have more questions and curiosity as she gets older.

I really don't think my brother tried to steal your car.

How can Rachel be so sure? And if it wasn't Kane, who was it? A random burglar? Beth is struggling to accept that explanation. Her car is a ten-year-old Corolla as opposed to Pippa's top-of-the-range Audi next door, not forgetting all the faster, newer cars at the Sportsground. If someone wanted a getaway car or the thrill of a joy ride, there wouldn't be a contest.

I know he hasn't behaved well in the past ...

Understatement of the year. This is the man who left her destitute, and then did his utmost to destroy the home she'd cobbled together. Last time, Beth knew who had invaded their space, touched their things, violated their sense of security. This time – if Rachel's summation is correct – it's a stranger. Somehow that makes it worse, not knowing who she is dealing with, not having a face she can match to her fears.

They seem really happy together.

Kane and Georgia. Their names sound good together, more rhythmic than Kane and Beth, which is too monosyllabic. Has her ex-husband really 'turned a corner'? Beth's thoughts jerk back to her mother, how Linda became her better self after her divorce. Maybe Kane is the same. Maybe he has begun to flourish, too.

Her phone vibrates with another text. It's from Debbie.

Charlie just dropped a huge bunch of flowers to reception for you. He was super disappointed you weren't here. Wow, he is almost too good to be true.

18
Mia

Two years ago

Tara goes on another date on Wednesday night. A different guy to the one who picked her up on Saturday. Dark hair instead of fair. Blue car instead of black. Driving too fast, again. Skidding wheels when he hits the brakes. He gets out of his car, and Mia is surprised to see that he's older, mid to late thirties. He stands for a moment to survey the façade of the house, in the manner of a real-estate agent considering it for listing. His clothes (dark pants and sports jacket) and car (a Mercedes SUV) seem to support that sort of profession. He has a good look around before ringing the doorbell. Mia sees it all from the far side of the garden, where she has been picking some greenery for the house. She instinctively steps to the side so she's screened by one of the bushes; she sees him, but he doesn't see her. Not even when she extracts her phone from her back pocket, zooms in on the registration plate and takes a photo. She can't explain why she takes the photo, only that something about this man makes her feel threatened. His arrogant driving, for a start. The age difference, too.

Tara answers the door and a passionate embrace dissuades Mia from walking over to remind her about the gate. Instead, she sends a text.

Have fun. Don't forget the gate.

They spoke about it after the last incident, so Tara *shouldn't* forget. But Tara's memory is haphazard. She only half-follows Mia's directions on what food Elliot should eat, how much screen time he should have, what routine he should follow. Why should the gate be any different?

In an attempt to soothe her irritation, Mia inhales the scent of the greenery in her hand, cuts of fern and silver dollar eucalyptus. Tara said nothing about going out tonight but maybe she mentioned her plans to Ryan: she seems to confide more in him. It's a weeknight; does this mean she'll be groggy and hungover for Elliot tomorrow? No, Mia shouldn't assume the worst. Tara could be off to the cinema or even a romantic stroll by the lake.

'You need to remember what it's like at that age,' Ryan has said, numerous times. 'They don't want to stay home. *Anywhere* is better than home. *Anyone* is better than the people they live with.'

Mia has tried to resurrect memories of when she was Tara's age. At nineteen, she was in her first year at university and had been dating Ryan for two years. Yes, those were carefree days, but as far as she can recall they were far from wild. Money was short, which limited what they could get up to, and she wanted to do well in her degree; hangovers were unaffordable, inconvenient and rare.

Mia comes back inside and arranges the greenery in the tall glass vase that resides on the hall table. The vase was a wedding present; she and Ryan will be ten years married in a few weeks. It has been a good ten years, albeit a hard ten years. All the ups and downs of family life have drawn them even closer together. A second honeymoon would be a lovely way to mark the milestone. Maybe in a few months' time, when their bank balance is healthier.

Ryan passes through the hall, a fresh towel in hand for Elliot, who is in the bath.

'Looks good,' Ryan says, admiring her work with the eucalyptus and fern.

'Did Tara tell you she was going out?' Mia asks, while snipping one of the stems to get the right length.

'Yeah, she said she wouldn't be late.'

Point proven. Tara definitely prefers to confide in Ryan.

'It was a different bloke who picked her up just now. Did she tell you *that*?'

Ryan laughs. 'Yeah. I think our Tara is a bit of a player.'

'And he's a lot older than her. He's our age, at least.'

'Yeah, she said that.'

So, Tara is not just confiding about her social plans, she's divulging details of her love-life, too. Mia is unsettled by this. Is Tara trying to convey to Ryan that she's attracted to older men? Or is she trying to make him jealous?

Her husband continues on his way, his voice echoing from the bathroom as he coaxes Elliot out of the bath.

Mia goes to fetch a jug of water, making sure not to overfill the vase. Ten years. She has been one hundred per cent faithful during their marriage, and for most of their dating years, except for one small indiscretion in her second year of uni. She has always assumed that Ryan has been faithful too, despite being aware that other women find him attractive. Dark good looks and strong body, packaged with a caring nature. What's not to like?

Tara clearly fancies him. When she's not locked in her room, she seeks him out for conversation. They've been watching a TV show together: *Stranger Things*. Tara's got Ryan hooked on it; apparently she used to watch it with one of her sisters back at home. But this feels like another level: telling Ryan details about her boyfriends, blatantly letting him know that she's available, perhaps sexually active. Is having a 'player' in the house tempting fate? Has the thought crossed Ryan's mind?

120

Mia remembers reading somewhere that the seven-year itch is not really a thing. It's the ten-year mark that's the danger point, when most couples are at their unhappiest.

She picks up the water jug and the scissors, stifling the urge to stab the sharp point of the scissors into something.

~

Tara does not come home early as promised. Mia stays up late, engrossed in the Celeste Ng novel. The fact that the book keeps her interest is a measure of how good it is. She forgets about Tara for a couple of hours, forgets about the stresses of finding her feet at work, forgets about the reported ten-year itch. The family in the novel are so sharply drawn; Mia can already anticipate how the discussion will go at book club next week. Kellie and Heather will have opposing views, Mia will be somewhere in the middle. Book club usually involves heated debates, raucous laughter and far too much wine.

It's midnight when she closes the book, with about seventy pages left to read. Ryan went to bed hours ago. Does Tara have her key? *Where the hell is she?*

Mia is climbing into bed when she hears the sound of an engine outside, voices calling goodbye, tyres turning on gravel, and the engine fading into the distance again.

The front door slams shut. Mia badly wants to go out there. To see Tara and establish what state she is in. Has she been drinking? Did she have sex with that older man? A crash from the bathroom. Something dropped? Swearing by Tara. The flush of the toilet, water running from the tap, the bathroom door being opened and shut (none too quietly). More thuds and thumps until the girl is finally, finally in bed. Is this what it will be like when Elliot is older? Lying awake, waiting for him to come home, imagining the narrative of the night he has had from the noises he makes? Probably not. Deep in her heart, Mia knows that Elliot will be a homebody, one of those young adults who regards gaming as their social life.

~

Tara is as hungover as all hell the next morning. She stumbles into the kitchen, slitted eyes, reeking of alcohol and cigarettes.

'Are you even in a fit state to take care of Elliot?' Mia asks, not bothering to disguise how furious she is.

'I swear I didn't have that much. Only three or four. Must've been dehydrated. It was so bleedin' hot yesterday.'

Yeah, right. Blame the heat. Blame anything but her own recklessness and bad decision-making.

Tara disappears to the bathroom for an extended time. Mia checks her watch. She should really get on the road; she has a client meeting first thing. Tara isn't throwing up in there, is she? Probably not wise to leave until she comes out.

Mia is waiting, tapping her fingers impatiently on the counter, when Tara's phone – which is right next to her – lights up with an incoming text.

Hey there. Hope you had a good night. Just to let you know you left the front door unlocked and the gate open. Lucky we still had all our worldly possessions this morning. Ryan

Mia is stunned. Not just at the dire lapse in security and Tara's deplorable carelessness. Ryan's tone is friendly, jokey, intimate; it should be angry.

What other texts have they exchanged? How close have they become? Mia could check if she wanted to. She remembers Tara's passcode: 527527.

Tara, pale-faced and with a fine sheen of sweat on her forehead, has reappeared.

'I'll be fine once I have a Coke,' she declares, on seeing Mia's livid expression. 'Might make myself some Vegemite toast, too. Elliot, where are you hiding? Breakfast is outside this morning. I need lots and lots of air.'

Mia puts her bag strap on her shoulder. She feels betrayed. Ryan should have texted *her*, not Tara. Together, they should have decided the most appropriate course of action. Instead it feels like he has circumvented her. Let Tara off with a gentle rebuke when she deserves to be hollered at.

Well, Mia is not going to let Tara off so lightly. It's time to set some new rules.

'Listen up, Tara. Apparently, the front door was unlocked when Ryan left this morning, not to mention the gate.'

Tara's mouth forms a silent 'oops', which only serves to infuriate Mia further.

'I don't know quite what to say about the front door – how basic does it get? – but I do have a solution for the gate. Your friends can drop you at the end of the driveway. The walk will do you good. Might even sober you up a bit.'

If Tara wants to act like a child, then Mia will treat her like one, with privileges being taken away as a result of her misbehaviour.

Mia turns on her heel and walks out, Tara's hatred radiating behind her.

19
Ryan

Three weeks ago

He staggers through the next few days. Work, home, bed. At work he goes through the motions, concentrating just enough to get the job done and not cause an accident. At home, he and Mia are on tenterhooks. Waiting for the phone to ring, or – worse – a knock on the door. Waiting for Elliot to fall asleep at night so they can retreat outside and release all the things they've been bottling up. Sitting with feet dangling in the pool, having whispered conversations under the cloak of darkness. Mainly rehearsing their story, and trying to anticipate what the police will do next. In bed, he and Mia lie next to each other, a strained distance between their bodies. It takes him hours to fall asleep at night. The nightmares are waiting for him as soon as he lets go of consciousness.

On Wednesday Mia visits one of the library branches in Newcastle, using a fake name to purchase a guest ticket for use of the computer facilities. She trawls the internet for cases that have been solved as a result of a reward; not so many, it turns out.

'Apparently, very few police rewards are paid out. It's not as easy as it sounds to make a successful claim,' she reports back to Ryan.

'Then why offer all that money?'

'It's not about money, it's about publicity. Offering a million dollars generates new press coverage, catches the public's attention.'

On Thursday, Mia goes to a different library branch and uses a different fake name. This time her search is specifically on Siobhan McAllen. Interviews she has given over the last two years. Television, radio, newspapers, social media; Tara's mother has been very vocal.

'She's dogged,' Mia says to Ryan, later that night. 'She has never given up. I admire that, even though it makes things difficult for us.'

'Nothing about why she's so sure it wasn't an accidental drowning?'

'Nothing. Feels like a deliberate omission.'

Ryan hears Siobhan's voice replaying in his head: *A mother knows her child inside out ... All the small little things that make them who they are ...*

He hears her voice when he's in the car, when he's operating the forklift at work, even when he's playing with Elliot. How Siobhan enunciated her words, confidence underlying her anguish. Confidence that her instincts were correct. Confidence that she would find out what really happened. Confidence that there would be justice.

What does Siobhan know that they don't? Are the police operating on the same knowledge, or some other driving factor? Ryan is stunned that they crosschecked dates with his and Mia's employers. It's obvious that he and Mia are central to whatever investigation is occurring. It's obvious there will be further – more formal – discussions with police. It's obvious they're entering a tumultuous few weeks. At a minimum.

Elliot has picked up on the tension in the house, resulting in more tantrums, meltdowns and time-outs than usual. Ryan and Mia are not as patient with him, or as diligent about his routine, even though they're trying their best to act normal. With each passing day, the tension seems to ramp up another notch and their small family buckles under the pressure.

'They have nothing,' Mia whispers into the inky darkness as they lie in bed on Friday night. 'We need to keep remembering that.'

She's right. No body. No witnesses. A reward – no matter how large – cannot manufacture evidence. A mother – no matter how zealous – cannot make something from nothing.

For the first time all week, Ryan falls asleep almost straight away. He is immediately engulfed in one of his recurrent nightmares: the freeway, the burning truck. The traffic jam of all traffic jams. Black smoke. Searing heat. Rising panic. People out of their cars, walking up and down the bitumen, talking on their phones. Choppers hovering overhead, calling in details to news stations and media. Sweat trickling down his back. Smoke and anxiety clogged in his throat. How much longer?

An accident involving a fuel tanker, according to the radio. A fireball that has incinerated three other vehicles. At least four fatalities. A catastrophe.

The other drivers are on their phones, talking to family members and friends, killing the hours. Ryan has no one to call, no one he can talk to. He is alone. But he is not alone, and that is the true horror.

Flames and black smoke plume into the sky. The heat is intensifying. Everything seems brighter. The fireball is coming his way, destroying everything in its path.

But instead of running and shouting and trying to escape – which is how the nightmare usually ends – Ryan surrenders to the oblivion.

He opens his eyes with a deep sense of resignation. His Apple Watch blinks on his wrist: 3.05am.

Sleep does not come again. Through the dead hours he lies perfectly still, while Mia tosses and turns next to him. With each passing hour his thoughts become more certain about what they must do next.

20
Beth

Today

The car is gone. Even though she accepts this fact, she still phones the Police Assistance Line every day. The person who answers the call is generally sympathetic yet businesslike.

'The car has not been detected by highway patrol's number-plate recognition.'

'None of the abandoned or burnt-out vehicles over the last few days match its VIN.'

'We've reviewed CCTV in the area. Unfortunately, we have no images we can use to identify a person of interest.'

'Have you contacted your insurance company?'

Beth hobbles through the week, relying on buses that seem to arrive too early or too late, relying on her dad to help with Tilly. The school run puts Joe significantly out of his way, as well as impacting his start and finish times at work. At each handover, she profusely thanks and apologises to him.

The property manager arranges for a locksmith to change the locks without any charge; Beth is so grateful she gets teary on the phone. The house-alarm technicians are less generous: $600 for reprogramming the alarm and replacing the fobs. Beth pays the invoice with her rent money, putting her faith in the kindness of the property manager.

What am I going to do? she asks herself a thousand times a day.

Occasionally an optimistic voice pipes up: *The car might turn up. This could still turn out okay.*

Then the voice of reason: *You're deluding yourself. The car is gone.*

Tilly has a birthday party on Saturday morning in Merewether. At Pippa's insistence, Beth borrows her neighbour's car for a few hours. The Audi is a beautiful drive. Leather steering wheel, an excellent stereo system, and a sunroof that slides back to reveal a rectangle of perfect blue sky.

'I want a car like this one,' Tilly declares, perched in a car seat that is also courtesy of Pippa, who keeps it on hand for her grandkids.

Beth smiles at her daughter in the rear-view mirror. Their next car will be the very opposite of this. Their next car – if she can cobble some money together – will be an old banger, if she is lucky.

A bouquet of pink balloons tied to the letter box makes it easy to identify the house. Beth goes inside to introduce herself to the parents, a dozen squealing kids making the interaction brief. Two hours until Tilly needs to be picked up; just enough time to do the weekly grocery shop. But Beth doesn't turn back the way she came, which is the direction of the supermarket. She continues to the end of the street, takes a left and then a right, driving past familiar landmarks, including a playground she used to take Tilly to when she was little.

When Beth read the address on the party invitation, she must have made a subconscious decision to come back here. To see the house that was once her home. Eight years of her life, starting when she was in her early twenties and brimming with self-confidence, optimism and trust; finishing as a disillusioned and destitute single mother.

Kane and Georgia. They seem happy. Once again she is struck by the nice rhythm of their names when spoken together.

The house is Hamptons style, with a grey-and-white colour palette. Manicured front garden with the proverbial white picket fence: the picture of domestic happiness. And Beth was happy here, for the early years at least. According to Kane's sister, Georgia is happy, too. Probably too soon for her to notice anything amiss. How Kane avoids going to restaurants or spending unnecessary money. How he cares about cars, property and stock prices more than people. Has he suggested a joint bank account yet?

Beth can only hope that Georgia is more observant than she was, more clued in about money and the importance of not relinquishing control to someone else. Beth thought that her husband was being savvy, assumed that he had her best interests at heart. If it weren't for Tilly, she might still be living in that beautiful house, trapped, miserable and confused about what to believe.

There's movement at the house, the garage door trundling open to reveal two shiny cars. Kane's white BMW (an upgrade since the divorce – her ex-husband doesn't scrimp when it comes to himself), and a black four-wheel-drive that must belong to Georgia. Kane and a woman are standing to the side of the four-wheel-drive. Beth stares at the woman. Blonde shoulder-length straight hair. Tall. Well-dressed. As Beth watches, Kane leans in to kiss her.

That's one of the things that was so confusing. Kane, even when he was at his most controlling and miserly, always kissed Beth goodbye on her way to work or the shops, or even if she was just going to the park with Tilly.

'A kiss costs him nothing,' Caitlin pointed out once.

True. But a kiss, at its most basic, is a sign of caring about someone. This was the same man who was unperturbed by the fact that his wife couldn't afford a cup of coffee, not to mention sneakers that didn't have holes in their soles. This was the same man who resented every cent spent on Tilly, even to the point of insisting that the baby didn't need a pram. 'Waste of money. Wait until she's big enough for a stroller. We can carry her around till then.'

Again, it was Caitlin who summed it up. 'So you're telling me he has two investment properties and he's penny pinching over a fucking pram?'

Another thing that confused Beth: why did she feel so battered and broken when he'd never been violent and rarely raised his voice?

'Financial abuse is as real as physical abuse, hon,' Caitlin said gently.

Financial abuse: so there was a term for what this was, this day-to-day poverty and powerlessness. Kane wasn't being money-smart or plain old frugal: he was using money to control her life, and Tilly's. The behaviour had been there from the start, the obsession about keeping expenses to a minimum. Beth had found excuses and, even though it got annoying at times, she was grateful that he watched things so closely. But Tilly's arrival brought full illumination to the issue; Beth could no longer justify his behaviour.

'We're not poor, Kane. Why are you acting like we are?'

'Stop being dumb. Cashflow and assets are totally different things.'

'Kane, babies need stuff. Of course there are more expenses.'

'I didn't agree to a baby. The timing wasn't right. We should have waited.'

Beth is convinced that the timing would never have been right for Kane. He never bonded with Tilly, not as a newborn, not as a toddler, not even as a relatively independent and engaging preschooler. Where does Georgia stand on the babies front? Have they discussed it?

The black four-wheel-drive reverses out of the garage, down the driveway and out onto the road. Its blonde driver pauses to put on her sunglasses, affording Beth a close-up view. Georgia is not as young as she expected. Early thirties: still a fair bit younger than Kane but old enough to be appropriately wary in a new relationship. She glances at the house, seems to notice that the garage door has not been closed and leans down. The door begins to close, suggesting that Georgia is in possession of a remote control, suggesting that Georgia is more than just a visitor.

'Just don't let him near your bank account,' Beth says out loud. 'And whatever you do, don't accidently fall pregnant.'

~

Beth has every intention of driving away after Georgia leaves the house. She got what she came for. She has established that her Corolla isn't parked in Kane's garage or on the street outside. She even caught a glimpse of her ex-husband's new woman, proof that she exists.

But Beth doesn't drive away. She opens the door of Pippa's Audi and gets out. She smooths down her skirt and runs a hand through her hair before crossing the street and walking up the achingly familiar driveway. She rings the bell, at the same time noticing how badly her hand is shaking. Such an odd sensation to be ringing the bell of a house that was once her home.

Why is she doing this? Things have been settled with Kane the last few months. Why stir things up? Because she can't think of anyone else in the world who would want to steal her car. Because this man has left her destitute once before, and she simply can't allow it to happen a second time.

Footsteps in the hallway. Her heart hammering in her chest. A final pep talk under her breath.

Don't say you were in the area – he won't believe you. Just ask him if he did it.

The door opens and he recoils on seeing her. 'You!'

He's wearing designer jeans and a short-sleeved patterned shirt. His hair looks suspiciously dark, no sign of the usual flecks of grey. A new hairdresser or a home-dye courtesy of Georgia?

Beth is out of breath even before she starts speaking. 'Look, something happened, and I just need to ask you outright ...'

His expression is angry and mocking at the same time. 'Is this about the break-in at your place? Thanks for giving my name to the cops, by the way. You're fucking unbelievable, you know that?'

'My car was stolen on Monday,' she continues, her voice wavering. 'The thief tried a few times before they were successful. It seems they wanted my old Corolla when they had a choice of faster, newer, more valuable cars. I just can't imagine why. Then I thought of *you*.'

No matter what alibi he provided the police, the narrative fits with his obsessiveness, his fixation about balancing the books and being compensated for the car he lost at the time of the separation. It fits with his desire to show her that he still has control, that she is nothing without him. It fits with her deep-down fear that Kane will be there for the rest of her life, poised to leap out of the shadows and scuttle the building blocks of her new life.

The mocking has been replaced by unadulterated hatred. 'Fuck off, Beth. You're out of your mind ... I already *told* you ... stop blaming me for everything that goes wrong in your life.' Delivered in a perfectly calm tone. Then the door is closed in her face, decisively but without being slammed.

Beth is rooted to the spot by that same old confusion. His self-control, his refusal to shout, his deliberate way of moving and speaking. Is the venom in his tone down to her imagination? Is she actually out of her mind?

She finally turns and walks to Pippa's car, head down, suddenly fearful of encountering old neighbours. Then she drives away from her former home, her knees shaking so hard that she can't maintain a steady pressure on the accelerator. The playground that Tilly used to love is up ahead, a place to stop and recalibrate herself. God knows she had to do exactly that so many times before. Sitting on one of the metal benches, watching Tilly hurtling down the slide, unable to see a way out for them. Now, Beth pulls into one of the parking spaces and watches different children climb and slide, trying to find solace in the everyday normality of kids playing, laughing and crying.

He didn't even ask how Tilly is.

He would never admit it even if he had taken the car.

But the fact that Georgia is apparently living with him offers a degree of insight. She would've had something to say if her partner disappeared late at night, when the house break-in occurred. Likewise, she would have noticed a strange car parked outside the house – even briefly – or dodgy-looking visitors coming to take it off Kane's hands. At the very least, she would be sensitive to her partner's odd or preoccupied behaviour.

The fact that Georgia is 'living in' and the relationship is still at that stage where there is a need to present one's best self points to the thief being someone other than Kane.

So who is it, then? And *why*?

21
Ryan

Two weeks ago

Bethany Jenkins. Date of birth. Address. Photograph. Everything he
needs to know about the woman who bought their old car is here,
filed away neatly with the other documentation. There's a black-and-
white copy of her licence, as well as the notice of disposal submitted to
Transport for NSW, in which many of the same details are repeated.

The photograph is indistinct, but Ryan can remember her regardless.

'I'm Beth,' she said, offering the abbreviation of her name along with
her slender hand to shake.

Dark auburn hair, faint freckles smattered across her nose, white
sneakers, cut-off shorts: the 'girl next door' look. She was with an older
man – her father? – and a kid, a little girl whose hair was a frizzier
version of her mum's. The girl played with Elliot on the trampoline
while her mum and grandpa examined the car. Ryan remembers
resistance when the adults decided on a test drive – the girl wanted to
stay on the trampoline with Elliot. She needed to be persuaded that it
wasn't appropriate for her to stay behind. Elliot protested, too. And
being Elliot, his protest escalated into a tantrum.

Ryan presents the paperwork to Mia. 'It's all here. Hopefully, she's at the same address and hasn't sold the car to someone else. Do you remember the little girl's name?'

Mia scrunches her face while she thinks. No doubt she is remembering the children bouncing and squealing, forming a fast friendship within minutes of meeting each other. The girl was a couple of years younger than Elliot; he always gets on better with younger kids.

'Tilly,' Mia says, after a long pause. 'Her name was Tilly. It suited her. She was a cute little thing.'

~

Ryan takes a detour on his way home from work the next day. He has no fixed plan other than to drive past Beth Jenkins's house. Maybe the car will be parked in the driveway or on the street and he'll have his answer. Maybe he'll catch a glimpse of her, or the kid, and he'll have half an answer. He is nervous; he has been thinking about this all day at work. His preoccupation caused a few mistakes, picking the wrong product for one of the orders, getting some paperwork mixed up, earning a few irate words from Paul, his boss.

Now he's here: Cabbage Tree Avenue. Old houses and new houses side by side. Single-level and two-storey, large concrete driveways, established gardens. Kids on bikes, people walking dogs. It looks like the kind of street where the neighbours know one another, care about one another. It looks like the kind of street where a strange car parked for more than a few minutes would get noticed by someone. His first drive-by informs him that the house is a red-brick duplex: shared driveway and co-joined garages with white-panelled doors. Ryan glances at the time on the car's dash: 6.30pm. Does Beth work? What time does she get home every day? Is there a man on the scene? Her dad was with her when she bought the car and Ryan immediately assumed that she was a single mother, but maybe her partner had a legitimate reason he couldn't be there that day.

The street is a cul-de-sac. Only so many times he can drive up and down before drawing attention to himself. He navigates the turning circle, comes back down the street on the opposite side, barely doing thirty. Still nobody coming or going. The house could be empty for all he knows. Ryan keeps driving for a few hundred metres, before turning down a side street and parking outside a well-maintained weatherboard house. Time for a short stroll.

He walks as slowly and as inconspicuously as he can, but unfortunately the result is the same as before. There is no sign of life outside the two-storey duplex. If he were walking a dog, he could at least pause outside the house, but he has no option but to continue on, round the bend to the cul-de-sac, where a neighbour mowing his lawn gives him a polite nod. Ryan tracks back the way he came, pausing across the road for a few moments, under the guise of answering a phone call.

Do you still live here, Beth? Do you still have our car? How does it feel to drive? Ever experienced a sense of foreboding getting behind the wheel? Ever felt blind panic on being stuck in a traffic jam? Or had the sense that you are not alone?

Still a couple of hours' daylight until house lights need to be turned on, which would at least tell him if someone is home. But hanging around that long would risk getting noticed. As though to prove this point, a woman wearing gym pants smiles quizzically as she approaches, as though she is trying to place which house he lives in.

Ryan returns to his car and resists the temptation to drive past the house one last time. He'll return in the morning. Tilly is school age, which means that they'll probably be leaving the house between eight and nine.

~

The next morning, on Mia's advice, he brings forward the time to 7.30.

'Beth will have a job,' his wife states. Her certainty is puzzling; she doesn't know the first thing about Beth's working life. 'I bet Tilly goes to before-school care.'

Ryan doesn't ask Mia why she feels so sure; he trusts his wife's instincts.

He calls in sick to work, not having to fake a croaky voice. 'Sorry, Paul. I was feeling shit yesterday, hence all the mistakes. Hope a day's bed rest will see me good.'

His boss is unimpressed. 'Not a good day to be sick, mate. We've got shitloads of orders to fill.'

The warehouse is a tough, unsympathetic place to work, with the unofficial expectation that employees soldier on through colds and other minor illnesses. Ryan has gone into work many a day when he should've been home in bed. On balance, he is owed this sick day.

'You actually *sound* sick,' Mia comments, when he hangs up the phone.

That's because he feels genuinely ill. His arms and legs are weak and shivery. He skips breakfast, baulking at the thought of cereal or toast. Is he really going to spy on a defenceless mum and her kid? Assuming they still live at the address, still have the car, what is he *actually* going to do about it? Steal it? Destroy it? What if he is seen? Or caught in the act?

He is still asking himself these questions when he parks a few hundred metres from Beth's house just after 7.30. There is only one way out of Cabbage Tree Avenue; Beth and her kid will need to pass this way at some point. His car is not visible if she looks out her window; neither is it visible to any of her immediate neighbours. There is a fair amount of activity on the street at this hour: cars reversing out of driveways, their drivers hopefully preoccupied with thoughts of the day ahead; a few passers-by, wearing suits and carrying laptop satchels, hurrying to the closest bus stop. Ryan convinces himself that people are too busy to notice him.

While he waits, he listens to talkback radio and scrolls through ABC News on his phone. His car window is open, so he can hear approaching vehicles and it's not necessary to stare ahead the whole time. There's a steady stream of cars, all colours and sizes, but at 7.50 he glances up to see the shape and colour he has been waiting for.

'There you are. Good morning, Beth.'

His hand reaches for the ignition, the engine charging to life. When the dark-grey Corolla has passed – with a flash of Beth's pale face and curly hair – he executes a U-turn and follows.

~

Beth Jenkins works in a busy clinic off Hunter Street called Wellbeing and Sports Massage Therapy. Her daughter, Tilly, goes to school at the local public primary school, about three kilometres from where they live. Mia was correct: Tilly attends before-school care. The little girl dragged her feet on the way into the single-level building, shoulders sagging under the weight of her schoolbag, her mum ushering her along. Ryan was parked across the street, watching, ready to pretend that he was looking at his phone if Beth happened to glance his way. She didn't.

Now he and Mia are sitting at home, outside on the patio, having a debrief. They've been avoiding conversations inside the house, for fear of police bugs. The midday air is thick with heat and the shriek of cicadas. Everything feels off kilter. The fact that Ryan is here at home instead of work. The hungry-sick feeling in his stomach; he is yet to have anything to eat today. Not to mention the surreal conversation with his wife.

'The car is garaged when Beth's at home and parked in a public car park when she's at work. This isn't going to be easy.'

'It is if you have the keys,' Mia points out. 'Then you're simply jumping in and driving off.'

'Accessing the keys means breaking into the house. When Beth and her kid are at home.'

Mia reaches across to squeeze his hand. 'None of this is pleasant. It's just something we have to do.'

True, and he has already proved that he can do things he never dreamed of doing. He is half-exhilarated, half-appalled by this morning's events. Trailing Beth's car through suburbia, striving to maintain a careful distance. The nervous wait while she went in and out of the childcare facility. Temporarily losing sight of the car at a busy intersection and having to take an educated guess that she had turned left. Once he had her in his sights again, the hardest thing was making sure he didn't get left behind at traffic lights. This involved some creative lane-changing, and sometimes getting a little too close for comfort. Terrifying but in a weird way thrilling, too. If he could remember Beth's face, he had to assume there was a risk that she could remember his.

You're being a good driver, Beth. Just don't look in your mirror, okay?

Beth drove her car decisively but carefully. She maintained a safe distance from the car in front and always stopped at orange lights. She only changed lanes when necessary, indicating well in advance and checking her blind spot.

Ryan felt a huge sense of relief when their tag-along journey ended at the Sportsground car park. He followed her through the entrance and waited to see which row she chose before taking the next one along. The rest of the escapade was by foot and a hell of a lot easier. Beth's steps were short and fast in her flat slip-on shoes. A ten-minute walk to her workplace, the glass doors affording him a view of Beth greeting the blonde woman behind the counter, before slipping on an aqua-coloured tunic: obviously her work uniform. Ryan went to a nearby café and called the number of the clinic, requesting a five-thirty appointment, claiming that he'd hurt his back at work and Beth had been recommended by a friend. The woman who answered the phone said that Beth's last appointment was at five, and it was already booked. Was tomorrow any good? Ryan replied that he 'would see what he could do', and hung up. He now knew what time Beth finished work, and approximately what time she would reach Tilly's childcare. He could even visualise her arrival at the centre, hurrying through the steel gates in her black jeans and t-shirt. He made two further calls, to a chiropractor and another massage therapist, to support his story of having a sore back.

'What's the best way to break into the house?' he asks his wife now, blinking on hearing the absurdity of his words. 'Hope she's stupid enough to leave a window open?'

'Beth is too careful to leave a window or door unlocked.'

That strange certainty from Mia again, but, in this instance, Ryan agrees with her. Beth *is* careful; he witnessed that this morning, watching her driving. She's someone who keeps to the rules, maybe even relies on the rules a little too much.

'So that leaves what?' He sucks in a breath of muggy air. 'Picking a lock? Smashing a window?'

'Can't smash a window if they're in bed upstairs,' Mia muses. 'You know, this doesn't need to be done all at once.'

'What do you mean?'

'Beth will have spare keys for the car – we gave her two sets, remember? You break into the house during the day, when they're not at home, and take the *spare* keys – with any luck, she won't even notice they're missing. Then you take the car from the car park – there's no need to return to the house.'

The seeds of a plan. Ryan feels a flare of admiration for his wife's problem-solving skills. Shame that her skills are being used for a criminal act instead of a salaried job.

'Good idea ... But if I smash a window or damage a lock, Beth will check to see if anything is missing. And she'll be on alert, probably let the police know.'

Mia shrugs. 'Then no sign of forced entry, if we can help it.'

Ryan needs a more detailed plan; how, exactly, are they going to pull this off? He also needs food; he's starting to feel lightheaded. He realises that he forgot his medication this morning, which probably hasn't helped.

'Let's go inside. I'm finding it hard to breathe.'

The kitchen is at least ten degrees cooler. Ryan opens the fridge and gathers what he needs for a ham and cheese sandwich. Mia heads to the coffee table, where they keep a stash of magazines and old issues of the local newspaper. She begins to flick through the stash.

'What are you looking for?' he asks, as he butters bread.

Her response is vague. 'I remember reading something somewhere ...'

Ryan assembles his sandwich and after a few bites his equilibrium is restored. He'll return to Beth's street this afternoon, see what he can learn about the next-door neighbours. The houses are co-joined, which means that breaking glass or suspicious behaviour would be especially noticeable. Hopefully, the neighbours are at work most of the day, too. Hopefully, they're the disinterested rather than the nosey types, although he has the sense that it's a close-knit neighbourhood.

'Aha!' his wife exclaims, intruding on his thoughts.

Mia, a triumphant smile on her face, is holding up a dog-eared newspaper.

She slaps it down on the counter, pointing at the headline she wants him to read:

Thieves remove roof tiles to break into family home.

22
Mia

Two years ago

The house has an unpleasant atmosphere in the following days. Tara goes through the motions of taking care of Elliot, a 'fuck you' expression on her face whenever Mia imparts instructions. Mia tries to focus on what's important: transitioning Elliot back to school – first day back is next week – while maintaining her performance at work. Back to school means back to Elliot's medication and its myriad side-effects, back to a more regimented and demanding routine, and back to her child feeling overtired and overwhelmed in the evenings; a few extra tantrums are on the horizon. Tara will get the school bus with him in the mornings and afternoons – tedious for Tara but an adventure for Elliot, who has always been driven to school. In between school hours, Mia will set Tara some tasks – cleaning, laundry, some basic prep for dinner – which should ease her own domestic load. On the work side, Mia will have to continue learning, concentrating hard and putting her best foot forward. There is still a lot to get to grips with at Citiware, each day revealing new aspects to her job. Just when she thinks she is getting a handle on things, something new pops up and it's back to Geoff for direction. She is lucky that her new boss is so supportive and kind.

'Ask me anything,' he says regularly. 'I'd rather you ask me twice or three times than not ask at all.'

Despite his reassurances, Mia is well aware that she is under scrutiny. She has to remind herself that it's nothing personal: it's natural to keep a close eye on new employees, to evaluate whether they'll last beyond the probation period.

Lucky Tara. No probation period or pressure to impress. No threat of her job going to someone else. No juggling between work and family. But she's too young to realise how easy she has it, too self-absorbed to see the big picture. Hopefully, Elliot returning to school will make the job more appealing to her. Yes, there is the pain of bussing it there and back, but her reward is six hours a day without her young charge.

Mia can only imagine what Tara is relaying back to her friends and family in Ireland. Probably all sorts of derogatory statements about Mia and her obsession with routine. Probably exasperated anecdotes about Elliot and unbridled relief at his imminent return to school. What does she say about Ryan? Has she admitted to her friends back home that she finds him attractive?

The weekend finally comes around and Saturday morning is luxury: no handover before leaving for work, no need to worry about Elliot's welfare throughout the day, no bored or 'fuck you' expression to deal with. Tara, as is her habit, spends half the day in bed. Mia keeps busy with all the housework that didn't get done during the week; the truth is that Tara creates more mess than Elliot. At 3pm the Irish girl appears, yawning and stretching, before making herself some Vegemite toast, for which she seems to have developed a taste. The next two hours are spent getting ready to go out. A shower that goes on for half an hour and empties the hot-water tank. Fake tan, with residue left behind on the towels that Mia placed in the bathroom only that morning. The air in the bathroom and outside her bedroom is thick with chemicals: a toxic mix of hairspray, perfume and nail polish.

'Ready?' Ryan asks, when she totters into the kitchen at 5.30. They are seated at the table, having an early dinner, which Tara declined when asked if she wanted something to eat before going out.

'Yeah. How do I look, Elliot?'

'You look *gorgeous*,' her son says, his reply sounding coached.

'Am I going to find a hot man tonight?'

He giggles. '*Hundreds* of hot men.'

Good lord. What sort of ideas is she putting in his head? He is at an age where things stick: the notion of 'man hunting' and implied sex; the visual of Tara's skimpy dress and vampish make-up.

'Want to come for a ride to the station?' Ryan asks Elliot.

'Yes. Yes. Yes.' Elliot jumps to his feet. His meal isn't anywhere near finished.

There is suddenly a lot for Mia to process. A lift to the train station that was prearranged between Ryan and Tara without any mention to her. A sudden tightness to Tara's expression, which suggests that she would prefer that Elliot did not come along. Elliot's half-finished meal, tangible proof of a different set of rules now that Tara lives here.

'Hang on a minute. What about Elliot's dinner? Tara, can you catch a later train?'

'Yeah, but I'll be, like, seriously late.'

Now Tara is looking upset. Who is she meeting? That arrogant older man or someone new? One thing is for sure: it can't be anyone so important that they can't wait a half-hour.

Ryan opens one of the kitchen cupboards and produces a Tupperware container. 'Elliot can take his dinner with him. How about a picnic in the car, mate?'

Elliot whoops and Tara's face brightens. Because Mia is looking closely, she catches the girl mouthing 'thank you' to Ryan. Getting a 'please' or 'thank you' from her is a rarity; it appears she saves her manners for Ryan.

Less than a minute later, the front door slams and Mia has been catapulted from a pleasant family meal to sitting alone, seething. She begins to tidy up, gathering plates, scraping leftovers into the bin. Her arms feel strangely rigid. There is a hard lump of fury in her chest.

Tara has not only been confiding in Ryan, she's been colluding with him: everything about what just occurred points to them being allies. Even Elliot seems to be edging over to Tara's camp. Fascinated with the view she affords into the world of 'grown-ups', a world consisting of alcohol, hangovers and boyfriends. Elliot is not ready for that; he has neither the emotional intelligence nor the maturity. Tara is damaging his innocence, in the same flippant manner in which she's trying to damage Mia's marriage.

Mia has underestimated the girl. Even joked to Kellie that Tara's infatuation is a positive thing, making the job more engaging. She realises now that the attraction is no laughing matter. Tara is selfish, conniving and devoid of morals. Ryan is responding to her. Even Elliot is responding.

Mia and Ryan need to reassess the parameters of her employment and establish rules and boundaries.

I want her gone. The thought comes to Mia unbidden. *I don't want her presence tarnishing my husband, or my son, or my home. I. Want. Her. Gone.*

But it's pointless thinking those kinds of thoughts. She might want Tara gone, but the truth is she can't do without her.

~

Mia wakes up early on Sunday morning, her eyes popping open. What was that sound? Dawn is seeping through the crack in the curtains, shrouding the room in grey light. She listens for a moment and hears it again: the sound of someone retching. Her first thought is that it's

Elliot and she leaps out of bed. Previous vomiting bouts have involved numerous changes to bed linen and clothes: a sick child and extra laundry are more than she can handle right now.

But it's not Elliot who's kneeling over the toilet bowl in the bathroom. Tara looks up when she hears Mia come in. Her face is deathly white, yesterday's eyeliner smudged under her eyes, giving her a ghoulish appearance.

'Dehydration again?' Mia asks pointedly, staying safely near the door.

Some dry heaving in response. Then muttering. 'Never again ... Never, ever, ever ...'

The vomiting bout over, the girl rises from her knees, flushes the loo, and goes to the basin. She lowers her head to the tap, takes a mouthful of water, spits it out and repeats the process. The effort seems to sap her of the little strength she has; she leans heavily on the edge of the vanity.

'Never felt so baaaaad in my life.' A declaration to her reflection rather than Mia, who is standing just inside the door.

The girl in the mirror has lank hair, half-closed eyes and a sickly skin tone; she looks like she might keel over.

Mia finally feels a flare of sympathy. She wasn't one for hangovers at Tara's age – she was far too focused and sensible – but she has suffered the occasional clanger. The awful nausea and dizziness. The inability to hold a thought for longer than a few seconds. The cold sweat, weak limbs and slow reaction times.

She'd be the most hard-hearted person in the world not to feel some sympathy. 'Come on. Back to bed. I'll get you a glass of Coke and you can sleep it off.'

Mia guides her down the corridor to her room, the door still open after her hasty exit. She helps her into bed: there's a smell of stale booze in the room – at least it's not vomit. Minutes later she returns with a glass of icy-cold Coke and some Panadol. She holds the two tablets in the palm of her hand, to make it easier for Tara to manage.

'Never again,' she croaks, before flopping back against the pillows.

Mia smiles tightly and closes the bedroom door behind her.

No point in going back to bed. She is wide awake, might as well start her day. She pauses on her way to the kitchen, to regard the front door: did Tara remember to lock it? The doorknob doesn't budge when she tries to turn it: locked. What about the gate? How *did* Tara get home last night?

Instead of going to the kitchen and making herself a coffee, she decides to take a walk, slipping on sneakers from the shoe rack in the hallway. Sneakers and pyjamas: one of the benefits of living off the beaten track is not having to care about being seen.

The air outside is fresh and still, poised for the day to begin. Mia folds her arms around herself – her pyjamas are summer ones and it's a few degrees cooler than she expected. She makes her way down the driveway with long, determined strides. Gravel crunches under her feet. Birds chirp in the wattle and magnolia trees. Mia takes deep breaths of scented air in an attempt to clear her tangled thoughts.

What are we going to do about Tara? Am I expecting too much of her? Will everything settle once Elliot's at school? Do I really need to worry about her and Ryan?

Mia is sure her husband would not be attracted to the shivery, pathetic creature in the bathroom this morning. As for the orange-skinned, bejewelled and shoe-teetering version last night? Hardly. Ryan would never choose someone so artificial or brash. Understated and sophisticated, that's his type. *Mia* is his type.

The gate is locked. Well, that's something at least. Mia didn't hear an engine, so Tara must have taken her advice and asked whoever it was to drop her at the gate. Mia has an amusing image of the girl staggering up the driveway in her platform shoes. She's smiling as she turns around to return to the house. Presumably Tara took off those ridiculous shoes, although the gravel wouldn't feel nice in bare feet. Whatever she had on her feet, Tara *had* made it home, and aside from her head and stomach – which are far from optimal right now – she is in one piece. The gate is locked and maybe, just maybe, Tara has learnt her lesson.

Mia is only a hundred metres into the return walk when she notices something foreign at the edge of the driveway. Silver, glittery, instantly familiar. She bends down, picks it up: Tara's phone in its garish case. The phone screen has a long scratch on its surface; she must have dropped it last night, too drunk to notice. Mia presses the home button and the passcode screen immediately lights up. She tells herself that she is only entering Tara's passcode – 527527 – to ensure that the phone is properly working. It is.

She looks around her, illogically checking for someone watching, bearing witness. Of course there isn't anyone watching. It's just her and this phone – and a choice. Option one: turn off the phone and return it to its owner, who should be damned grateful it's been found (it could have been left in any bar or nightclub in Newcastle). Option two: see this incident as fate, offering the chance to decipher Tara's intentions about the future and to prepare accordingly.

Mia's conscience puts up a protest. *You shouldn't invade her privacy. How would* you *feel if someone read* your *personal messages?*

But doesn't she have a right to know exactly what she is dealing with here? Is Tara making serious moves on her husband? Has she been sending a litany of complaints to friends and family back home? Is she planning on backing out of their contract before the agreed six months are up?

It's a contest: Tara's privacy versus Mia's job, husband and financial security.

No real contest. Mia sits down on an old tree stump and opens up Tara's Messenger.

23
Ryan

One week ago

Nothing goes to plan. Waiting until Beth's elderly neighbours go out, knees quaking as he climbs the ladder: he has never been good with heights. Clambering across the roof tiles, terrified of falling, even more terrified of being seen, questioned, exposed. All for nothing because the internal door between the garage and the house is locked. It's a simple lock but that doesn't change the fact that he doesn't have the know-how to jemmy it. He is barely back in his car with the ladder stowed in the boot when the neighbours reappear.

The second time round he opts for the protection of darkness and entering on ground level. He has practised how to jemmy a lock and believes himself more prepared. He gets a bigger shock than anyone when the alarm begins wailing; Beth must have heard him downstairs and activated it. He should have prechecked for its existence: dumb, dumb, dumb. Another close escape. Another step closer to having a nervous breakdown.

Stealing Beth's handbag and keys from the clinic is by far the most ambitious plan. Ironically, it goes without a hitch: not a soul in reception to stop him. Now Ryan is driving the Corolla down a dirt road, which is off a quiet side road, which is off a lonely section of main road about fifty kilometres from the freeway. No houses or buildings or even farmland anywhere in the vicinity. After studying dozens and dozens of aerial shots, Mia settled on this area and it's just as remote and desolate as it looked online. Ryan is following Mia's written directions; his phone has been switched off since leaving home. A couple of kilometres down this dirt road, there's a sandstone platform where they'll burn out the car. The photos show adequate clearing so nearby trees or shrubs shouldn't catch alight: the last thing they need is to inadvertently start a bush fire. If the car shell is found at a later point, it can of course be identified by its VIN, which would make police suspicious. But suspicion is one thing, evidence is another. Despite scrupulous cleaning and scrubbing, Ryan and Mia were never 100 per cent confident that they'd eradicated all the evidence. And fire, according to Mia's research, is better at destroying DNA and trace fibres than water is. Her initial plan was to submerge the car in the lake, in a spot along the foreshore that was deep enough, vehicle accessible and suitably remote. But the internet reported tussles between the water police, the Roads and Maritime Services and the council as to whose responsibility it was to wrench vehicles from the water. If the vehicle is stolen, it's the water police's responsibility. If the vehicle poses a navigational risk, the RMS are responsible. Environmental concerns are the council's problem. Bottom line, the chances of the vehicle remaining submerged are slim – one of the relevant authorities would recover it. The fact that trace-fibre evidence and DNA can survive months of water submersion was another big deterrent.

Mia is waiting at their pre-arranged meeting spot, deep in the bush. She gets out of her Ford and points to where she wants him to go, a wordless 'Come on, let's get this over with'. The sandstone plateau is to the left of the track, beyond a thin layer of bush and scrub. The little car bumps over the undergrowth. The edge of the rock scrapes the underside but thankfully there's enough clearance to keep going.

Mia strides towards him, the hose and jerry can in her hand. Like him, she is dressed entirely in black – tank top, leggings and a cap shielding her upper face from the afternoon sun. She looks like a sleek actress from a movie set. He has the strange urge to kiss her, but her mouth is set in a thin line of concentration.

He pops the bonnet, and by the time he gets out to help, she has already attached the hose to the fuel line.

'Turn on the engine,' she commands.

The fuel oozes satisfyingly through the hose and into the jerry can. This is necessary to avoid an explosion that someone might hear or see from a distance. As it is, there should be enough combustible liquids and materials in the car to facilitate a hot, evidence-destroying fire.

Mia has a quick look inside the car when the fuel tank is drained.

She holds Beth's handbag aloft. 'This is hers?'

'Yeah. We should burn it.'

She shakes her head. 'I want the chance to look through it.'

He doesn't have the strength to argue with her; they mustn't waste time. He takes the jerry can around to the boot, where he splashes some petrol about. This is the area that needs to burn the hottest.

'Step back,' he says, giving his wife the can to hold. She takes three or four steps backwards.

He lights the match from what he perceives to be a safe distance, lobs it into the boot. Then he takes Mia by the arm, moves her further back.

'We should leave,' he says, his arm settling around her waist.

He feels her resistance before she voices it. 'I want to see it burn. I want to be sure it's done properly.'

And so they wait, Mia setting the timer on her watch. Vivid orange flames quickly consume the boot of the car. The bumper pops off, landing on the rock with a bang. The rear tyres explode, with a flare of white and a sound like a gunshot that makes Mia jump, then laugh. The fire transitions into the main cabin of the car, the air filling with the acrid smell of burning rubber and plastic. The windows shatter in a spectacular fashion, thousands of tiny crystals falling to create a carpet of glitter.

Watching the car burn is unexpectedly cathartic. Ryan wanted to get rid of it straight after the accident, but Mia argued it would look too suspicious. 'What? You want to pretend it's been stolen and make an insurance claim? Insurance companies employ detectives, Ryan. They don't want to pay out so they investigate, probably in more detail than police investigate. It wouldn't take them long to uncover that our previous nanny is missing, presumed drowned. They could easily make a connection.'

At Mia's insistence, they hung on to the car until enough time had lapsed for a disposal not to be deemed suspicious. Six months after the accident, they placed an innocuous advertisement on an online site, and two weeks after that they sold the vehicle to an oblivious Beth Jenkins.

Maybe now that the car is gone, Ryan's nightmares will cease. The fire is in the engine now, popping and hissing, thick black smoke curling upwards. The whole car is engulfed with hot, irreversible flames: the job is essentially done.

'We really need to get out of here,' he says.

Mia checks her watch. 'Wow, that only took four minutes ... We should have time for a cup of coffee before school pick-up.'

~

Mia drives on the return journey, pressing hard on the accelerator, the tyres spinning as they seek traction on the dirt. Trees rush towards them and separate at the last minute. Ryan is suddenly overwhelmingly exhausted. He breathes a sigh of relief when they finally exit the dirt road. Mia slows down to take a long, scrutinising look in the direction they came from.

'Well, at least you can't see any smoke from here.'

Then she puts her foot down and they fly along the dead-straight country road, as empty of traffic as it was on the journey in. The car feels like it is skimming the road surface. Ryan feels like he is in a dream.

'Slow down, babe,' he murmurs. 'The last thing we need is to get pulled over.'

'I'm doing the limit,' she insists.

She is not doing the limit; from this angle, the speedometer is at least ten over. Mia has a habit of speeding and flatly denying it when challenged.

He studies his wife's profile. Her black tank top and tanned shoulders. Her tattoo: the tree.

'The roots are the most symbolic part,' she said proudly, after she got it done. 'They represent how grounded we are. The three of us. We can withstand anything.'

It's a nice sentiment, but is it true? Ryan feels the opposite of steady as the car whizzes towards home, his wife's knuckles protruding as she grips the wheel. He stole someone's car and set it alight in an area susceptible to bush fires. Both crimes could see him sent to jail but that's not the full extent of what he's done. He broke into Beth Jenkins's house, he followed her, spied on her and her young daughter. Eighteen months ago, he sold her a car that had a dark, rotten history.

Mia joins the main road with barely a glance at the oncoming traffic, then immediately overtakes a car she perceives as going too slow. Ryan grips the door bar. For a while, as they watched the car burn, he felt a sense of peace – but it didn't last longer than the four minutes it took the Corolla to become engulfed.

The guilt and shame of what he's done to Beth. In addition to Tara, poor, poor Tara. All their excuses and crazy justifications. For the sake of Elliot and their family unit. For the sake of love.

As Mia overtakes another car, the speedometer at well over a hundred and twenty, Ryan makes a silent resolution. He has done his last terrible thing. No matter what happens from here, he is done.

The question is, will Mia allow him to be done? They call themselves a team, but she is the leader, the mastermind, a force he cannot stop.

He blinks and sees a bright-yellow warning sign already upon them. *Reduce speed. Dangerous bend.*

For a moment Ryan fantasises about the car losing control, skidding and pirouetting off the road into oblivion.

A high-speed crash. Two dead. Then they would be done.

Mia takes the bend with no issues. She accelerates again.

The faster she drives, the more certain he is that the past is catching up with them.

24
Mia

Two years ago

Tara's messages are even more venomous than Mia imagined. A digital outpouring of complaints and resentment, fired off without filter to her mum, siblings and friends.

OMG. She is such a controlling cow. Can't even make the kid a sandwich without her laying down rules.

She's more fucking obsessive about Minecraft than Elliot is. She needs to chill out. Computer games teach kids all kinds of skills.

Not allowed to have friends come past the gate now. Next she'll be locking me in my room.

Mia is appalled. What must Tara's family and friends think of her? Do they believe that she's the sociopath portrayed in the messages? Surely they must know that Tara is not in danger of being locked in her room. Surely they can see that Tara is exaggerating, being grossly unfair.

Mia is just a regular mum, concerned about her child's diet, screen time and safety.

Ryan is painted more positively, which is no great surprise.

He's too good for her. How did such a nice guy end up with such a miserable cow?

Ryan drove me to the station again. Had a nice chat. I like making him laugh.

Great craic last night. Ryan still up when I got home. He made me drink some water so head not too bad this morning. Nice that he's watching out for me.

The messages confirm that Tara doesn't intend to stick around. The job is boring. Elliot is annoying. The isolation is 'doing her head in'. She talks about travelling to Queensland or Sydney while the weather is still good. Staying in a hostel would be fun, with people her own age who are up for a good time. A waitressing job at a beachfront café or bartender at a busy pub, where she could meet some hot guys. *A few more pay cheques and I'm outta this shithole.*

Of course, Mia can share none of this with Ryan. He would be furious if he knew what she'd done. The phone is back in Tara's possession, but the messages remain seared into Mia's brain. She can't admit the full truth to her husband; she tries a more roundabout way instead.

'Do you ever wonder what she says about us to the people at home?' she asks, moving Tara's dirty dishes from the sink to the dishwasher.

Ryan is wiping down the benchtop. Her question doesn't cause him pause. 'Nope.'

'Not even slightly curious?'

'She thinks we're a dull married couple. The same thing we thought about thirty-somethings when we were that age.'

A dull married couple! His words, not Tara's. Should they be making more fuss about their ten-year anniversary? There are still a couple of weeks in which to organise something special, a romantic meal or even a night away. Mia puts the thought aside to deal with another time, when she is less exhausted and preoccupied.

'I don't think she's going to stick around, Ryan. I think she hates it here. What are we going to do?'

This does cause him pause. 'Elliot's back to school Thursday. That will make things easier. Let's wait and see what happens, eh?'

Elliot being back at school is not going to change anything, other than buy them 'a few more pay cheques' worth of time. Tara is aiming to stay in a hostel, work in a café or bar, and socialise every night of the week. The messages are black-and-white proof that they're living on borrowed time.

Make sure you give notice, Siobhan advised her daughter in one of the message strings. *Don't leave Mia and Ryan in the lurch.*

A few weeks' notice is not going to change anything either. Their location and Elliot's unsuitability for before-and-after-school care are huge impediments.

Mia forces a smile for her husband and stifles the urge to divulge just how much trouble they're in.

~

The rain begins as Mia is going to bed on Wednesday night, thrumming on the roof, gushing down the gutters. By Thursday morning it's entrenched and Elliot's return to school is a wash-out. Mia delays her departure for work and drives Elliot and Tara to the end of the driveway, releasing them into the elements with a golf umbrella and a promise that the bus is mere minutes away.

157

She has just arrived at work – fifteen minutes late, which Geoff noticed although he did nothing more than throw her a sympathetic smile – when a text arrives from Tara. *Bus twenty minutes late. Elliot had massive tantrum outside school gates.*

Oh dear. Not the start to the school year they were hoping for. Poor Elliot. Going back to school is always stressful. The strain of trying to keep to all the rules, to sit down for long periods of time and to maintain focus on things he is not especially interested in. The anxiety of a new teacher and whether they'll be cross or nice, inflexible or understanding. Mia feels the same anxiety. She spoke to the principal at the end of last year, requesting Mrs Walsh, who has a reputation for being firm but kind. The principal took her comments 'on board' but 'couldn't make any promises'.

Mia tries to concentrate on her work, putting her worries about Elliot to one side. Her day is comprised of a few tricky meetings, a lot of phone calls and the shock resignation of the onsite expert in one of her largest projects.

'Damage Control 101,' Geoff says, on hearing about the resignation. 'Maybe we can convince him to stay – call HR to see what we can offer. Soothe the client – they love this guy, they're going to be upset. And get on to the recruiters ASAP. Let's see the calibre of candidates in the market.'

Quite a lot to ask of someone who has only been in the job a few weeks. Mia does the best she can. By the end of the day HR are working on a counter-offer, and the preferred recruitment company is checking their database for potential candidates. The client, however, is in a panic: they can't visualise the project being completed without this individual. An 8am emergency meeting is scheduled at their premises tomorrow morning.

Elliot doesn't get Mrs Walsh, he gets Mr Patel. He chatters about his new teacher's star chart and class rules, displaying excitement about a tepee at the back of the classroom.

'Is the tent for reading or playing?' Mia asks, stifling a yawn.

'It's the Thinking Tepee. It's only for people who need to *think*. I went there twice.'

Mia becomes more alert. Two time-outs? Or was Mr Patel giving Elliot the opportunity to self-calm?

'Henry wouldn't let me sit next to him and Eliza said I was the most annoying boy on Earth.'

No improvement on the social front, then. Mia sits and listens while Elliot purges about the day's events. Finally, when everything has been recounted, she allows him some time on Minecraft as a reward for getting through the day. At least Tara has made a start on dinner, a pot of potatoes bubbling on the stove and a roast chicken in the oven, as per Mia's instructions. The girl disappeared from sight as soon as Mia came in the door – probably on her phone sending more venomous messages.

Mia looks around the kitchen. The packaging for the chicken has been left on the benchtop, droplets of raw chicken juice visible on the grey marble. A closer glance at the potatoes reveals that they haven't been cut to the right size and will take twice as long to boil. Mia bins the packaging and disinfects the bench. As she moves around the kitchen, she notices that the floor tiles are sticky underfoot. Tara's list of tasks included mopping. The mop and bucket have been left out, implying that some attempt was made. What kind of detergent did she use?

Ryan arrives home soon afterwards, and they all have dinner together. Tara is surly. She has looked at the weather forecast for the next week – it is meant to rain every day! – and is not impressed.

'I didn't realise it could rain like this in Australia,' she says, an accusing undertone to her voice.

'We get less rain than most parts of the world,' Mia points out, jabbing some chicken with her fork.

Ryan smiles. 'It always rains in February, when all the kids are back at school, cooped up inside. Poor teachers.'

Tara doesn't give a toss about the teachers, or the kids. She can only see things from her own perspective. 'Does it rain like this *everywhere* in Australia?'

'Well, Queensland is worse than New South Wales at the moment,' Ryan says. 'They're in the middle of a cyclone and we're only getting the tail end of it.'

Maybe Queensland is losing its appeal as her next destination? It's the first proper rainfall since Tara's arrival; there is really nothing to complain about. No doubt her family and friends have already heard all about it. Mia wouldn't be surprised if she was somehow to blame for the weather as well as everything else.

After dinner, Mia calls Tara aside and thanks her for preparing the meal. She mentions the danger of salmonella, and the care required when dealing with raw meat and its packaging. Then she asks – using a light, non-judgemental tone – which detergent was used to mop the floors.

Tara shrugs. 'I didn't know what to use so I just squirted in some dishwashing liquid.'

Well, that explains the stickiness. Mia shows her what to use next time – the container with *Floor Cleaner* blatantly printed on it – and resigns herself to having to redo the floors once everyone has gone to bed.

~

Friday is just as wet as Thursday, with the added problem that Mia has to leave early for the meeting with her client; she can't even offer a lift to the end of the driveway. Elliot has another tantrum outside the school gates, and a couple of time-outs in the Thinking Tepee. Tara forgets that she has rice cooking on the stove and burns the base of the pot. Wet umbrellas and jackets are dumped in the hallway. The smell of damp plastic and burnt rice greets Mia when she comes home after a long, stressful day.

With an exhausted sigh, she starts to tidy up the carnage. Tara is old enough to know better. Why hasn't Siobhan taught her daughter basic cleanliness? What did Tara do with wet jackets and umbrellas in her mother's house? Did they miraculously disappear from wherever she dumped them? Did Tara *ever* cook a family meal or help with the housework? It certainly doesn't seem like it.

With the wet jackets hung to dry, Mia salvages what she can of the dinner. She substitutes noodles for rice and is only slightly mollified when everyone cleans their plates. Ryan bathes Elliot while she tackles the burnt pot, scouring its base furiously. As she scrubs, she becomes more and more angry towards Siobhan. Tara's mother is to blame for some of this debacle. To paraphrase Geoff: Parenting 101. Ensuring they don't kill themselves (or others!) from food poisoning. Hammering home the importance of locking doors and turning off appliances. Basic standards of cleanliness and tidiness. Fairness and decency in their dealings with others.

Make sure you give notice. Don't leave Mia and Ryan in the lurch.

Bloody Siobhan. What parent tells their kid it's okay to renege on a six-month contract? This is Tara's first proper job. She should be grateful for the opportunity, and mindful of getting a good reference at the end.

Mia's fingers are raw from scrubbing; the base of the pot still has a hard veneer of black. She leaves it soaking in a mixture of vinegar and baking soda and takes a deep breath. Rising voices can be heard from the bathroom: Elliot starting to melt down; it has been an overwhelming couple of days. Mingled with Elliot's wails and Ryan's soothing reassurances is a humming sound: the hair dryer. Is Tara going out tonight? For some reason this makes Mia even more furious.

Mia's phone beeps from where she left it on the kitchen counter. She turns to pick it up with an angry swipe.

Don't forget book club tonight. Wine and nibbles waiting for you. Xx Kellie

Damn! Book club. Mia *had* forgotten, comprehensively forgotten. She hasn't even finished the book, despite finding it so engaging at the start. There simply wasn't the time, or the headspace. Book club is the last thing she needs right now. She wants to hit something, scream as loudly as she can, before burrowing down for a long sleep. Book club is also *exactly* what she needs. Something to distract her from the difficult week she's had. The support and humour of Kellie, Heather and the others. The numbing effect of a few glasses of wine.

She runs into Ryan, Elliot and Tara in the hallway. Elliot's face is tear-streaked, his chest heaving in his cotton pyjamas. Tara is dressed to go out, her hair sleek and shiny, her clothes and shoes laughably unsuitable for the weather conditions: it's still pouring down.

'Tara needs a lift to the station,' Ryan begins breathlessly, glancing at the Irish girl before meeting his wife's gaze.

Mia takes a moment to think, to recall what she read in black and white: the words, thoughts and opinions of the young woman standing in the hallway, one knee jutting out, portraying sultriness, impatience and disrespect.

He's too good for her ... I like making him laugh ... It's nice having him watch out for me ...

A sense of anticipation is swirling with Tara's strong perfume. Being alone in the car with Ryan is what she wants, yearns for. More opportunity for chats, in-jokes, intimacy. More opportunity for something to happen.

Some damage-control measures are required.

'I'll take Tara,' Mia announces. 'I forgot about book club tonight. If we leave now, I'll only be a little bit late.'

25
Ryan

Today

When he looks back on that night, he casts around for different things he could have said or done to change the outcome. Maybe he could have insisted on driving Tara to the station, dropping Mia to book club on his way. Maybe he could have dissuaded Mia from going to book club at all, by pointing out that she was perilously tired, or that Elliot needed one-on-one time with his mum before going to bed. He could even have suggested to Tara that it wasn't a great night for going out, that the pubs would be half empty and Ubers scarce and expensive. Tara valued his opinion; she might have changed her mind.

Instead he said a distracted goodbye, and concentrated all his energy and ingenuity on getting Elliot down to bed. Poor kid was equal parts exhausted and hyperactive. It took an hour of wailing, lashing out, consoling and coaxing before his son finally relented to sleep. Then Ryan, feeling ragged around the edges, got himself a beer from the fridge and collapsed on the couch. The TV was on – a property show – and he remembers being unable to follow whether the couple featured were upsizing or downsizing. Mia's words from earlier in the week replayed over and over in his head.

'I don't think she's going to stick around ... What are we going to do?'

At the time, he had been quick with reassurances, not admitting that he was worried, too. Tara had all the hallmarks of someone who wanted out. Those questions yesterday about the weather in other parts of the country – it was obvious she was considering different places to live. To add to his worries, a letter from the bank, reminding them that their mortgage would be reverting to full repayments as of next week. Luckily, Mia's first monthly salary would also hit their bank account next week. His wife earned a lot more than he did: a few of those fat salary payments would turn things around. The question was, how long could they coax Tara to stay?

Ryan got himself another beer, and drank it while staring sightlessly at the television. Mia looked like she was at breaking point tonight. No surprise there. Juggling the demands of a new job with a child who relied on her so heavily for emotional regulation. Processing all the new job-related information while maintaining attention to detail in terms of Elliot's activities and welfare. The fact was, Tara didn't have the capabilities they'd expected of her. Hopelessly messy, clueless about kids and cooking; in many ways it was like having another child in the house. Despite all this, Ryan liked the girl. Her indefatigable desire to socialise and have a good time. The energy she invested in her make-up and outfits – he automatically smiled when he saw her dressed to go out. Her funny little sayings and accent. She brought some fun and colour to their rigid, monochrome existence.

He must have fallen asleep after that second beer, exhaustion overtaking him. When he woke up, Mia was shaking him vigorously. Water dripping down her face. Wild-eyed. Screaming.

'I've killed her. Oh my God, I've killed her.'

Ryan thought he was having a nightmare. Until he realised it was real. Horrifically and irreversibly real.

26
Mia

Today

When she looks back on that night, she can pin everything that went wrong on one thing: the departure from routine. The usual arrangement was that Ryan would drop her to book club, and one of the husbands or other women would run her home. She never took the car because there was always wine. She never took the car because she deserved at least a few glasses of that wine. Book club was her only social and intellectual outlet. They met once a month; she was always disappointed on the rare occasion it was cancelled.

What else does she remember about that night? Tara's surliness on the drive to the station. Rain pinging off the windscreen, making it difficult to see the road ahead. Unable to fathom Tara's desire to go clubbing on a night like this, before drawing a parallel to her own desire to go to book club: the craving for social contact and escape. Mia remembers making a run from the car to Kellie's porch, shaking rainwater from her jacket before hanging it up. That first glass of wine gliding down easily, having an instant effect. The warmth in her cheeks, the glow of the women's friendship. Sheepishly admitting that she hadn't finished the book. Their laughter and understanding.

After the book had been discussed – Kellie and Heather had predictably opposing views – the conversation moved along to kids, husbands and family life. At some point Mia held court about Tara: the burnt rice, raw chicken juice and sticky floors.

'Does she still have the hots for Ryan?' Kellie had asked, or something along those lines.

Mia rolled her eyes. 'Her face fell when I said I'd drive her to the station. The thought occurred: maybe she engineers her social life so they have alone time in the car? Maybe it's not the pubs and clubs that she likes the most. Just the car journey there.'

Heather left early and offered Mia a lift, but she wasn't ready to go home. Sally's husband came to pick her up, two sleepy kids in the back seat, providing room for one extra passenger. Michelle was the obvious choice, as she lived in that direction.

'I'll wake Dino up,' Kellie offered. It was after 1am. They were finally ready to call it a night.

The rain was still coming down hard. Mia tried to calculate how many glasses she'd had: three? Four? Whatever it was, she'd been here for hours and had plenty to eat: Kellie always over-catered. No need to wake up Dino, or Ryan for that matter. Half the drive home was comprised of Kellie's driveway and her own: only a couple kilometres of main road to negotiate.

The main road was deserted; she didn't encounter a single vehicle on the way. She drove with care, well below the speed limit: visibility was terrible. Within minutes she reached the gate of their property and had to duck in and out of the rain a couple of times, fantasising about a day in the future when she could do the job with the click of a remote-control button.

Back in the car, flicking a strand of wet hair from her eyes, she put the gearstick into drive and took off a little too fast. It was the relief from getting off the main road. Possibly adrenaline after a good night out. Or the desire to get inside, out of the awful weather. Whatever it was, she was going up the driveway faster than she usually would, oblivious to the problem looming ahead.

A blurry silhouette that she saw too late. A flash of bare legs and a red umbrella: Tara. Tyres skidding on the gravel. A sickening thud on the bonnet.

Then a one-way conversation in the teeming rain.

'Tara, for fuck's sake. What were you doing standing in front of me like that? Just because you can see me doesn't mean *I* can see *you* ... Tara, *Tara?*'

Other memories. The awkward angle of Tara's head. The trickle of blood from her ear, diluted by the rain. Her small feet, bare, with red toenails. Where the hell were her shoes?

'What were you doing? What the fuck were you doing? Didn't you hear the car? Why didn't you step aside? Why the fuck didn't you get an Uber like a normal person?'

No response from those blue-tinged lips. No rise or fall in her chest. No detectable pulse in the rain-sluiced skin of her throat.

'Don't give me that shit about being dropped at the gate,' Mia wailed, straightening the girl so she was fully flat on the ground. 'That obviously doesn't apply in weather like this. Where is your *fucking* common sense?'

Putting one hand over the other, she pressed down forcefully on Tara's chest. Thirty compressions. Two rescue breaths.

Tara had zero common sense, that was the problem. And Tara had no answers or justification for her actions, because she seemed to be dead.

'Don't do this to me ... They'll say it was the wine or speed – it's *always* the driver's fault ... Tara? *Tara?*'

Another thirty compressions. Two breaths. Still no answers.

27
Beth

Today

Charlie is Beth's first client on Monday morning – he usually tends to book either the first or last appointment of the day, depending on his work schedule. She gives him a warm smile when she sees him waiting in reception, long legs stretched out and crossed at the ankles, a frown on his face as he reads something displeasing on his phone. His face clears when he looks up and sees her. Blue-green eyes light up behind the lenses of his glasses. A responding smile.

Beth leaves him to get settled in the treatment room, paying a quick visit to the bathroom to comb her hair and apply lip gloss.

Why are you doing this? Just because he was kind last week? Even if he was interested, you can't afford to date him. You don't have the money for restaurants or drinks or movies.

'Hi there,' she says, closing the door softly. 'How've you been?'

'Fine. Fine.' He's lying on his front, turning his head to watch as she prepares the hot stones. 'But what about you?'

He has texted several times during the week, asking for news and offering lifts. She responded, to thank him for the huge bouquet of flowers, and supply updates – *Still no news, not looking good!* – while resisting the temptation to accept lifts from him. Charlie works long hours – hence the need for weekly stress-relief massages – and lives in the opposite direction to her. The fact that he is even offering is a testament to how kind he is.

'I'm going to give it until the end of the week. If there's no news, I'll just have to buy a banger to see me through.'

'What's your budget?'

'A thousand.'

He whistles in what could be either admiration or disbelief. 'I did some tinkering with cars when I was at uni. Buying old cars, stripping them for parts – it wasn't a bad way to make money.'

'I'll keep in mind that you're an expert on old bangers ... Now quit talking and relax.'

~

Beth has a cancellation at midday and phones Caitlin, asking if she's free for an impromptu lunch.

'Sure,' her friend replies with gratifying enthusiasm. 'I'm always up for lunch. Where do you want to go?'

'A park bench somewhere,' Beth says drily. 'I'm broke.'

'Let me treat you, hon. We could go to that new place on King Street.'

'No thanks. I have a delectable ham sandwich in my bag. Can't wait to eat it with a steel bench biting into my thighs.'

Caitlin, like the good friend she is, doesn't push the issue. The two women meet fifteen minutes later in Civic Park, roughly midway between their workplaces.

Caitlin is holding aloft a container of salad. 'I was trying to get out of eating this. The fact that you're broke is a bonus for my diet.'

Beth rolls her eyes because the notion of Caitlin being on a diet is preposterous. Her friend is wearing a long sheath dress, her honey-coloured hair tumbling down her back. As usual, there is no point being envious. Her radiance is a salve for what has been a grim week.

Beth takes a small bite from her sandwich and chews mindfully. The weather is warm, without being too hot, a few puffy clouds filtering the sun. A light breeze plays with her hair and clears some of the noise from her head. Her appointments are almost always back to back, making it necessary to eat on the go. Free or cancelled appointments rarely coincide with lunch hour. It's nice sitting here among the trees and greenery, eating at a more leisurely pace and watching the lunchtime bustle of workers cutting through the park.

Caitlin, echoing Charlie, asks if there is any news and chokes on a mouthful of salad when she hears Beth's budget for a replacement car.

'Oh, hon, that's not going to be enough. I can lend you some money.'

Like most social workers, Caitlin is poorly paid and it is especially generous of her to offer.

Beth smiles her gratitude. 'Thank you, but no thank you. I have a meeting with Shepherdess Finance tomorrow. I need to explain how I have a car loan but no car! And I need to brazenly ask for another thousand. I mean, they're a charity, so let's test how charitable they really are!'

Caitlin's fork is poised mid-air, some unappetising green leaves attached. 'Oh, hon, it's rotten luck.'

Beth swallows. 'It's not rotten luck, that's the annoying thing. My car was targeted. I just wish I knew why.'

'And you're absolutely certain it's not Kane playing his games?'

'As sure as I can be about anything to do with Kane.'

Caitlin takes a moment to think. 'Has your car been anywhere out of the ordinary the last few weeks? Maybe someone mistook it for someone else's car and put something in it? Cash or drugs or something they now want back.'

Caitlin's theory sounds like a plot from an action movie or a novel.

'It's been nowhere unusual. Work, school, grocery shopping, a few visits to Dad's.' Beth manages another smile, although there is really very little to smile about. 'And I think I would have noticed a mysterious package or otherwise.'

'Not if it was tucked under the bonnet or in the spare-tyre compartment or someplace you wouldn't usually look. Hey, you should Google crimes in the area ... Or ask the police to do their job and consider links to other crimes.'

Beth sighs. 'From what I gather, the police don't actively investigate stolen cars. They wait until they turn up, either passing one of their patrol cars on the highway, or found abandoned somewhere. Looking into petty thefts in the hope of finding a link sounds unlikely to me.'

'That's the point, Beth. If it was *petty* it wouldn't be worth the trouble. It would have to be something big.'

Caitlin has a point. How big is 'big'? Thousands of dollars' worth of drugs? A weapon of some sort, or evidence of a serious crime? Maybe the fact that the car is gone is for the best. She and Tilly could have been in danger.

Beth closes her eyes and suppresses a flare of panic. She and Tilly are safe. Car-less and penniless, but safe. That's the most important thing.

'You know, I don't want to talk about it anymore. It's the first thing I think about in the morning and the last thing at night. Let's talk about something more fun. Tell me about your new boyfriend.'

It transpires that Caitlin's new boyfriend has already been ditched. Poor sod didn't even last the month.

'He just wasn't right,' Caitlin says, waving her hand dismissively.

'How exactly?' Beth asks, bemused. 'Is anyone *ever* going to be right?'

'He wasn't ...' Caitlin is still searching for the specific fault. 'He wasn't very ... Oh, I don't know ...'

Beth laughs. 'Good thing I didn't waste any brain cells remembering his name.' She retrieves her phone to check the time. 'I should be getting back.'

Caitlin's eyes are fixed on something in the mid distance. 'Do you know that woman?'

Beth looks around, her eyes sweeping a group of office workers walking past. 'Which one?'

Caitlin jerks her head towards the next bench, about twenty metres away. A woman is sitting there alone. Long dark hair curtaining the side of her face. Slender tanned arms and legs. She's dressed casually in shorts, t-shirt and sandals – obviously not an office worker.

'She turned away when she saw us looking,' Caitlin says thoughtfully.

'Mmm ... mysterious.' Beth stands up and stretches. 'I'll have a closer look as we pass.'

There is a rubbish bin next to where the woman is sitting, and so Beth has a reason to slow down and take a harder look. She drops her sandwich wrapping into the bin, repeatedly glancing at the woman, whose head is still – stubbornly – turned away. Glossy hair, linen shorts, a nondescript shopping bag resting by her feet. It's hard to pinpoint her age without seeing her face. The only distinctive feature that Beth can see is a tattoo on her upper arm: a tree.

A jolt of recognition. She has seen that tattoo before, but she can't immediately recollect where or rather *who*. She falls into step next to Caitlin, linking arms with her.

'I think I do know her but it's obvious she doesn't want to be seen. Maybe an ex-client who has gone somewhere else. They always get embarrassed about it, scared of hurting my feelings.'

28
Mia

She stays frozen for a good five minutes after they leave, not even daring to turn her head to confirm that they're safely out of sight. Finally, with a plummeting sensation in her stomach, she slowly stands up and reaches down for the shopping bag. Then she starts walking in the opposite direction, using every ounce of willpower not to break into a run.

Beth's friend saw her. She caught her staring. Ryan will be furious.

This is what comes from trying to do the right thing. Ryan told her to leave it alone; she should have listened to him. Oh God, why didn't she *listen*? What was she trying to achieve with this stupid expedition?

To prove to herself, to the universe, that she isn't a bad person.

The bag was a faux-leather Target one, worth no more than $30 or $40. Inside, Beth's purse, containing a twenty-dollar note, some coins, her licence and other cards. Loose at the bottom of the bag: an almost empty lip-gloss, a worn-down eyebrow pencil, and a notebook that Beth used for shopping lists. It was the latter – those carefully written lists, with a dollar amount assigned to each item – that pulled at Mia's conscience.

Beth Jenkins either got a kick out of scrupulous budgeting or was living a hand-to-mouth existence.

'She's poor, Ryan,' Mia said, the handbag sitting on the table between them. 'We've stolen from somebody who has to count every cent she spends in her weekly grocery shop. That $20 note in her purse is the equivalent of $100 to someone else.'

Ryan shifted uncomfortably in his seat. 'Look, at least it's a cheap bag and won't cost a lot to replace. And at least we haven't tried to rack up anything on her credit cards. These are small losses, in the scheme of things. The big loss, the car, will be covered by insurance. Sometimes the insurers pay more than the car is worth and you end up ahead. So dump the bag and move on. Okay?'

Mia stared at it mutinously. 'She'll have to get a locksmith.'

Ryan reached across the table, for her hand. He squeezed it. Hard. 'Let it go, babe. Compared to all the things we've done, this bag means nothing.'

But Mia couldn't let it go. One of her failings is her tendency to get sidetracked by minor details. She wanted this bag to go back to its rightful owner. Maybe Beth hadn't forked out for a new driver's licence yet, or hadn't yet thought about getting her locks changed. Maybe Mia could save her some money and a lot of inconvenience by returning the bag to her.

She'd wiped the faux-leather clean of fingerprints and placed it in a reusable shopping bag, which she intended to leave in one of the food courts near where Beth worked. A security guard would notice the bag, find Beth's details on her licence, and it would be returned in due course. A simple plan. Until she'd seen Beth and her friend walking down Hunter Street. Until, acting entirely on impulse, she'd turned around and followed them to Civic Park. Until she'd stared too long at Beth eating her homemade sandwich and come to the notice of her sharp-eyed friend.

Now, unfortunately, she can't right this particular wrong. She has taken enough of a risk as it is.

It's okay. There was no eye contact. Beth didn't even see my face. Chances are she wouldn't remember me anyway.

At the next rubbish bin, Mia stops and discards the shopping bag, pressing down firmly, pieces of half-eaten food and other foul rubbish caving in on top of the bag.

'There,' she mutters, wiping her hand on her linen shorts. 'Gone.'

Sometimes, good intentions backfire. God, does she know all about that!

~

That night, Mia has a vivid dream about Beth and her friend. They're in the park again, and Mia confronts the two women as they walk along, arm in arm. She offers Beth her handbag, saying, 'I thought you'd want this back.' Beth screams and recoils. Her friend looks equally disgusted.

'What kind of person are you?' she hisses, putting a protective arm in front of Beth.

Their reaction is confusing, until Mia glances down and sees fat grey maggots crawling out of the handbag and up the bare skin of her arms. She wakes with a scream on her lips, an itchy sensation on her arms, and that phrase resounding in her head: *What kind of person are you?*

She is a mother. A loving, committed mother who would do *anything* for her son.

She is a wife. A loving, committed wife who has supported her husband through the best and the *very worst* of married life.

She is an analyst, who evaluated the details of that tragic night and saw fault on both sides. Tara couldn't drive: if she'd been a driver, she would have been more aware of the risks with such bad weather. Tara had been drinking, not properly tuned into her surroundings or the fact that she might not be visible to the oncoming car. Tara had been wearing those stupid, impractical shoes: she could have got out of the way quicker if she'd been wearing more sensible footwear. As for Mia, she had been driving on autopilot, slightly intoxicated, and possibly going too fast for the conditions.

She is a pragmatist. Tara was dead, which was truly awful, but they needed to think 'Damage Control 101'. Nothing could bring Tara back, but there was a lot they could do to salvage their family life and future.

She is a planner. All her project management skills, her brainpower and fanatical attention to detail, were employed in the aftermath of the accident. Planning what needed to be done, down to each tiny step. Creating a timeline and communication plan. Making sure they left no incriminating evidence.

She has a conscience. Trying to return Beth's bag is proof of that. And Siobhan. My God, the lengths she went to for that woman. Trying to give her some level of solace: Tara had died happy and carefree (albeit foolishly, swimming intoxicated on an unpatrolled beach). Trying to give her closure: Tara was *definitely* dead, not missing (which would cause false hope and never-ending trauma for the family). Mia even went as far as giving the Irish mother an iconic beach as her daughter's final resting spot. Bondi Beach was infinitely more glamorous than a gravel driveway on a country block west of Newcastle. Bondi Beach was somewhere the family could hold a memorial, if they wished, or visit sometime in the future to remember Tara.

I am a good person, Mia declares silently, the darkness of the room pressing down on her. *I've just had some shit luck.*

She tries to fall back asleep, but the sensation of crawling maggots won't go away.

29
Beth

The meeting with Shepherdess Finance goes better than expected. The loan officer listens to her story and seems sympathetic when she explains why the vehicle wasn't fully insured. He even suggests that she apply for an extra $1000, to give herself 'some breathing space'. The loan amendment still needs to be approved but nothing about the loan officer's demeanour suggests that it won't be. Beth leaves the city-centre office feeling lighter and immensely grateful that charities like this exist. A real bank would laugh in her face.

She texts Caitlin on the bus home: *Looking good for the $$$. Hopefully back on the road soon!*

Charlie has been sending messages throughout the week, attaching links to various cars listed for sale online. Some of the messages are funny. A link to a bashed-up Ford missing two of its tyres, with the caption: *I can see you in this one!* Other messages are more serious in tone. *This Holden Commodore is an option. The Commodores have legendary engines.* It's great that Charlie wants to be involved and seems to be enjoying the challenge. Beth is more than happy for him to do the legwork. She can already tell that he is a lot more knowledgeable than her dad, who helped her buy the Corolla.

As the bus wrangles with rush-hour traffic, Beth finds her thoughts slipping back to that day eighteen months ago. Joe's car crunching on the gravel of the seemingly endless driveway, Tilly wide-eyed with interest.

'Is this place a *farm*? Do they have *animals*?'

It didn't look like a farm; there were no sheds, fencing or animals in view. Just one of those large country blocks, with the single-level brick house set a long way back from the road. The property was well cared for, apart from the rusty gate at the entrance to the driveway. *Please shut the gate*, the sign said, and so they did.

There was a trampoline in the front garden with a boy – who appeared to be a couple of years older than Tilly – manically jumping up and down. Tilly couldn't get out of the car fast enough to join in. Beth remembers watching her daughter scramble onto the trampoline, jumping side by side with the boy, shrieking with joy. If only that lack of self-consciousness and ease with strangers extended into adulthood.

The boy's parents were standing at the doorway, well-dressed and attractive. Beth and Joe shook hands with them, and they walked as a group towards the car. Joe asked some perfunctory questions about when it had last been serviced and if it had been in any accidents. Beth found her eyes drawn away from the car to the couple, who took it in turns to answer. The husband had dark hair, deeply tanned skin and a strong body. The wife had dark hair too, swept back into a high ponytail, and a heart-shaped face. Everything about her was tasteful and elegant. Her navy skirt and whiter-than-white top. Even the tattoo on her upper arm. A small tree, with a floret of branches and roots in stark black ink.

Now Beth can't recall the names of either the husband or the wife. The kid was called Elliot, that much she remembers. Poor thing had a huge tantrum when Tilly was summoned for the test-drive. The extent of the tantrum seemed at odds with his age. The soothing words and quick intervention by his mother implied behavioural issues.

When they got back from the test-drive, there was no sign of the woman or the boy. Beth made an offer of $500 less than the asking price and to her surprise and delight the good-looking man immediately accepted.

~

Joe and Tilly arrive home at the same time as Beth, meeting each other on the driveway. Tilly scuttles out of the car and Joe winds down the window.

'I won't come in, love. I've a few things to do at home.'

'No problem, Dad. I think they're going to approve the extra finance.'

He smiles, and the tiredness on his face evaporates. 'That's good news, love.'

Beth is tired too, with a dull headache from the jerky, airless commute on the bus. She disarms the alarm with her new fob, unlocks the front door with her shiny new key, and steps inside with trepidation. Her eyes sweep the hallway and then the kitchen, to make sure that everything is as she left it. She tells herself that the new alarm and locks ensure her safety but her thumping heart is evidence that she doesn't fully believe it. When will she feel safe again?

Dinner is a stir-fry, which she starts to cook immediately, hurriedly chopping vegetables and meat, urging the rice to cook faster. Afterwards it's bath time and then the dreaded reading time, to which Beth has been devoting extra attention these last few days. Tilly is also being taken out of class for additional one-on-one reading help, with an emphasis on phonics and sight words, but Beth cannot detect any discernible improvement. Tilly stammers her way through the first few easy sentences of the reader.

'I don't know this word,' her little girl says repeatedly, without even trying to sound it out.

Page one takes an inordinately long time to get through. Page two is even more excruciating. They don't make it as far as page three – the recommended minimum. Tilly has relatively good comprehension and vocabulary but immense problems with reading the individual words. Beth fears her daughter is falling further and further behind the rest of her cohort.

Once Tilly is in bed, Beth begins to clean up downstairs, methodically stacking dishes in the dishwasher. Does Tilly need professional help? How much will professional help cost? The loan officer talked about giving herself some breathing space. He must have been able to tell how hard she is finding it, how there is a constant flutter of panic in her chest. It has always taken a degree of ingenuity to make ends meet, to ensure Tilly has everything she needs while having enough leftover for rent and other bills. The car being stolen is too big a loss to absorb. There are no small sacrifices or cutbacks she can make to cover that loss. It's just so unfair. Why? Why? Why? She stops suddenly, the plate she was holding slipping into the dishwasher rack with a clatter.

That woman yesterday. The woman who Caitlin said was staring at her. The instant familiarity of her tattoo. If it were a rose or a butterfly or something equally common, she wouldn't have given it much thought. *But a tree. A small tree.*

Beth dries her hands and hurries towards the half-size filing cabinet she keeps in the playroom-slash-office. It doesn't take long to find what she is looking for: she has always been scrupulous about keeping records.

The good-looking couple were called Mia and Ryan Anderson. It's not just the tattoo, now that she thinks about it. The woman's physique and hair colour were similar, too.

How odd if the woman yesterday *was* Mia Anderson. Was she staring because she recognised Beth but couldn't figure out where from?

Does she have any idea that the car they both owned is gone without a trace?

Beth puts the paperwork carefully back in its file and slides the drawer shut with her foot. She returns to her chores, wiping down the kitchen bench, taking out the recycling, and packing Tilly's lunchbox for tomorrow. She is smearing butter on a slice of bread when she stops again.

Did Mia and her husband want the car back for some reason? Is there a miniscule possibility that they're the ones who stole it?

No. No. Too outlandish. Too far-fetched.

Kane's voice chimes up in her head: *You're being a paranoid bitch; you need to stop blaming innocent people.*

~

Despite her best efforts not to be a 'paranoid bitch', her suspicions percolate overnight and at work the following day. She can't get Mia and Ryan Anderson out of her head. What is their story? They seemed like a close couple on the day she went to inspect the car. Ryan had his hand around his wife's waist as Beth and Joe pulled up outside the house. When Elliot had his tantrum, Beth noticed that his parents shared a look of solidarity before Mia calmly intervened. Mia had done most of the talking about the car – apparently, she was the main driver – but when she got sidetracked with Elliot, Ryan stepped in and completed the sale. A true team.

After she gets Tilly off to bed on Wednesday night, Beth types *Mia Anderson* into the search engine on her laptop. There's Mia Anderson the basketballer, Mia Anderson the recruitment consultant, Mia Anderson the poet and Mia Anderson the ecologist. The poet and basketballer dominate the first few pages of results. Beth clicks in and out of LinkedIn profiles and is searching for a solid ten minutes before she finds Mia Anderson the project manager. Long dark hair, clear navy eyes, a crisp white business shirt. *Message Mia Anderson*, the screen prompts. No, she does not want to message her. Not yet.

Next she tries the husband, Ryan. Bizarrely, another basketballer of the same name. Plus a baseballer, a footballer and a contender on *The Bachelorette*. She can't find the good-looking man she remembers on either LinkedIn or Facebook. Not unusual: Beth doesn't have a LinkedIn profile either and only uses Facebook to post pictures of Tilly for her grandmother's benefit in London.

It's getting late. Beth had six back-to-back massages today and her arms and shoulders are feeling the effects. There are chores needing to be done before she goes to bed. What is she hoping to achieve here? She stands up and stretches. But instead of organising the laundry, she heads towards the filing cabinet again. She locates the Transfer of Registration, takes the paperwork back to her laptop. This time she Googles the address of the previous owners, which is outside Morisset. The search returns some aerial images of the house, set well back from the road, and reminds her of the fact that it's a 45-minute drive away.

A couple of hours later, in bed, Beth is wide awake and still thinking about the couple. According to Mia's LinkedIn profile, she's a project manager. What kind of projects does she manage? Construction? Technology? Where does she work? In Newcastle, close to Civic Park? Ryan's lack of a professional profile suggests that he isn't the corporate type. This fits with Beth's first impressions. He had the physique of someone who does physical work for a living. He seemed extra conscientious when completing the disposal paperwork, in the manner of someone not used to dealing with forms and admin. More than anything, Beth had the sense that he was unwaveringly loyal to his wife and child. She even remembers a pang of envy.

The same questions remain. Was the staring woman in the park Mia Anderson? Was her presence something more meaningful than a random encounter? Do Mia and Ryan want their old car back for some reason?

There is no way to know, besides asking them.

~

The approval from Shepherdess Finance comes through on Thursday and the money lands in Beth's account on Friday.

Car shopping tomorrow morning, Charlie texts, when she lets him know that the funds have arrived.

Charlie has narrowed it down to three options, and seems energised when he rings her doorbell, just after 10am on Saturday morning. Tilly is delighted to see him, flinging herself forward for a hug.

'I'm happy to see you too,' he says in a bemused tone, meeting Beth's eyes over Tilly's head.

He drives them to each address, the first one a car yard and the other two private addresses. The vehicle at the car yard is a possibility, albeit at the top end of Beth's budget. They immediately disregard the second vehicle due to an ugly dent on the side panel that the seller forgot to declare. Beth laughs out loud when she sees the third car, a Holden wagon. Originally dark-green in colour, its bonnet is now silver, the driver's door is red and the side mirror is blue. The car has obviously been involved in a few prangs with no money wasted on spray painting the new parts to the original colour. Tilly loves the multi-coloured effect and instantly labels it 'the rainbow car'.

Charlie does a thorough inspection, assessing the condition of the tyres, the engine and all the internal controls. When he's satisfied, they take it for a test-drive, popping Tilly's car seat in the back.

'How does it feel to drive?' Charlie asks, sounding slightly anxious.

'It feels solid,' Beth replies, then glances at her daughter in the rear-view mirror. 'I think we've found our new car, pumpkin.'

183

Their 'new' car is far from new: it's twenty-two years old and has a staggering 230,000 kilometres on the clock. Beth signs the paperwork and makes the online bank transfer. A smile twitches her lips as she drives it home, Charlie following in his black Volkswagen.

'It gets a lot of second glances,' she grins, as they survey it again in her driveway. 'It'll be hard to steal this one without getting noticed.'

'The engine is all that matters, the rest is cosmetic.'

She looks up at him. 'Thank you. Thank you for doing all the research and making this so much easier.'

'No problem.' He pushes his dark-framed glasses further up his nose. 'I enjoyed it.'

An awkward silence. Tilly is unusually quiet, her eyes darting between them.

Beth swallows nervously. 'Do you have time to come in? I could make you lunch as a thank you.'

He blushes. She has embarrassed him. 'Sorry, I told my girlfriend I'd drive her somewhere this afternoon. I really should go. I'll see you during the week, okay?'

Now Beth is the one who's blushing. He has a girlfriend. Of course he does. How stupid for thinking a guy like him – kind, intelligent, nice-looking – would be single. She must have missed the clues that there was someone special in his life. Missing the clues is a habit of hers.

Pippa and Ian are coming out their front door and provide a welcome distraction. Their eyebrows shoot up when they see the car.

'This is our new car,' Tilly says proudly. 'It's the rainbow car.'

'Well, it's certainly colourful,' Pippa says diplomatically. 'It looks like a very nice car.'

Ian gives it a nod of approval. 'You can't go wrong with Holdens of this era.'

Beth remembers her manners. 'Pippa, Ian, this is my friend Charlie.'

Her neighbours shake hands with Charlie and then set off on their walk. Charlie says goodbye, and Beth hops into the car, to drive it into the garage. It is significantly longer than the Corolla, leaving only a small margin between the front bumper and the garage wall, but that's barely a quibble.

She and Tilly go inside, and Beth is immediately glad that Charlie turned down her invitation. The sparse furniture. The obvious lack of ornaments, pictures, possessions. Charlie knows that money is tight, hence his efforts to help her find a bargain-basement car. But coming in here, seeing how she and Tilly live ... well, that's another level of knowing.

Beth begins to make lunch: tuna-and-salad sandwiches. Tilly is upstairs, pottering and humming to herself. Beth retrieves mayonnaise and a packet of spinach from the fridge and is confronted with more evidence of their meagre existence: largely empty shelves.

She is happy about her new car. Happy and relieved and grateful. So why this huge effort not to burst into tears?

30
Mia

Ryan has been withdrawn all week. Mia has tried to give him the space he obviously needs, cognisant of their different coping mechanisms. While she felt clear-headed and invigorated after burning Beth's car – the last of any potential evidence destroyed! – Ryan felt depleted. But he was the one who had trailed Beth, who had broken into her house a couple of times, who had snuck into the clinic to snatch her handbag, and who had driven the stolen car from the city to their meeting spot in the bush, every kilometre of the way fearing that he might get pulled over and exposed as a thief – at the very least.

It's been a gargantuan effort on his part and Mia respects that. So, she is granting him this time to recover, to come back to himself, to come back to her. She hasn't mentioned that she and Beth almost came face to face at Civic Park; that would only stress him out more. Neither has she mentioned the most recent video-clip of Siobhan McAllen on RTÉ News, talking to reporters in Dublin.

'The Australian police are making progress. Having a large reward certainly prompts people's memories. I'm hopeful we'll have some answers soon.'

Siobhan is bullshitting. Pretending that there's progress when there obviously isn't. How can there be progress without a body, without evidence? The only memories that can be prompted are Mia's and Ryan's. Nobody else can begin to imagine what actually happened.

But Mia can understand the Irish mother's gnawing grief. She only has to imagine losing Elliot, how devastating that would be. There would be *no point in anything.* No point in getting up in the mornings, working, eating, existing. Certainly no point in offering crazy amounts of money as a reward. *The outcome can't be changed, Siobhan. No matter how much money or publicity you drum up, the outcome is still the same: Tara is dead.*

Mia grieved for Tara, too. She thought about her morning and night, and practically every minute in between. She missed the girl's quirks and contradictions, which had become part of the beat of everyday life without them noticing. The dreadful mess she left in the bathroom, while at the same time being so pedantic about her appearance. Her general surliness, at odds with her ability to laugh that harsh little laugh of hers at random moments. Mia can still hear that laugh, even though her recollection of Tara's face has started to blur. There was the fact that Tara was so very easily bored. Her messages to her family and friends attested to this: *Bored out of me feckin' mind.* But nature, of all things, piqued her interest. The water dragon who lived in the pool-equipment shed: she named it Denis and spoke about it affectionately, like it was a family pet. The cicada shell she found on the patio: *What the holy fuck is that?* The photos she took of native animals and birds and posted on Instagram. For someone who was supposedly bored out of her mind, she paid attention to the natural world around her. And how could they ever forget her phobia about vegetables and healthy food? Mia had never met someone so unadventurous with food. This from the same girl who once boasted to Ryan that she had tried more than thirty different types of gin.

'If at first you don't succeed, try a gin,' Ryan had quipped, and Tara had laughed her abrasive laugh and blinked her spiky eyelashes at him.

Yes, Mia grieved for Tara, too. It was quite shocking how much she grieved. That's why she went to such lengths to give Siobhan closure, the solace of being able to visualise her daughter's final resting spot. She wanted Siobhan to have parameters for her grief, to help contain it. The worst type of grief is the bottomless kind, the 'not knowing what happened' kind.

In addition, Mia wanted Tara's demise to be removed from Newcastle, to be removed from them: the family she had worked for. She wanted any police investigations to be targeted on Bondi Beach and its surrounds, not her home. To make this happen, she had to use all her project management skills, and every ounce of courage, strength and ingenuity that she possessed.

~

Mia hunkers down to do some studying on Sunday morning. She has been neglecting her online course, thrown off track by the reward and the reopened investigation. It's imperative that she refresh her skills and apply for some suitable jobs: preferably part-time roles with flexible hours. She hasn't worked since Tara was here, her foray into the workforce woefully short-lived: just the one pay cheque in the end. If it weren't for Ryan's mum, they'd be in financial dire straits. Dianne came to their rescue two years ago, gifting them a significant sum of money.

'Just concentrate on that precious child,' she said at the time, waving away their offer to treat the money as a loan rather than a gift. 'He needs one of you at home.'

For the last two years, Mia *has* concentrated solely on Elliot, and it is incredibly validating to see how much he has improved: there is a direct correlation between their son's behaviour and the time invested in him. Now a window of opportunity has opened up: what promises to be a stable couple of years until Elliot starts high school (when things could get rocky again). Mia wants to use this window to return to the corporate world, to prove her worth on a professional level; her worth as a mother has been proven beyond doubt. And the money Dianne gave them is starting to run out.

The house is exquisitely quiet; Ryan and Elliot have gone into town, to return some books to the library. Her course is not difficult – she already knows most of the syllabus, it's just a matter of proving to prospective employers that her knowledge is up to date. She is answering some chapter review questions when she hears the rumble of an engine. Ryan and Elliot? She hoped they would stay out longer than this – usually a trip to the library extends into a walk around town and a milkshake or some other treat.

Mia frowns as a car comes into view through the window, a strange car with a mish-mash of colours; it looks like it belongs on the scrap heap. Wrong address, or someone trying to sell her something? She is suddenly conscious of being alone in the house, without knowing what specific time Ryan and Elliot are due back. She is deliberating on whether or not to answer the door when the driver gets out of the car. Auburn hair tied back into a messy bun. Long floral hippie-style dress. Mia's breath catches in her throat. Beth Jenkins.

Why is she here? What does she want? *Does she know something?* The bell resounds throughout the house and Mia reminds herself that there is no requirement to answer. But how else will she find out what Beth wants? How else will she determine how much Beth knows? Because one thing is certain: she hasn't turned up here for nothing.

Mia gets to her feet slowly, her mind galloping at a hundred miles an hour. That heap-of-shit car – the insurance company obviously didn't pay out. Beth is out of pocket, most likely angry. Beth is also alone. Did she tell anyone she was coming here today?

Mia takes a deep breath, arranges her facial expression, and opens the door.

'Can I help you?' she asks quizzically.

Beth offers her hand, along with a self-conscious introduction. 'Beth Jenkins. You probably don't remember me. I bought your car. The Corolla.'

Mia carefully manages each expression. Surprise. Wariness. Confusion. *What's brought you here?*

With a show of reluctance, she takes Beth's hand. Her grip is both soft and strong.

'Was there a problem with the car?' she asks, her gaze flitting to the dilapidated wagon parked at the top of the driveway.

'No problem.' Beth's smile is restrained. 'I loved it. But someone else did too – it was stolen two weeks ago.'

Mia manufactures a sympathetic expression, before reverting to confusion. *Explain why you are here!*

Beth wets her lips, noticeably nervous. 'Look, this probably sounds crazy but I'm here now so I might as well plunge in. The person who stole the car made a few attempts before they were successful. They seemed to want my car and no other, which was suspicious. My friend suggested that maybe the car had been involved in a crime. Maybe drugs or something else incriminating had been left in it. I—'

Beth is interrupted by the sound of another approaching car. Ryan and Elliot? A familiar small white car emerges from the corridor of trees. A distinctive pouf of brown hair behind the wheel: Dianne.

Mia strives to stay calm. 'I think this one must be lost. Excuse me a minute.'

She hurries towards the car, positioning herself so Dianne has to stop further away than she would otherwise have done. Her mother-in-law winds down the window.

'What's the matter?' she asks, her face mostly hidden behind large sunglasses. 'Who's that you're talking to?'

Thankfully, Beth is turned sideways, and doesn't see Dianne's stare.

Mia gestures and points in the direction of the main road. 'I'll explain later. I need you to pretend that I'm giving directions. Turn around and go back the way you came.'

Any other mother-in-law would protest or at least ask more questions. But Dianne and Mia have a deep-rooted trust in each other. The older woman promptly rolls up her window, executes a neat three-point turn, gravel crackling under the tyres.

Once the car is safely out of sight, Mia walks back to Beth, wearing a bemused smile. 'Sorry about that ... Where were we? Oh yes, you think we left drugs or other criminal evidence in the car!'

Beth blushes violently. 'No, no, of course not. Look, I'm sorry, I shouldn't have come.'

Her words and actions are at odds with each other. If she shouldn't have come, then why is she standing steadfast, making no move to leave?

'Did I see you at Civic Park last week?' she asks, a tremor in her voice. 'I thought I saw someone who looked like you.'

Mia takes a millisecond to think and decides there is little point denying it. 'Yes, I was at Civic Park last week. I'm sorry if I inadvertently ignored you.'

Beth's blush deepens even further. 'My friend and I had just been talking about the car. She noticed you staring at us.'

Mia shakes her head. 'Staring into space, more like. I was feeling overwhelmed. Sometimes sitting still and absorbing nature puts me back on track ... How is your daughter?'

'My daughter?' Beth, just as she intended, is thrown off track. 'Ah ... She's good. Just started Year Two. It's hard to believe.'

Mia nods and leaves a small pause before delivering her final statement. 'Elliot has started Year Five. He has ADHD – school, and everything else, is a constant struggle. So, if you saw me staring into space or acting strangely, it's just because I was having a moment. I promise you I'm not a criminal, Beth. I'm a mum, just like you are, and some days it's a damned hard job.'

31
Beth

She drives away from the house a little too fast, gravel spraying as her tyres seek traction. Why did she come here? What did she hope to achieve? She established that Mia Anderson was the woman at Civic Park. So what? And she established that Mia Anderson sometimes finds being a mother incredibly difficult. Doesn't everyone?

At the end of the driveway, Beth gets out to open the gate. On the other side, she has to get out again, to close it. Funny to think of that lost driver going to the same effort ... all for nothing. How often do people come up the Anderson driveway by mistake? Mia seemed very quick to intercept the driver. Beth had the sense that she was being intercepted, too. That sudden question about Tilly: *How is your daughter?* It felt slightly threatening, as though Mia was making a point.

Beth accelerates along the road, her thoughts drilling down on Tilly, who is spending the morning with Grandpa, fishing. The Andersons' trampoline was standing in the front garden, invoking memories of Tilly and Elliot bouncing, squealing and instantly bonding. Elliot didn't seem to be at home today, and neither did Mia's husband. If Tilly had come along, she would have sought permission for a quick bounce, and no doubt asked questions about Elliot's precise whereabouts. The little girl would have asserted her presence, in the way that children do, even the shy ones. For some reason she can't yet articulate, Beth is glad that her daughter was not with her today.

Beth is driving through Morisset now, the town bustling with people and traffic, a train pulling into the station as she stops at the lights. People cross in front of her car: two well-dressed old ladies, a young couple with a pram, a dark-haired man with his arm around the shoulders of his dark-haired son. Beth squints at the father and son: not Ryan and Elliot, as far as she can tell.

The lights change to green and she presses on the accelerator, the old car taking a few moments to respond. There is a lot more to Morisset than she realised. A good variety of shops and restaurants and, of course, the train station, offering a vital connection to either Newcastle or Sydney: small city or big, depending on what one wants, or needs.

The town is behind her now and the wagon is chugging along the single-lane road, bush to the left-hand side, Lake Macquarie to her right: blue-green and shimmering under the midday sun.

As the road weaves along the shores of the lake, Beth realises something else. Mia Anderson said that absorbing nature helped make her feel less overwhelmed. If that was the case, then why sit in a busy city-centre park when she has all this boundless nature virtually on her doorstep?

~

Caitlin comes around on Sunday night, for dinner. Tilly, although tired after her day out with Grandpa, is thrilled to see her 'fun' godmother. They play dress-ups while Beth prepares a simple chicken casserole for dinner. Caitlin is transformed into a princess via a tiara, numerous beaded necklaces and a length of tulle fabric draped across her shoulders. Liberally applied pink lipstick, rainbow eyeshadow and glitter blush complete the look. Caitlin, bless her kind heart, plucks a Disney Princess book from Tilly's bookshelf and capitalises on the mood to squeeze in some reading practice.

'Stunning make-up,' Beth comments to her friend when she calls them to eat.

She grins good-naturedly. 'My future prince would find me irresistible if only he could see me now.'

Tilly's eyes begin to droop halfway through the meal, her food barely touched.

'Too much sun and fresh air.' Beth scoops her out of her chair. 'Of course, no fish to show for their efforts. Come on, pumpkin, time for bed.' Beth carries her upstairs. 'Oh my God, you are heavy! You're getting too old for this.'

Beth is exhausted herself. She can't believe she drove all the way to Morisset this morning, as though she didn't have a thousand better things to do with her time. She just felt the need to do *something*. She wanted the person who took her car to know how much it has affected her. Was that person Mia Anderson? Is it ridiculous to still have this niggle?

'You did *what*?' Caitlin asks incredulously.

Tilly is sound asleep. The dishes have been cleared, Caitlin's dramatic make-up wiped off, and they are sitting down with a glass of the wine Caitlin brought as her contribution to dinner: a crisp Sauvignon Blanc.

'I drove out there,' Beth admits in a sheepish voice. 'I know it was random. I know it was stupid. I was acting purely on instinct.'

'So you just rocked up. Wow! What kind of reception did you get?'

'The wife was at home – Mia. She was ... I am probably reading too much into this, but she was ... a bit passive aggressive, if I'm honest.'

Caitlin's eyes widen before she consumes a large gulp of wine. 'Okay, so now you're worrying me. This is the same woman who was staring at you in the park?'

Beth nods. 'I asked about that and she admitted to being there. Staring into space, apparently, not at me!'

'Are you sure? Maybe you should mention this woman – Mia – to the police.'

'You mean report her for being at the park the same time as me? I can't do that. Police need hard evidence, not vague suspicions.'

Now Caitlin is tutting. 'If you were hellbent on going all the way to Morisset, you could have asked me to come along. Or Charlie.'

'It was completely on a whim,' Beth tries to explain, even though she knows Caitlin is right. 'I assumed you were enjoying a lazy Sunday morning and I'm sorry to report that I'm not on those terms with Charlie. Helping me buy the car was a one-off. He has a girlfriend.'

'Oh,' Caitlin says, her face falling in disappointment.

'Yes, *oh*. My radar with men continues to be terrible. I'm just hoping I wasn't too obvious ... Debbie was right when she said he was too good to be true!'

Caitlin gives her a sympathetic hug. 'Don't be so hard on yourself, hon. It's easy to misread the signals.'

An hour later, they've finished the bottle of wine and Caitlin calls an Uber.

'Promise me no more detective work on your own. I'll call you during the week. Bye, hon.'

Beth locks up, double-checking all the windows and doors. Once upstairs, she activates the alarm and decides to wait until the morning to shower.

Five minutes later she's in bed, lying rigidly on her back, staring into the dark. Her body is bone-tired, but her mind is restless, dissecting the weekend. She is the owner of a very strange-looking, very old car and an extra $2000 in debt. She is acutely embarrassed about Charlie and self-loathing for misreading his intentions. These realities are contributing to the noise in her brain, but it's Mia Anderson who is causing the most clamour. Self-possessed, smooth, condescending: *I promise you I'm not a criminal, Beth. I'm a mum, just like you are …*

The most disturbing thing was how she somehow managed to make Beth feel intimidated. Mentioning Tilly out of the blue like that. Knowing full well that Tilly is her weak spot.

Beth spent eight years of her life married to someone who deployed the same sort of manipulation tactics. Someone who didn't need to shout or lash out in order to incite fear or compliance. Someone who had a black belt in mind games.

Something about Mia Anderson reminds Beth of her ex-husband. Mia and Kane seem to be the same personality type. Precise. Manipulative. Unnerving.

32
Ryan

He is aware that Mia is concerned about him, aware that he has regressed, aware that he needs to pull himself together. He forces himself out of bed in the mornings and through the minutiae of his daily routine, repeating the mantra: *there is no body, there is no evidence, there is nothing to dread.* His head believes these words to be logical and true, but his soul doesn't. Dread infuses every moment of the day and night. His body is leaden. His thoughts are on a constant loop. Last night's nightmare looms behind his eyes: drowning in an unidentified body of water, the current pulling him down, his ability to swim mysteriously disabled.

Mia tries to nurture him out of his depression, making his favourite meals, massaging the tension from his shoulders. Then she drops a bomb: *Beth came to the house.*

Fuck, fuck, fuck! This means trouble. Beth is upset about her car; her suspicions are aroused. How long before she hears about the million-dollar reward and puts two and two together?

There is no body. There is no evidence. Beth can be suspicious all she wants.

Ryan's subconscious can't be controlled through mantras or positive thinking, hence the continuing nightmares. Mia soothes him when he wakes in the middle of the night shouting and thrashing.

'Shush. It's okay. There's nothing to worry about.'

Wrong! There is *everything* to worry about. Beth Jenkins: who thinks her car might have been involved in a crime. (Full marks for having the nerve to call to the house. Zero marks for not having the intuition to run in the opposite direction.) The police: trying to second-guess what leads the detectives have and what might be their next step. Last of all, and most of all, he is worried about Mia. He can see that she is weighing up the Beth situation, the project manager in her kicking in, determining how she can mitigate this growing risk. And this is what he dreads the most.

On Monday morning, Ryan is driving on the freeway and the dread is so strong it feels like a presence in the passenger seat, murmuring lethal suggestions.

See that tanker coming up the inside lane? Pull in front of it at the very last moment. Then this will be over.

Don't want to ruin another life? Fine. Put your foot to the floor and veer into the cliff face. One-car accident. Perfect.

Elliot? His parents are criminals of the worst kind. He'll be better off.

Ryan is not far from where the fireball occurred when his phone rings, cutting off the nagging voice in his head. It's an unfamiliar number, yet he knows, deep in the pit of his stomach, exactly who it is.

'Good morning. Detective Sergeant Amy Goodwin here. Just seeing if we can arrange for you to come in for an interview.'

An interview, not a chat. Does this mean it will be recorded? Will he be read his rights?

He swallows. 'Where?'

'The station at Morisset. I presume that's the most convenient for you?'

'I'm on my way to work,' he points out, not sure if he is expected to take the next exit and turn back home.

'Later is fine. How's 6pm?'

Six doesn't leave enough time for peak-hour traffic. They agree on six-thirty.

Ryan phones Mia as soon as the call is ended. He strives to get his tone right, imagining his voice being replayed to an audience of detectives, or future jury members. He needs to sound both cooperative and curious.

'Babe, that detective just called. She wants me to come in for an interview.'

Mia's response is the perfect blend of surprise and concern. 'Really? Any idea why?'

'Nope. I'll miss Elliot's bedtime. Tell him I love him lots and I'll see him in the morning.'

End on the loving-father note, to disguise the fact that their conversation is full of innuendo if not many words.

Ryan hangs up with a weird sense of relief. The waiting is over. The end is drawing near. There is a job to do. No matter how tired and rattled, he must rally himself to do it to the best of his ability.

There is no body, there is no evidence, there is nothing to dread.

Who is he trying to fool?

He spends the rest of the drive visualising the interview room at Morisset station, Amy Goodwin's deceptively friendly face, and what questions she might ask of him.

~

The police station is a relatively large establishment considering the small size of the town. Ryan has walked past it a thousand times but has only been inside once before: to give the swab. He parks his car in the commuter car park across the street, and uses a tissue to dab the sweat from his face before getting out.

The officer at the reception desk, an unsmiling woman in her fifties, is expecting him and shows him to an interview room at the back of the station. The room is nondescript, windowless, claustrophobic. He sits down, concentrates on his breathing. At lunchtime, he went to the library closest to work and researched his rights. He does not need to agree to this interview and legal advice is strongly recommended. But in the interests of appearing cooperative, here he is. Also, what better way to gain insight into what the police actually know, if anything?

The door opens. Detective Goodwin sweeps into the room, holding a manila file close to her chest. Stavros, her ginger-haired colleague, follows and shuts the door.

Using a businesslike tone, Detective Goodwin informs Ryan that the interview will be recorded and that he has the right to remain silent.

Ryan shrugs. 'I just want to help in whatever way I can.'

To his embarrassment, his stomach grumbles, but nobody seems to hear it. Goodwin is looking down at her notes, Stavros is adjusting the recording equipment. His hunger is the only thing about the setting that feels real, and he actually wonders what Mia has made for dinner. His wife is a good cook; she is good at everything she turns her hand to. Project management. Being a mother. Covering up an accidental death. Her mind is always thinking ahead, planning and plotting into the future, her intellect far superior to his own. Even at school, where they began their relationship, she was always looking beyond that term's exams, beyond their HSC, beyond university. The dumbest boy in the school dating one of the smartest girls. Of course, he knows now that he wasn't actually dumb: learning was just harder for him than other kids, a problem with how his brain was wired, just like Elliot.

He is lucky that Mia is so forward-thinking. The night it happened, when she burst into the house – clothes sodden, borderline hysterical

– her logic had already kicked into gear. She had made the conscious decision not to call an ambulance. At first, he assumed it was an oversight, and on seeing Tara's eerily still body, he pulled out his phone to make the triple-zero call.

Mia's hand shot out to stop him. 'They'll charge me for this. I could get *years*.'

'You don't know that for sure,' he countered. 'It was an accident.'

'There's a magistrate in Newcastle imposing *maximum* sentences,' she cried. 'It was in the paper.'

Ryan had no knowledge of the magistrate Mia was referring to or the specifics of the cases that had merited maximum penalties.

'It's too late to save Tara,' Mia insisted, gripping his arm in desperation. 'But we can save our family.'

That's why he is here. That's why he has done all the terrible things he has done. To save his family. To save Mia, because she is the lynchpin that holds them together.

Hopefully, today's questions will be relatively simple, covering topics he and Mia foresaw and rehearsed. Hopefully, this won't take long and soon he'll be home, eating whatever dinner is on the menu tonight, each mouthful filling the emptiness inside him.

'Ryan, thank you for coming today. We appreciate your cooperation. We want to ask some questions about the nature of your relationship with Tara McAllen. Please be aware that the purpose of these questions is to paint a broader picture. We are not here to make moral judgements.'

Ryan's brain is already scrambling. He came here expecting more questions about their DNA being found on Tara's belongings, or perhaps her exact movements during her last days in their employment. Worst-case scenario – an inference to Beth Jenkins's stolen car.

Detective Goodwin registers his puzzlement and leans further across the table, eyes narrowed. 'Tara sent texts to friends, being open about the fact that she was attracted to you. She mentioned late-night chats, intimate conversations in the car, the fact that the two of you liked the same things ...'

There's a pause in which Ryan assumes he is expected to speak. 'We did like some of the same things. There was a show on Netflix – *Stranger Things* – that we were binge-watching together. She'd tell me about her boyfriends, what pubs she'd been to, how many drinks she'd had ... I was half friend, half father-figure, someone she could confide in ...'

'Did you send each other messages by text or other apps?'

'Sometimes. Like, she'd text during the day if she needed to ask something and Mia wasn't contactable. And she'd send photos of Elliot playing Lego, or of the water dragon, who lived in our pool area, sunning himself. That sort of thing. Nothing inappropriate.'

'Did you talk to Tara about problems in your marriage?'

'No.' Ryan feels heat on his cheeks, even though he is technically telling the truth. He never once complained about his marriage to Tara; however, she did make a few disparaging comments.

'You shouldn't let her boss you around so much,' she murmured one night. The atmosphere in the house was fraught following a colossal meltdown from Elliot and terse words from Mia, who believed the incident could have been avoided had Ryan intervened sooner.

'She *is* the boss when it comes to Elliot,' he'd explained with a wry smile. 'She has done all the reading, all the research. She's in charge of the complicated decisions about medicine and side-effects, the ongoing negotiations with the school, how to get the best out of Elliot. I'm in charge of play, bath time and bed. We joke that she is "strategy" and I'm "operations".'

Tara snorted. 'If you're "operations", what does that make me?'

'You're operations coordinator, I'm operations supervisor ... How does that sound?'

'Pretty shit.'

Just thinking about the banter and warmth of that distant

conversation is enough to make him feel emotional.

Detective Goodwin is staring at him. 'Can you tell us if you and Tara McAllen were involved in a sexual relationship?'

'*No.* Absolutely *not.*' He is close to tears, takes a deep breath to regulate himself. 'Tara was practically a kid. I did not find her attractive in any shape or form.'

Ryan has only ever had one 'type'. Dark hair, navy eyes, golden skin. Ferocious intellect.

He is devoted to his wife. Blindly, dangerously in love with her.

33
Beth

'All these years I've been rushing around like a headless chook, stressed and sore and not realising that the answer to my problems was right in front of my nose. I admit it – if my staff hadn't bought me a voucher for Christmas, I'd never have come here. All I can say is, thanks to them and thanks to you, Beth, I'm a new woman.'

Lydia, the owner of the café across the street, came for her first massage in January, the voucher in hand and an 'I'm not sure about this' expression on her face.

The experience was transformative, putting her back in touch with her body and the importance of taking care of it. 'It was like a light bulb went off in my head ... I'm on my feet all day, I've always struggled with my back, I'm getting older, I need to take care of myself.'

This is Lydia's third massage, and she has also taken up ocean swimming and yoga classes. Beth has heard many times from clients how resolutions about exercise, mindfulness and diet are often prompted by a simple massage.

She squirts coconut oil onto her hands. 'Let's get started, Lydia.

Make those arms nice and floppy ... That's good ...'

Lydia stops talking and relaxes beautifully, allowing Beth to do her job to the best effect. A lot of the businesses in the vicinity are owned by people like Lydia and Debbie: sole traders who work long and physical hours, for small profits. It's nice to be able to support one another.

At the end of the massage, Beth gives Lydia some privacy to get dressed and quietly exits the room. The waiting chairs in reception are empty; her next client isn't due for another five minutes.

'Fancy one of these?' Debbie asks, holding up a muesli bar.

Beth accepts the offering gratefully. She will be eating on the go, today.

Lydia emerges, pink-faced and reaching for her purse. She is a small woman, carrying a few extra kilos from all those years of not taking care of herself. While Debbie processes the payment, Lydia assesses the state of play across the street.

'Better get back to it. Already starting to get busy, I see.'

Beth and Debbie automatically look across and note the small queue at the coffee counter.

A thought suddenly occurs to Beth. 'Lydia, do you have CCTV at the café?'

Lydia stores her credit card away in her purse. 'Yes, just a basic system, though. More of a deterrent than anything.'

'Would you still have footage from two weeks ago?'

'I should do. Why?'

'My handbag was stolen. I'm just wondering if our doorway is visible on your camera.'

Lydia nods. 'Pop in after work and we'll find out.'

~

Beth calls her dad to see if he can pick up Tilly from after-school care. She feels guilty – now that she has transport again, she should be asking less of Joe – but she is motivated by the same sense of injustice that drove her all the way to Morisset. Thankfully, the café is a lot closer. By the time she gets across the road, the place is empty. Chairs are stacked on tables and a CLOSED sign is stuck to the door. She knocks, and Lydia – looking a lot more harried than this morning – appears from a back room to let her in.

'The monitor is set up here, next to my computer. There's a file generated every day, which backs up onto this drive. Which day did you say it happened?'

Lydia opens the relevant file, shows Beth how to operate the software, and leaves her to it. 'Take your time. I still have heaps of cleaning to do.'

There are two cameras, one pointed at the cash register and counter area, and the other covering the doorway. Next to the doorway is a section of window, and through the glass is a view of the clinic across the street. The video quality is poor: this is a cheap, unsophisticated system. Even the faces of the café patrons are blurry and indistinct as they come through the door.

Beth fast-forwards until the time stamp on the recording is five minutes before Mary's appointment on the morning of the theft. And this looks like her, entering the frame from the left-hand side. It's a side profile, and the quality is awful due to the distance, but her outline and clothing look about right. She pats her hair before pulling open the door and disappearing inside the clinic. Beth fast-forwards again, her eyes trained on the clinic door. How far into the treatment before Mary started to feel faint? Fifteen or twenty minutes?

'Shouldn't the police be doing this?' Lydia says, pausing at the doorway of the tiny office, cleaning spray in one hand, a cloth in the other.

'Too small-fry for the police,' Beth murmurs. 'Imagine if they had to do this for every stolen handbag in the city. Having said that, it wasn't just my handbag, it was my frigging car, too. Hold on ... here we are ...'

She hits pause, rewind, replay, and squints at the fuzzy figure opening the clinic door. 'This must be him.' The man is wearing a baseball cap and carrying a reusable shopping bag. He disappears through the door, and reappears less than a minute later. 'And here we are. I bet my handbag is in that shopping bag. Thieving bastard.'

Lydia comes further into the room, frowning at the monitor. 'Rewind again. What direction did he come from? ... Shit, Beth, he came out of *here*.'

It's true. Beth was so focused on the clinic's door, she didn't notice that the suspect started his journey from the café. More rewinding. Video of when he entered the café, about fifteen minutes before. Better quality but impossible to get a clear view of his face. His baseball cap is low on his head. His chin is pointed downwards. He seems to be slightly broader across the shoulders than Kane, but it's hard to be certain. He orders a coffee at the counter and sits with his back to both cameras. Dark-coloured t-shirt. A glimpse of closely cut hair, visible between the baseball cap and the back of his neck. He sips his coffee intermittently, his phone never leaving his other hand. Is he waiting for a call? No, he is monitoring the time.

Beth exhales a shaky breath. The thief wasn't an opportunistic passer-by. The thief was sitting here across the street, waiting for a certain – pre-agreed? – amount of time to elapse.

This proves what she already knew. It wasn't a random theft. Far from it.

34
Mia

It was an Oscar-worthy performance. Feigning that she didn't recognise Beth to start with. Diverting Dianne who had chosen that window of time for one of her ad hoc visits. Conjuring up an explanation for why she was at Civic Park. Then finishing with a flourish: *I promise you I'm not a criminal ... I'm a mum, just like you are ...*

She lied. She *is* a criminal. Her list of crimes is long and damning, and she is more startled than anyone that things have turned out this way. Mia used to be someone who kept to the rules, who followed processes and procedures to the T, who prided herself on being a cut above everyone else. Becoming a mother changed all that. Being mum to Elliot, with all his challenges and quirks, required a drastic readjustment of rules, priorities and her ambitions in life. These days it comes down to one simple objective: she wants her son to have the best life possible. That's why she didn't call an ambulance or the police on that awful night. She would have been breathalysed and charged. Only that week she'd read the article about the fed-up magistrate in Newcastle imposing custodial sentences for run-of-the-mill mid-range offences.

There was a dead girl on her driveway; this was far from a run-of-the-mill offence. On top of that, there was the financial cost to consider. At least a couple of thousand in penalties, in addition to astronomical legal fees: a lawyer, a barrister and other experts deemed necessary to defend the indefensible. She and Ryan would need to sell the house to cover the costs. The loss of their house, Elliot's safe haven, and the loss of all the progress they've made with him. Mia is keenly aware of how much her son needs her to stay on track. She manages his routine, she is the interface with his teacher, she is the mastermind of all the specific tasks that improve his attention span, his social skills, and his ability to follow instructions. Ryan would not be able to manage alone, corners would be cut, and Elliot would regress.

Technically, she is a criminal, but she doesn't feel like one. She is just a mum who will do anything – *anything!* – to keep her child safe and on track to live his best life. Tara was dead, there was no changing that fact. Elliot was alive, tucked up in bed, out of the rain and away from the horror unfolding on the driveway. *Elliot needs his mum. He needs stability and routine. He needs the house with its generous space and garden to burn off his endless energy.*

Beth is a mum, too. What was her little girl's name again? That's right: Tilly. She was a bossy thing, younger than Elliot but calling the shots within minutes of being on the trampoline. What would Beth do if she were in Mia's shoes? Would *she* commit an unthinkable crime if it guaranteed her daughter's wellbeing? Has she ever been faced with an *impossible* situation, a brutal choice between two horrendous alternatives?

Beth seemed taken aback at the mention of her daughter. She apologised again, repeating that she shouldn't have come. She got back into her car – a hideous-looking thing – and manoeuvred it back and forth, engine grunting, gears clashing, until it was facing in the correct direction. Mia frowned at the rear of the car, its back bumper sporting a sizeable dent, and stayed on the front patio long after it had gone out of sight. Was that the end of it? She hoped so. She hated to think what they might have to do if it wasn't.

~

On Tuesday morning, Mia receives a phone call similar to Ryan's: Detective Sergeant Goodwin requesting her attendance at Morisset Police Station for an interview. Two phone calls and interviews in as many days; the police are giving the impression of momentum.

She is still processing the details of Ryan's interview last night, heartened by the fact that the police suspect an affair between him and Tara. Let them go down as many dead-ends as they want, anything to divert from the truth. She agrees to come in directly after dropping Elliot to school.

'You look pretty, Mummy,' Elliot says, noticing the change from her everyday clothes.

'Thanks, buddy. That's sweet of you.'

She has chosen to dress conservatively: floral summer dress, wedge-heeled shoes, hair pinned back over one ear. She needs to produce another Oscar-worthy performance.

The interview room is small and bland. Amy Goodwin uses a clipped tone as she goes through the formalities. Yes, Mia is aware that she has the right to remain silent and doesn't have to agree to the interview. Yes, she is also aware that legal advice is recommended. Like everything in life, it's a balancing act. Weighing up the need to appear cooperative with the risk of saying something that could be used as evidence against her. Weighing up her desire for information with the torture of not knowing the shape and thrust of the investigation. Weighing up the cost of legal advice with the cost of making a rookie error.

Detective Stavros states the start time of the interview, 9.15am, and asks the first question.

'Mia, for the sake of background information, can you tell us when and where you met your husband?'

'We met in high school. We started dating in Year Eleven. We were both seventeen.'

'And you've been together exclusively since then?'

'Mostly. A few short breaks here and there in the early years. Trying to convince ourselves that we should diversify.' She smiles and shrugs. 'I guess, your soulmate is your soulmate, regardless of what age you are.'

'How would you describe your relationship today?' the detective asks, his face and tone empty of expression. Either he doesn't believe in soulmates or he's too focused on his next question to properly listen.

'We love and respect each other.' She meets their eyes in turn, challenging them to disagree. 'And we're devoted to Elliot and would never do anything to jeopardise his happiness.'

'Have there been financial pressures to contend with?'

'Yes, some. But no more than many other families.'

'And Tara McAllen was hired two years ago so you could return to paid work and improve the family finances?'

'Yes.'

Mia resists the temptation to elaborate: Tara wasn't what they hoped for; she had a detrimental effect on their finances in the end. But the less said, the better.

A pause, then the detectives swap roles, with Amy Goodwin asking the questions. Her style is more animated, which Mia prefers.

'Can you tell us what time you and your husband left for work in the mornings when Tara was living with you?'

'Ryan always left before me. He commutes to Sydney, I only had to go as far as Newcastle,' Mia explains, before providing the approximate times.

'And in the evenings?'

'Same deal. I got home between 5.30 and 5.45, Ryan would come in an hour or so later.'

The female detective gives her a scrutinising stare from across the table. 'How often was your husband alone with Tara?'

'Not very often. He gave her the occasional lift to and from the station, as did I, but that was about it.'

'Your husband admitted that he and Tara chatted a few times when she came home late. Tara's texts to her friends corroborate this fact.'

Mia issues a slight smile. 'A few late-night chats are hardly evidence of a torrid affair. Ryan was concerned about Tara leaving the front door unlocked. He stayed up to reassure himself that the house was properly secured.'

'Was your husband having a sexual relationship with Tara McAllen?' Amy Goodwin asks with staggering bluntness.

'Absolutely not.'

'Did you find out about their affair and have a confrontation with Tara?'

'*No.*'

'Jealousy can be a powerful emotion,' the detective perseveres. 'Things can escalate and suddenly we've done something we never imagined we'd do. Did a confrontation with Tara result in her death, accidental or otherwise?'

Mia is genuinely shocked. She gathered that the police were going down this path but never imagined being presented with a question as explicit as this.

'Look, I am trying to cooperate, but these questions are both offensive and preposterous. I trust my husband 100 per cent – I can assure you that nothing was going on between him and Tara, and I had no such "confrontation" with her. The last I saw of Tara was the day she departed for Sydney. We parted on cordial terms even though she'd left us horribly in the lurch.'

'We appreciate your cooperation,' Detective Goodwin says, sounding sincere. 'Right, Mia, we're going to show you some CCTV footage now. It's from the hostel where Tara was staying in Bondi.'

Mia nods, tries to keep her alarm contained. *What about the hostel in Bondi?*

Detective Stavros positions his laptop so everyone around the table can see the screen.

'We have a few different videos of Tara ... See, this looks like her, entering the hostel's kitchen.' The video is grainy and washed of colour. 'We can't actually see her face, because her head is tilted down, but her mum recognised the sweater. It's a rather unique brand and style.'

The sweater is an oversized leopard-print one. Mia remembers it all too well. The cheap-quality fleece. The make-up stain on the cuff. Tara's cloying perfume ingrained in the fibres.

'Yeah, that looks like her sweater,' she ventures.

Detective Goodwin bestows her with another all-seeing stare. 'The thing is, it was thirty-four degrees at the time this footage was recorded. Not exactly sweater weather ...'

Mia nods again and murmurs, 'Maybe the air-conditioning was up too high.'

'Maybe,' Goodwin says, not even trying to sound convinced. Stavros closes the file and opens another, the screen filling with more grainy footage. A girl walking down a corridor, a striped towel wrapped around her torso, on her way from the pool or the shower. 'Tara's hair is obscuring her face, so still no clear shot of her facial features, but we're almost certain that this is the same girl as the first clip. The towel also matches the one Tara left behind on the beach.'

Mia looks up from the screen and into the female detective's appraising brown eyes. 'I can't really say. The towel isn't very distinctive, unlike the sweater. Can I ask why you're showing me these videos? Are you needing help confirming that the girl is actually Tara? I can't see her face any more than you can.'

'Mia, I'm showing you this particular clip because I want to draw your attention to something. Can you zoom in, Martin? Thank you. Perfect.'

The screen is frozen on the girl's upper arm, the cursor pointed at what appears to be an irregularity on her skin. Mia's heart goes into freefall.

She manufactures a look of utter confusion. 'Sorry, I don't understand.'

'Unusual place to have a bandaid, don't you think? Not a part of the body where you'd expect to get a cut or a nick.' Now those all-seeing eyes are trained on Mia's upper arm, and the small tree she had tattooed after Elliot's birth.

The tree was to signify strength, growth and family roots. Mia needs every ounce of that strength when she hears the detective's conclusion.

'I am putting it to you that the person in this CCTV is *not* Tara McAllen. I am proposing that the person in this footage is *you*, masquerading as Tara.'

35
Ryan

Mia devised most of the plan. He listened, desisted, appealed, even cried. But he ended up deferring to his wife, as he always does. They stayed up all night, going back and forth, debating the difficulties and risks and how best to mitigate them. Mia employed her seven-step process, a problem-solving methodology she learned about on one of her university courses. Recognise and define the problem. Gather facts and make assumptions. Define end states and establish criteria.

'Tara *cannot* die on our property. The police need to be focused on a place that's as far away from here as possible.

'And she can't up and go out of the blue – her mum has already advised her to give notice.

'Let's have her work out her notice period – two weeks sounds about right. Tara can send messages and communicate with everyone as normal during the two weeks. She can be excited about her upcoming adventure, a little bit sad about leaving us ...'

Ryan stared at his wife incredulously. 'That's impossible. We'd need to get into her phone.'

The phone had survived the accident, ensconced in Tara's water-resistant handbag, its landing cushioned by a nearby bush. But having the phone in their possession and being able to hack into it were two different things.

This was when Mia admitted to already knowing Tara's passcode and having previously read her texts and messages. Ryan listened with horror. The poor girl. How many violations had they inflicted upon her?

The rain stopped around three in the morning.

'We need to move her,' Mia declared. 'Before dawn breaks, before she becomes stiff.'

They wrapped the body in a large blue tarp. There was only one place they could store it to prevent decomposition: the chest freezer in the garage. Plastic baskets and frozen meats emptied onto the gritty concrete. Bending the knees to fit her in. Layers of frozen products reinserted over the top. Frantically searching for the key that locked the lid, a key they'd never had reason to use before. Relocating the excess frozen food to the kitchen fridge.

'We'll have some of these chops for dinner tonight,' Mia said, leaving one of the zip-lock bags to defrost on the counter.

Ryan felt vomit rush up his throat and ran for the sink. All that came up was a pathetic dribble of yellow bile.

~

The planning continued through the next two weeks. Hair dye purchased with cash, to tint Mia's hair from dark-brown to black. Experimentation with tanning products and make-up, and deciding which clothes fitted best. Mia and Tara were of a similar height and physique. Tara was bonier, with sharp elbows and a prominent collarbone. Best to cover up whenever possible. Hence the sweater in thirty-four degrees.

Of course, the entire plan hinged on the carefully constructed messages to Tara's mother and friends.

Resigning tomorrow. Wish me luck.

Mia and Ryan took it okay. They knew I was unhappy. Agreed two weeks' notice.

Booked the hostel. So excited. Sydney here I come.

Mia laboured over the wording, using Tara's previous messages as a guide to the syntax. On day four, she woke up to an alarming text message from Ciara, one of Tara's sisters.

Hey Bitch, you forgot my birthday!

A sibling's birthday is hard to forget, having celebrated together during all those formative years. How would Tara react? Contrite or defensive or laugh it off? Mia decided that contrite was the safest option.

OMG! So sorry! Happy birthday. Miss you!

The sister responded with a string of emojis. Then she tried to call. Mia cut off the call, sent a text.

Sorry, can't talk, busy with the kid.

In some ways Tara's messages were the easiest part of the project, as was deciding which hostel to book in Bondi. The rest had to be done without leaving a digital footprint. While Ryan was at work and Elliot at school, Mia did the rounds of libraries in Newcastle, using their computer facilities to find out a raft of information. She discovered an app for locating security cameras, using a phone's camera and flashlight to detect hidden devices. She researched burials at sea, and the depth of the ocean beyond the Sydney Heads: three kilometres. She researched hire rates for boats, as well as security deposit and licence requirements. She even researched how long a frozen body takes to defrost, but of course neither of them foresaw the truck accident on the freeway.

There's no denying that Mia's planning was meticulous, even down to Tara's spending habits.

'We need to make sure her bank and Opal cards are being used. She would be out and about, as per usual.'

So Mia used the debit card in the pharmacy and supermarket in Morisset, buying the type of items Tara would buy: nail polish, lip balm and sanitary products. She wore Tara's clothes, fixed her hair so it was obscuring her face, and practised using the app on her phone to locate security cameras. On the Saturday night following the accident, she had a night out in Newcastle, buying gin and cheap wine at a few different bars, before catching the train home. Ryan picked her up from the station. She was drunk and jubilant.

Of course, Elliot asked questions about where Tara was. They used a variety of different explanations.

'Tara is feeling sick ... Mummy will take care of you today.'

'Tara is staying at her friend's house for the weekend.'

'Tara is moving to Sydney, Elliot.'

A moment of horror when their son found one of Tara's wireless earbuds a week or so after the accident.

'Look, look, it's Tara's.' The dirty white plastic was pinched between his delicate fingers. It must have got caught in Tara's clothes, dislodging in the garage without them noticing. The tiny earbud could be full of incriminating evidence. Was the brown staining from dirt, or dried-in blood, or even brain matter?

Ryan praised Elliot and promised to post the missing earbud to Tara in Sydney. Lucky that kids with ADHD never focus on anything for very long. Elliot accepted everything they said at face value, his mind already jumping ahead to something else. It was heartbreakingly easy to fool him. Tara was not sick or at a friend's house or moving to Sydney, as was her dream. She was dead, frozen solid in the freezer chest in the garage.

Then the planning phase was over and it was time for execution. Elliot went to stay with Dianne for a few days, on the pretence that they were celebrating their wedding anniversary. Without their son's constant activity and questions, it was easier to stage 'Tara's' departure for Sydney. It rained on the day she was leaving.

Mia wore one of Tara's oversized hoodies, paired with leggings and sneakers. She took Tara's phone and left her own at home, which meant that she'd be uncontactable after the drowning.

'You need ID to purchase a prepaid sim,' she stated, when Ryan suggested buying two cheap phones so they could remain in contact. 'Too risky.'

The car journey was largely silent, the person sitting next to him half-Tara, half-Mia. The clothes, the perfume, the jewellery, the hair: Tara. The intelligence, determination and bravado: Mia. Ryan navigated the turning circle at the train station and came to a reluctant stop.

'I can't believe we're going through with this!'

'We have no choice.' Mia didn't lean across to kiss him goodbye; she was already in character. 'See you in three days.'

Mia did a superb job in Sydney. Kept away from security cameras as much as possible. Acted the part of the Irish tourist, mixing sightseeing with a great deal of socialising (she was even mimicking the flat Dublin accent by the end). On the final day, she ran all of Tara's clothes through the hostel's washing machine, using the hottest setting: aiming to remove as much DNA as possible, while aware that some would inevitably survive. Despite the hot, humid weather, Mia had only one shower the whole time she stayed at the hostel. She didn't use the pool, simply because the fewer clothes she wore, the more dissimilarities that were revealed.

Now Mia is telling him that she was captured on the security camera outside the hostel's shower room.

'Don't worry, you can't see my face,' she says. 'They're identifying Tara purely on the basis of the sweater and the beach towel. The sweater stands up, but the towel is too generic. For heaven's sake, every second beach towel in Bondi has stripes of some sort, and every second girl in that hostel had dark hair.'

'But they zoomed in on the bandaid?' Ryan checks again.

'Yes,' she concedes, before squeezing his hand. 'Have some faith, Ryan. Our plan is not going to fall apart because of a stupid bandaid.'

'Are you sure about that?' he asks weakly.

She nods her head once, the way she does when she wants a discussion to end soon. 'I actually laughed when they suggested I was masquerading as Tara. It felt like the most genuine response to something so outlandish.'

36
Beth

Beth uses Lydia's computer to email the café's video footage to the police, quoting her case reference number. She has realistic expectations; at the end of the day, the footage is blurry, the clothes are nondescript, and the baseball cap does an effective job of hiding the man's face. Not much to go on, really.

At work, she unearths the patient questionnaire that Mary completed before her massage. According to the form, she was suffering from tension headaches, but Beth is starting to doubt whether this was true. She phones the contact number listed on the form, an automated message immediately kicking in.

'Telstra advises that the number you have dialled is incomplete or incorrect. Please check the number and dial again.'

Beth hangs up with a grimace, then asks Debbie's permission to send a copy of the form to the police.

'I guess it's okay.' Her boss shrugs. 'Hopefully, we're not breaching any privacy laws. Or falsely accusing the woman.'

Beth lines up her phone to take the photo and sends it off with the case reference number, and an accompanying message: *This is the client who had a medical episode, which resulted in our reception being left unattended. The phone number listed seems to be missing a digit. Maybe this is a deliberate error?*

'What next?' Debbie asks with a concerned expression. 'It's all very well playing detective, Beth, but you don't want to put yourself in any danger.'

Beth raises both hands to show that she is done for now. 'I know, I know. Doing this stuff makes me feel better, less of a victim, but I understand there's a limit to what I can do ...'

The phone rings, cutting her off. Listening to Debbie's side of the conversation, it sounds like another cancellation. Three today, all short notice, offering little opportunity to fill the appointment with someone else.

'What's going on?' Debbie shakes her head in dismay.

'Is it one of mine?'

'Yeah. Your 3pm.'

Acting purely on instinct, Beth uses her phone to Google the clinic. The first thing she notices is that their rating has skydived from 4.7 to 3.1.

'Uh oh. This doesn't look good.'

Debbie is peering over her shoulder as she clicks on the reviews. A spate of one- and two-star ratings, all posted in the last couple of days.

Overpriced. Don't waste your money.

Nobody answers the phone. Too hard to make a booking.

Therapist Beth was uncommunicative and didn't care that she was hurting me.

Blood rushes to Beth's face. She has never received anything but glowing online reviews. Has she been uncommunicative or unintentionally rough with a client? Or is someone trying to sabotage her reputation and the clinic's business?

~

Charlie is her last client of the day and she can tell that he immediately notices that something is wrong. It's as though he can see right through her professional smile to her battered soul.

'You okay?'

'Just tired.'

He's a client; it's not fair to burden him with her worries. And it's true: she *is* tired. She's also anxious and defeated. Who left those reviews? Genuine clients with real grievances? Or someone who wants to make her feel threatened and worried? Kane? The problem with having a devious, vindictive ex is that you can never be sure when they'll strike next.

Charlie's neck and shoulder muscles are as tight as ever. Beth works hard at them, using her thumbs and the hot stones. He groans into the face cradle.

'You okay there?' She pauses, uncertain about how to interpret the groan; the reviews have rocked her confidence.

'Yes. Great. Keep going. Honestly, Beth, you're a legend. Definitely the best massage therapist in Newcastle.'

Charlie has always been effusive with his praise, and she usually barely listens. Today it means the world to hear him say nice things.

'Not according to Google reviews.'

'What do you mean?'

'We've had all these bad reviews. I'm actually mentioned in a few of them. I don't know who these people are. Nobody said they were unhappy.'

He jerks his head up from the table. 'Can I see?'

'No, you cannot see. You're in the middle of your massage. Now shush. We shouldn't be talking.'

'Let's talk when you're done.' He rests his face back in the cradle and the rest of what he says is muffled but at the same time comforting. 'I can help.'

Thirty minutes later, Charlie is dressed and hunched over Debbie's laptop in reception, reading the reviews.

'Mmm ... Definitely looks like the handiwork of trolls.' He stands up straight, pushes his glasses further up his nose, and addresses Debbie. 'You should always respond to negative reviews. Don't get defensive – just say you're sorry they've had a bad experience. Ask for more information. When was their appointment? Would they care to talk about the problem? This way, other customers can see that you are making a genuine attempt to rectify the issue – if it *is* a real issue. Trolls won't want to talk or give specifics and potential customers will see through this.'

'Thanks, Charlie.' Debbie's face is pinched with worry. The business runs on tight margins, with barely enough revenue to cover rent and salaries. Late cancellations are particularly painful. It's not their policy to charge a cancellation fee; most of the time the client has a good excuse.

His smile is kind. 'I'll make sure to add my own five-star review. Ask your regular customers to do the same. Eventually the positive reviews will drown out the negative ones.'

'I will. Thanks again, Charlie.'

Beth checks the time; she needs to get going if she's to make after-school care. While Debbie and Charlie are talking, she retrieves her bag from the treatment room, its new safe-keeping spot. She hitches it on her shoulder, enjoying the feel of the soft tan leather against her bare arm. Pippa had the bag sitting in her cupboard and insisted Beth take it as a replacement. *Here. I never use it. You're doing me a favour.* So generous of Pippa.

Charlie finishes up with Debbie, and he and Beth leave together.

'Are you parked in the Sportsground again?' he asks, pausing outside the clinic. 'I can walk with you.'

'Sure. I need to hurry, though. I'm always one of the last parents to arrive at the school.'

'How's the new car going?'

She laughs as they stride down the footpath. 'As you know, it's far from new, but it's going well. I can't thank you enough.'

'A welcome break from my day job. Listen, I was looking at car parts last night, and came across this Bluetooth system on eBay. I could wire it up to your stereo. Then you could stream music and make hands-free calls, just like a modern car ...'

Not having Bluetooth is a major downside of the wagon. She gives him a sideways look. 'How much?'

'A hundred. Bargain. I think I can manage the installation. If not, I have a mechanic friend I can ask for help.'

It *is* a bargain. But she still needs a moment to think about it, do the sums.

'Sure.' She decides that Bluetooth isn't a luxury; it's a necessity. Especially on days when she's running late to pick up Tilly. 'Thank you. Being able to make calls again will be great.'

Charlie's long legs make little of the ten-minute walk to the Sportsground. They stop at the entrance.

'Thanks again for giving Debbie some advice.'

'No worries.' He pushes his glasses into place, and their eyes meet. A moment of connection before he becomes Mr Management Consultant again. 'It's really common. Excellent businesses getting smashed online. Sometimes it's competitors trying to get an edge. Sometimes it's personal, someone out for revenge because of some small slight. And sometimes it's totally random: the troll is from a different country, has never even set foot in the place.'

Beth wonders which one it is in this instance. She can't shake the feeling that it's personal. Her name is mentioned.

Surely, not the handiwork of someone from a different country?

37
Mia

The library is busy, students, seniors and a few oddly dressed homeless people competing for the computer facilities. She has to wait her turn, trying not to let her impatience show because the aim is to be as invisible as possible. Such a pain to have to take these measures – the trip into the city, and already fifteen minutes of waiting – but she can't be careful enough these days. A recorded police interview. A direct accusation: *I am putting it to you that the person in this CCTV is* not *Tara McAllen.*

Mia might have outwardly laughed at Detective Goodwin's deduction, but inside she was aghast. Her hair was dyed the exact same shade as Tara's; there were no clear shots of her face; she was even wearing Tara's clothes, for heaven's sake. What had made the police look beyond the superficial? What had made them trawl through blurry footage to zoom in on an arm, specifically the outline of a bandaid? Was it Siobhan's insistence that something was amiss? The *inconsistencies* she keeps referring to. If only Mia knew what those inconsistencies were.

Finally, it's Mia's turn, one of the homeless clientele pushing back his seat and vacating a booth. An unwashed smell lingers in his wake, catching at the back of her throat. She uses an anti-bacterial wipe to clean the keyboard: she has done this often enough to expect this kind of thing.

On the positive side, she's online at last, and anonymous.

Wellbeing and Sports Massage Therapy: she is pleased that the clinic's previously excellent rating has taken a dive. Beth's boss will have noticed and should be asking questions by now. Beth will be feeling confused, alarmed, perhaps a little defensive. Other reviewers have said positive things. What has she done wrong?

Turning up at Mia's house: wrong.

Asking if the car had been involved in a crime: perilously wrong.

The last thing Mia needs is Beth poking her nose in, providing police with another piece of the puzzle: the role of the car. Beth needs to stop the amateur detective work. She needs distraction.

Mia deftly creates a new Google Account; she has about ten of them now. *Share your experience to help others*, the screen prompts.

Mia thinks for a moment, then types:

Hard to recommend this place. Beth, the therapist, was quite rude.

Then she smiles with satisfaction as she clicks on POST REVIEW.

~

On the drive home, the sun beams down from a cloudless crayon-blue sky. Perfect weather for the beach, for the lucky people who don't have work or other responsibilities. Mia's thoughts drift to Bondi, those incredibly vivid few days when she was one of those people. What was surprising, and weird, was that she actually enjoyed being Tara. She expected to be tense, constantly looking over her shoulder, scared that she'd slip up; instead she felt young, carefree, as though she was on an unexpected holiday. No housework, no immediate money problems, no managing Elliot. Of course she missed her son, and was worried about how he'd get on without her, but there were hours when she didn't think about him at all, hours that were consumed with sun-bathing, playing on Tara's phone, reading second-hand books from the hostel's library, and getting deliciously drunk. The weather was hot, and she swam in the ocean every day, cooling down and at the same time researching what part of the beach she would use to get in and out of the water when the time came. The logistics weren't hard to work out. Drinking beforehand at the hostel bar, pretending to knock back several gin and tonics, then a public statement that she was going for a swim. Clothes – including that horrid sweater – and towel left on a quiet, treacherous stretch on the southern end. Goggles tucked into her hand, she waded through the white-wash. Discreetly slipping on the goggles before diving into the first set of waves. The cool embrace of the water, the strong pull of the rip, yielding to it, trusting that it would deliver her to the sandbank. Finally, compact sand under her feet. Getting her breath back, her bearings, before freestyling towards the rocks, cutting and scraping her legs on the scramble out of the water. A small backpack hidden in the bush beyond the rocks. Quick change of clothes: Lycra pants, runners, hat. A swimmer transformed into a woman out for a walk. And so she walked, she powered along the coastal path all the way to Bronte Beach, where she and Ryan had arranged to meet. It was fully dark by the time she reached Bronte. She sat on the grass and waited, and waited and waited. Back in the hostel, Helena, an English girl she had befriended, noticed 'Tara's' empty bed around midnight. She assumed her friend had met someone on the beach, gone to an impromptu party or something like that. It was late afternoon on the next day before the alarm was raised, and the clothes were found on the beach.

Those days in Bondi offered a glimpse into a parallel life, a life with no husband, no child, no responsibilities. Mia found herself in those days, or maybe it was more that she recovered herself. Her strength. Her focus. Her ability to enjoy nature, her own company and even her body. Sex seemed to be on offer with practically every male – and some females, too – in the hostel. She contemplated it, decided that she wanted this time solely to herself. She swam. She read voraciously. She boozed and flirted but came home alone, finishing the night with her hand between her legs, an orgasm summing up the perfection of each day.

I am proposing that the person in this footage is you, masquerading as Tara.

Mia denied the accusation, and even risked a laugh, although she is not laughing now. Amy Goodwin has managed to piece together some of what happened. That's alarming, and more than Mia expected. On the plus side, there is no body, and no real evidence.

A bandaid is not enough to secure a conviction. A distinctive tattoo would be another matter, though. Thank heavens she had the foresight to cover up her little tree – strength, growth, roots! – with a rectangle of flesh-coloured plastic.

~

Ryan is pale when he gets in from work. No matter how much she reassures him, he seems convinced that they are about to be exposed, charged, taken into custody. He needs to snap out of it. The telltale slump of his shoulders, the guilt clouding his eyes, his lethargy and jitteriness combined: he is starting to give himself away.

Despite all this, he still manages to salvage something for Elliot. A quick game of cricket before dinner, a game of airports afterwards, then supervising an excruciatingly drawn-out bedtime routine. Their son is ten years old and should be able to stay on track with shower, reading time and lights out. But Elliot is not like other children and that's why they're in this awful mess. If their son had been like other children, Mia could have thrown herself at the mercy of the justice system, taken whatever punishment was coming her way.

If our son had been like other children, we wouldn't have needed Tara in the first place.

No point in thinking thoughts like these.

Finally, Elliot is in bed and they go outside to talk, as is becoming their habit. The air is heavy and humid, the temperature still in the mid-twenties.

Mia begins with their biggest problem: the bandaid. 'I can plant the idea of Tara getting a copy tattoo, claim that she admired mine and wanted the same. I've Googled tattoo parlours in the Bondi area. Plenty for Tara to choose from. The bandaid could be to protect it from the sun or infection or whatever ...'

Ryan seems to be only half listening, her words dissolving into the dark around him.

'Hey, can you *listen*? This is important. We need to treat these discussions like they could be our last, like one of us could be arrested tomorrow.'

This makes him pay attention. He straightens in his seat. Looks at her face instead of somewhere over her shoulder.

'Do you *think* we're going to get arrested?' he asks, the panic in his voice so tangible she can almost reach out and touch it.

'No. I just want your full attention.' She smiles, to prove she isn't overly concerned. 'Moving on to Beth. We need to distract her, get her worrying about something else. Hopefully, her boss is giving her grief about the reviews. But I think we need to up the ante. Something closer to home.'

'What?' Ryan croaks. 'What are you saying?'

She leans forward, puts her hand on his knee: a commandment. 'I'm saying that we need to get back inside Beth's house.'

38
Ryan

'You want me to do *what*?'

'Break into the house.' Mia's fingers are digging into the bare skin just above his knee. 'Snap the flexi hose under one of the sinks. Preferably upstairs, so there's maximum damage – you'd be shocked at how much water comes out of those things. Beth will have a huge mess to deal with. The car – and who stole it – won't be top of mind.'

'No, Mia ... *just no*.'

'Yes.' Her fingers curl, and now he can feel her nails sinking into his flesh. 'It's *necessary*.'

'It's not necessary. We've taken the car, destroyed whatever evidence was left. You want to wreck her house, too?'

'I want her to stop thinking about us,' she hisses into the dark. 'I don't want to find her on my doorstep again. Or worse, walking into a police station with our names on her lips. We're on their database, Ryan. Any suggestion that we stole the car and hey presto: Amy fucking Goodwin has another piece of the puzzle. Short of murdering Beth Jenkins, this is the best I can come up with!'

He knows, from her cold determination, that she has thought about it, weighed it up, actually considered murdering Beth.

All he can do is appeal to her sense of logic.

'Beth has a house alarm.' He can still hear the wail, feel the bloom of panic in his chest. 'I can't do it.'

'I bet she doesn't put on the alarm when she pops next door. You said she was friendly with the neighbours?'

Fuck! She has already begun to formulate a plan; when Mia devises a plan, she is almost impossible to stop. He summons all his strength.

'No.' He is firm, resolute, frightened. 'I already told you. I've done my last terrible thing.'

'This isn't an opt-in or opt-out,' she exclaims, sarcasm coating each word. 'We're in this *together*. We need to do everything we can to protect ourselves.'

'*No.*'

'Think of Elliot. Do it for him.'

He thinks of their son, his dark hair resting against the white cotton of his pillow, eyes closed, his body at rest after a day of relentless activity.

'No,' he says simply.

Mia is not used to this. He always gives in, acquiesces to her stronger personality and superior intelligence.

'I'll do it myself, then.' She stands up, her fury radiating through the dark air. 'It's always down to me, isn't it? Why is it always *me*? Why can't you ever come up with a plan and make things fucking happen?'

~

His wife's plans aren't as brilliant or as infallible as she thinks they are. Exhibit A: the day Tara 'drowned'. The nightmare on the freeway. Trapped in the traffic jam, the heat from the blazing fuel truck combining with the high temperatures. Tara's body defrosting in the boot, releasing odours, gases and damning DNA. Ryan had no way to contact Mia to let her know about the truck accident and the horrendous delays. 'Tara' had left her phone at the hostel, Mia's phone was back at the house, and so Mia had sat on the grass in Bronte, getting more furious and frustrated and concerned as the hours ticked by.

'Where the fuck have you been?' she screeched, when he finally turned up, just after midnight. 'I've been here for *hours*. I didn't know what to do.'

He explained about the fireball, the incinerated cars, the complexities surrounding the removal of the burnt-out truck and repairing the melted bitumen. All in all, it had equated to more than an eight-hour delay.

She listened without fully comprehending. 'Let's get the hell out of here.' She went to pick up her backpack. 'Where did you park?'

He put out a hand to stop her. More explaining: the fact that he'd been too late for the boat-hire place.

Mia recoiled. 'Jesus Christ. You mean she's still in there?'

Ryan hadn't dared open the boot to determine how bad things were. A pungent smell had started to seep through to the cabin of the car. That told him enough. In hindsight, they should have wrapped the body in something other than a tarp: a giant cooler bag, perhaps, to counteract the intense heat and slow down the defrosting process.

'We can sleep here.' He gestured to a nearby picnic shelter, its square white roof glowing in the darkness. 'The boat place opens at 7am. I called them when it was clear I wasn't going to make it in time. They were really understanding – the truck accident was all over the news. The boat we booked isn't available tomorrow, but we can get a slightly more expensive one. They'll only charge us the difference in rate.'

Mia glared at him, furious that he had used his phone, unwilling to accept that her plan should have included two cheap phones with prepaid sims (purchased with false ID or whatever it took), so they had the means to contact each other. At the very least, they should have had a Plan B in the event of serious delays.

That night in the picnic shelter was the second-worst night of his life. They sat on the cold metal bench, barely talking. Mia was still angry; Ryan was choked with self-disgust. The park around them was full of ominous shadows, threatening sounds and the scream of his thoughts.

What were they doing? This was madness. This was evil. They were out of their minds.

At some point, Mia stretched out, rested her head on his lap, and slept. Ryan couldn't contemplate sleep. Tara was decomposing in the boot of the car. He wanted to unfurl that suffocating tarp, hug her back to life, beg her forgiveness.

Mia opened her eyes as the sun started to appear on the horizon. Orange, yellow and pink reflected on the water.

'Happy anniversary,' she whispered after a few moments.

With a jolt, he realised that she was right – they were married ten years. Looking out to the horizon, he saw flashes of their wedding day. His new wife glowing in her elegant silk dress. Exchanging the rings, his hands shaking uncontrollably, hers steady. The photos, the speeches, his relief when the formalities were over. All the while unable to believe his luck that this extraordinary woman wanted to spend the rest of her life with him.

And here they were. Not the happy-ever-after he envisaged. A living nightmare.

Mia sat up on the bench, kissed him lightly on the lips. 'Let's go for an anniversary swim.'

It was a good suggestion: they had an hour to kill, and his skin was crawling at the thought of what was waiting in the car. Wading into the sea in their underwear. Dunking his head to clear his thoughts. The cleansing effect of the waves and the unsoiled early morning. Afterwards they bought takeaway bacon-and-egg rolls. They were washed. They were fed. They were as ready as they'd ever be.

Ryan drove with the windows down and the radio up high. The car's licence plates were splashed with mud, something he had done (on Mia's instruction) before leaving home to make it more difficult for cameras to capture the rego. Did the mud-coated licence plates look suspicious in this well-to-do part of Sydney? He and Mia were wearing caps and large sunglasses. Did they look like they were about to commit a heinous crime?

It took fifteen anxiety-filled minutes to get to Rose Bay, holding his breath for much of the journey, turning to the open window every time he needed to inhale. Ryan had used his boss's boating licence and credit card to make the booking, counting on the fact that Paul wouldn't notice the cards missing and they could be returned as easily as they'd been 'borrowed' (Paul always left his wallet in an unlocked drawer in his office). The credit card was only required to hold the booking; Ryan had already organised to pay in cash. All going well, Paul would be none the wiser. All going well, there would be nothing to link the boat hire to Ryan. Except for that unavoidable phone call from the freeway, to advise them he'd been delayed.

Mia did most of the talking with the young woman at the boat-hire office.

'Thank you for being so accommodating about yesterday.' A flash of Mia's most charming smile from beneath her cap. 'We're so excited. It's our wedding anniversary. Ten years!'

Producing Paul's licence, counting out the cash for the hire fee and security deposit, before a tour of the boat and a rundown of the safety instructions.

'My husband just needs to get some stuff from the car,' Mia said airily. 'He's planning a big day!'

The administrator turned her attention to the next customer, who had been waiting a few minutes and was obviously keen to get out on the water. They needed to act quickly; the car park and jetty were clear but wouldn't remain that way for long.

Ryan had attached a makeshift strap to either end of the tarp. A few beach towels carelessly thrown over and it looked like a folded-up shade structure. He braced himself for the weight, tried not to let it show on his face, while Mia trotted ahead, carrying a picnic hamper and snorkelling gear. Ryan was glad she was there. Her natural charm, the fluency of her lies, the aura of having it all under control: there was no way he would have been as convincing on his own.

Ryan drove the boat carefully out of the bay, endeavouring to portray experience when all he had to rely on was taking the occasional turn at the helm of friends' boats over the years. Once they were safely clear of the expensive vessels moored in the bay, he advanced the throttle. Mia stood next to him, squinting at the horizon, smiling when hit in the face by a shower of sea spray.

Inside the picnic basket were cleaning products, a garbage bag for the tarp (to be discarded somewhere on land), and a shroud in a degradable canvas material: Mia had hand-sewn the shroud, sowing barbells into the corners to ensure rapid sinking and permanent submersion of the body.

They cruised to a stop fourteen nautical miles beyond the Sydney Heads. Dark-navy water lapped the sides of the boat, hinting that the continental shelf was behind them: they had reached the desired depth.

'We need to be quick.' Mia knelt down, and unceremoniously started to unfurl the tarp. 'We're not supposed to take the boat out this far.'

Ryan sucked in a wave of nausea. The smell was horrendous, the tarp slick with brown liquid. He placed the shroud over Tara's head, and wiggled it down, somehow avoiding eye-contact with her mottled face. A final act of self-preservation.

The shroud was a dead weight to lift, Tara's bloated body and the barbells combined.

'One, two, three ...' Mia gasped as she lifted her end. 'Jesus.'

A definitive splash as Tara hit the water. Straight down, down, down, the weights doing their job. Landing on the ocean bed, dislodging sand and sea life. The gases would soon leave her body. Sea creatures would move in. Nature would take its course.

'Rest in peace, Tara,' Mia murmured as she leaned over the side, her hypocrisy leaving him speechless. Then she became businesslike. 'Turn the boat around.'

He steered them back around the Heads, to their permitted zone within the bounds of the harbour. The sky was pale blue now, the sun higher with the promise of another hot day to come, and the water glittered and glinted and rippled. The beauty provided a sharp contrast to the horror of what they'd just done.

They anchored near Watsons Bay, washed the tarp by immersing it in the sea, before folding it tightly to fit in the garbage bag. Then they scrubbed the deck of any potential body fluids using bleach, water and the sheer force of their guilt.

When there was nothing left to do, Ryan fell apart. Sinking to his knees, rocking, his body convulsing with sobs and shame and regret.

What had they done? There was no way to justify this. What had they done?

'Shush.' Mia held him as he howled and ranted and grieved. 'It's over. We can put it behind us. It's over.'

Now he hates himself. For being bullied into carrying out Mia's macabre plan. For allowing himself to be comforted on the boat. For yielding to the soft, reassuring kisses that turned into anniversary sex, the boat bobbing on the surface of the water while Tara's shroud was already being circled by curious fish three kilometres deep.

He hates himself. He has never been able to forgive himself. Or Mia.

39
Beth

The smell of baking fills the house; Beth is hoping it will mask the bareness. She doesn't like being critical of her home – every item has been carefully considered, bought second-hand or on a shoestring budget – but she imagines Charlie living in an urban apartment on the waterfront (or wherever management consultants live) and can't help wincing every time she looks objectively at the old-fashioned table and chairs, the saggy sofa and the faded rug.

She's jittery, constantly checking the clock. He said he would drop by around midday with the new Bluetooth system – another hour to go. Tilly is excited too, repeatedly asking if the muffins are ready yet, and how long until Charlie is here.

'Let's bring some of these beauties over to Pippa,' Beth suggests as she extracts the baking tray from the oven.

A visit next door will calm them down and pass the time nicely.

Within minutes Beth is sitting on one of Pippa's kitchen stools, her hands cupping a mug of tea. Tilly receives a lollipop from the cupboard but is told to save it for later; the muffin is enough sugar for now! She gives the lollipop to Beth for safekeeping and departs, calling Fuzzy's name. 'Fuzzy-wuz, Fuzzy-wuz, where are you hiding?'

The muffins are warm and decadent: white chocolate and raspberry.

'Delicious,' Pippa proclaims. 'Is there a special occasion?'

'Just a friend calling over and nothing nice in the cupboard. I'm not as well stocked as you are!'

'Oh, I almost forgot!' Pippa suddenly straightens. 'I got that quote for the security cameras. Let me see if I can quickly find it.'

She rummages through a mound of paperwork on the sideboard. Then opens a drawer or two. 'Where on earth did I put it? Oh, never mind, I remember the approximate amount – about $500 each, including installation. That includes two cameras per property. What do you think?'

What Beth thinks is that she simply can't afford it.

She also thinks that her recent experience with security cameras hasn't been a good advertisement for their usefulness. A supervisor from the Police Assistance Line phoned yesterday, saying that the footage from the café had been reviewed and sent to local police, who will post it on social media in the hope that members of the public might be able to help. The supervisor was sympathetic yet forthright: given that the perpetrator was careful to angle his face downwards and was wearing nondescript clothes, a positive identification would be difficult to make.

Pippa reads Beth's thoughts. 'Let's leave it for now, shall we? We can talk about it again in a few months if your cashflow improves.'

'Thanks, Pippa. Sorry, I didn't mean to waste your time.'

The older woman waves a hand. 'I have all the time in the world, my dear. In the meantime, why don't you mention it to the property manager? You never know, the landlord might be willing to contribute.'

'I doubt it,' Beth smiles ruefully. She has been late with her rent too often to be asking for extra favours.

Thirty minutes later, after a second mug of tea, Beth opens her front door, ushering Tilly in ahead of her. She has time for one last tidy-up before Charlie gets here. It takes her a few moments to register the sound of running water.

'Did you leave the tap on upstairs?' she asks, stopping in her tracks.

'No,' her daughter replies indignantly.

Beth jogs up the stairs, Tilly trailing behind. The noise gets louder and louder. Oh God, this does not sound good.

'It's a fountain,' Tilly shrieks.

A jet of water is coming from the open ensuite door, arcing over the bed, some of it landing on the mattress, some on the carpet beyond ... some even reaching as far as the window and curtains. It's an astonishing sight: the sheer volume of the water, the incredible *power* of it, inconceivable that the pipework of a tiny sink could be the source. Beth is momentarily frozen, staring at the spectacle in shock. *All that water.* How long since it happened? How many litres pumped into the mattress, the carpet, the flooring beneath? Her brain finally kicks into action.

'Oh my God. Oh my God. Stay where you are, pumpkin. Mum needs to turn off the mains.'

She bolts down the stairs, out the front door and down the driveway. The water mains are on the nature strip, from memory. She's never had to think about them before, never had reason to turn the stiff tap with trembling fingers, never had to contemplate which way was OFF. Has she made it better or worse? Another sprint back to the house.

'Has it stopped?' she calls up the stairs to Tilly.

'Yes ... Mummy, the carpet is *squelching*.'

She can still hear water, albeit more of a dripping sound now. Leaving the front door open, just in case she needs to do another dash to the mains, she follows the sound, into the front room. Water is spooled on the wooden floorboards. The sofa and rug are obviously sodden. The plasterboard on the ceiling is sagging with a bellyful of water, large drips plopping down.

Oh God. This is big. The carpet and bed upstairs. The ceiling, sofa and floorboards down here. This is a disaster.

'Knock, knock. Anyone home?' a male voice calls out from the hallway.

Oh God. Charlie is here.

~

The plumber goes upstairs to fix the broken pipe, while Beth and Charlie try to deal with the mess downstairs. Towels are used to mop the excess water from the floorboards (Charlie predicts that they'll bow and need replacing). They drag the rug outside, squeeze out the excess water, and lay it flat on the driveway, in the sun. Tilly helps by carrying out the cushions from the sofa. Beth doesn't know if the sofa or her mattress are worth saving; she tries not to think about how many homes they've been in before hers.

'Your insurance company should replace them,' Charlie says in answer to her question.

Beth pushes her hair away from her face. 'I don't *have* contents insurance,' she replies faintly. 'All of this is second-, third- and fourth-hand. It didn't seem worth it.'

He blinks a few times. Beth tries to read his thoughts. Is not having home insurance as bad as, or worse than, not having car insurance? What would he say if she admitted that she didn't have health insurance either?

His smile is diplomatic. 'Well, the worst damage is to the floorboards and carpet, which are the landlord's problem.'

The *landlord*. Beth feels another wave of faintness. 'But am I at fault? Can I get evicted for this?'

Charlie's smile becomes more certain. 'It's a busted pipe. Totally not your fault. You're 100 per cent safe from eviction.'

She doesn't feel safe. She feels as though she is teetering on the edge of an abyss, about to plunge into the unknown, arms flailing uselessly. Her old furniture might not be worth much, but it will still cost money to replace: there goes the extra $1000 from Shepherdess Finance, her 'breathing space'.

Her front garden is starting to look like a cross between her living room and bedroom. Pippa appears, surveys the sad collection on the grass and driveway, and tuts, 'Oh dear, oh dear, oh dear.'

The plumber is next to join the group, striding through the front door, holding a piece of silver hose in each hand; presumably the two pieces were connected before the disaster. 'This is the culprit here.'

'What happened?' Pippa asks. 'Wear and tear?'

'Nope. Relatively new pipe and no sign of fraying or rust. Looks like a clean break, which is unusual ... I've installed a new flexi-hose. Just about to turn the water back on ...'

There's a roaring in Beth's ears. A falling sensation in her stomach. Hysteria in her voice.

'Can I have a look?' She juts out her hand to take the pieces of flexi-hose.

It's exactly as the plumber said: a clean break. As though someone took a set of cutters and clipped it right in the middle.

40
Mia

This is her week for getting things done, for moving forward. On Monday she finally finishes her online course and updates her résumé to include her new qualification. She spends Tuesday trawling through job ads and applies for two positions, one part-time and the other with flexible hours. Kellie has indicated that she's willing to pick up Elliot from school a couple of days a week. She's already at the school to fetch her own kids, and they all get on so well.

In the spirit of moving forward, Mia refrains from posting further negative reviews on Google. She doesn't expect to hear any more from Beth, whose house will be her priority. It was all too easy. Waiting until Beth and Tilly went next door. Letting herself in through the front door (unlocked, just as she'd hoped). Water gushing out at an astounding rate. She left the premises within a couple of minutes. Job accomplished.

Mia doesn't expect to hear any more from Beth, but the same can't be said for the police. However, she is prepared should there be a follow-up interview. At the end of the day – as she keeps reiterating to Ryan – they have *nothing*. No body, no evidence, no timeline. *Nothing*.

On her way into town to pick up Elliot from school, Mia receives a phone call from an unfamiliar number. A flutter of panic. A steadying breath.

'Hello, this is Mia.'

'Hello, Mia. This is Jane from the Nova Agency. We've just received your job application and were wondering if we could organise an interview this week.'

Mia is ecstatic, albeit unclear if the call is regarding the part-time job or the flexible-hours one; she can check when she gets home. What matters is they want to interview her, and their promptness implies an urgent need to fill the role. This should work in her favour. She has no notice period or current employer to take into consideration.

'I'd be delighted to interview. Just name the day. I'm available anytime this week.'

They agree on 10am Thursday morning and she hangs up with a sense of validation.

'Yes. Yes. *Yes.*' She whoops in excitement, and fist pumps the air.

The car flies along the country road and she feels in command of where she is going, something she hasn't felt for a long, long time. The Nova Agency is obviously keen – they made contact within hours of receiving her application! Maybe there's a skills shortage. Maybe they're worried that she'll be snapped up by someone else. Whatever the reason, she is just as keen as they are. She has *so much* to offer her future employer.

Unfortunately, Elliot's day has not been as good as her own. A heated disagreement over whose turn it was on the play equipment at recess. A visit to the vice-principal's office after disrupting class in the afternoon. A substitute teacher, therefore none of the usual 'calming down' strategies or special considerations.

Mia folds him into a hug, his growing body squirming with indignation and anger. Her instincts are to march into the principal's office, with its smell of lead pencils and bureaucracy, and bellow her disappointment and frustration. Why wasn't the substitute teacher properly briefed? It's an ongoing battle: constantly reminding the school how to get the best out of Elliot, fighting for consistency and fairness and understanding.

'Let's go home, huh? You can ride your bike and bounce on the trampoline, and I bet you'll feel better really fast! I'll talk to the school tomorrow.'

~

The news that she has an upcoming interview seems to have a positive effect on Ryan's mood, which has been brooding and obstinate.

'The advertisement says twenty hours a week, Monday, Wednesday and Friday.' She beams, prepared to put the disagreement about the water pipe behind them. 'I could do two short days and one long – I guess I'll have to play it by ear. I have a good feeling, darling. It's obvious they're in a hurry and, hey, I can start practically straight away.'

Ryan smiles for the first time in days but she can't help noticing the restraint in his smile and how exhausted he looks. The purple shadows lurking below his eyes. The pallor beneath the tan of his face. He hasn't been sleeping well, thrashing and shouting in the dead of night, his nightmares waking them both.

'Great news,' he says, his voice managing to portray both optimism and wariness. 'Fingers crossed that this is a new beginning.'

~

On Wednesday morning, Mia is relieved to see Elliot's usual teacher back in the classroom, looking both pale and preoccupied. At the last minute, she decides not to voice her disappointment about yesterday's events. The teacher looks decidedly under the weather, and the principal is always busy at this time of morning. She needs to get home, start preparing for her interview tomorrow. She crouches down, hugs Elliot fiercely, and tries to vanquish the flare of guilt that she is letting him down.

'See you, buddy. Try your best to be Calm Elliot today, not Cyclone Elliot.'

Back at the house, she rifles through her wardrobe. Once she has decided what to wear, she will go through some practice questions. Her work clothes are old but hopefully don't show it. Black trouser suit, suede heels, a few different tops to choose from. She slips off her shorts and t-shirt and steps into the trousers: a little loose on the waist but otherwise fine. The cream top first, which is perfectly adequate. Then the blue silk, which complements her eyes and is more vibrant. She pads to the ensuite, retrieves her make-up bag from the drawer. Foundation, pale-pink eyeshadow, mascara and nude lipstick. Back to the bedroom for the final touches: jewellery, shoes and jacket. She surveys her reflection.

'Hello, I'm Mia.'

She begins to question the woman in the mirror and listens critically to her answers. She modulates the tone of her voice, remembers to smile every now and then, while getting used to the feel of the jacket and the shoes, a professional armour that she has become unaccustomed to. She takes a walk down the hallway and does a lap around the kitchen, the shoes pinching her toes. She pours herself a glass of water, because the jacket is making her feel constricted and rather hot. The doorbell sounds and she startles, some water spilling from the glass onto her hand. Probably Kellie, dropping off surplus vegetables or eggs from the farm. Good timing: she can double-check with her friend about helping out with Elliot. Just a couple of days a week. Hopefully not too much of an imposition.

It's not Kellie. Detective Goodwin has a hard set to her face as she thrusts forward a document of some kind. Mia takes the document being offered and at the same time registers that the detective is not alone: a number of other officers are milling around at the front of the house, as well as several vehicles.

'Good morning, Mia. This is an occupier's notice. We have a warrant to search and enter your property.'

~

'We can sit somewhere while the officers conduct the search,' Detective Goodwin prompts, breaking Mia's horrified trance.

They go inside, sit at the kitchen table.

'Were you on your way out?' the detective enquires, giving her clothes a once-over.

Mia looks down at herself, feels an annoying trickle of sweat from her left underarm; now she'll have to wear the cream top tomorrow.

'Just an interview I was preparing for. Thought I'd dress up, get into character ... What on earth is this about?'

'As I said, we have a warrant ...'

'But on what basis?'

'On the basis that there are reasonable grounds to believe that Tara McAllen died here, somewhere on this property ...'

'*What?* That's *insane.*'

'Tell me about your tattoo, Mia,' Goodwin says pointedly. 'When did you get it done?'

'After my son was born ... How is my tattoo relevant? Is this about Tara's *bandaid?*'

A tight smile from the detective. 'We've had the images enhanced ... there appears to be the outline of something dark underneath ...'

'So? Look, Tara actually *liked* my tattoo. It's possible she went and got a copy one. I don't know, maybe it got infected, or she didn't want it to get sunburnt?' Mia laughs then, a harsh little laugh, not unlike Tara's. 'For heaven's sake, the tattoo was the only thing she liked about me. I was too boring, too strict, too focused on routine. If I were Tara's age, I would probably think the same!'

The detective mulls it over, her brown eyes intense in her freckled face. It's clear that she's deciding how much to reveal.

'How do you explain the changes in Tara's online activity?' she asks eventually.

'What do you mean?'

'A dramatic reduction in the number of social media posts in the weeks prior to her departure.'

Mia shrugs impatiently. 'Tara was *busy* ... probably for the first time in her life! She was packing, choosing accommodation, researching what to see and do.'

'No selfies taken during that time either, not even when she got to Bondi. Tara was the "selfie queen", according to her mum and friends.'

'She was growing up.' Mia is scathing now. 'Learning how to live *real* life instead of a fake virtual one ...'

The car is gone. The freezer chest is gone – dismantled and crushed for recycling a few weeks after the accident. Any blood or fibres on the driveway are long washed away. The fact is, there is nothing for the forensics team to find. No matter how scrupulously or desperately they search. No matter their theories about Tara's changed social media habits or whatever else.

Mia's sigh is audible and impatient. 'How long is this search going to take? What an unbelievable waste of time.'

Amy Goodwin has nothing more than a few scraps of circumstantial evidence, for which any number of explanations could be possible. And they both know it.

41
Beth

The industrial-grade dehumidifiers have been running sixteen hours a day; three machines are stationed upstairs, in her bedroom, and two downstairs in the living room. Sucking moisture from the carpet, the floors and the ceiling. Hindering her ability to move around the house, to clean and tidy. Infusing her thoughts with their noise.

Beth is allowed to turn them off at night, but the drone is hard to erase from her brain. She has been sleeping in the spare bedroom, the unfamiliar bed and her mounting anxiety resulting in hours of tossing and turning. Worrying about money. Worrying about their safety. Worrying about what to do from here. Echoes of the time when she was mustering the courage to leave Kane. The same helplessness and fear. Familiarity versus the unknown. Confusion and uncertainty muddying every thought and theory.

Did someone cut the flexi-hose? Is it the same person who has been leaving bad Google reviews? Is this related to the theft of my car? Bad luck or something more sinister? Someone who is known to me or a stranger?

On Saturday morning, Tilly is invited to go to the Wildlife Reserve with a school friend. She is picked up by her friend's mum – a high-energy woman whom Beth has met a couple of times before – just after 10am. Beth waves them off and turns back to face the dreadful whine of the dehumidifiers. She needs to get out too, before she goes crazy. She scoops up her car keys and her handbag.

Fifteen minutes later she is driving around the achingly familiar streets of Merewether. Past the shopping centre, the local park and red-roofed houses with their pretty front gardens. Her car attracts a few amused glances. She parks across the road from her old home, her heart thumping as she stares at the innocuous white picket fence. Each time something happens, she is drawn back here. Two years now since the overcast morning she bundled clothes and a few essentials into the back of the car. How much longer will it be before her thoughts – and suspicions – don't automatically turn to Kane when something goes inexplicably wrong in her life?

A sharp rap on the driver's window. Beth jumps, inadvertently lets out a scream. A familiar face is peering through the glass: Mr Zhang, her old next-door neighbour. Beth winds down the window, summons a smile.

'Hello, there. You gave me a fright.'

'Hello, Beth. So long since I see you! You want Kane?'

She wants Kane to leave her alone. 'No ... I ...'

'He's on holiday,' Mr Zhang announces. 'Hamilton Island. I'm watching the house.' A quick roll of his dark eyes. 'Home on Wednesday.'

The eye-roll is his way of letting her know that the house minding is a neighbourly duty rather than a genuine desire to help. When Beth lived here, Kane often dispensed curt feedback about optimal kerbside parking, preferred hedge heights, and the pruning of a shared tree. Mr Zhang listened politely but never warmly, and only acted when he saw fit.

'When did he leave?' Beth asks breathlessly.

'Last week. Nice for some, yeah?'

She manages another smile. Hamilton Island was meant to be their honeymoon destination, but there was a mix-up with bookings. They stayed at one of the high-rise hotels on the Gold Coast instead, which was nice but nothing special. Kane promised they'd go to Hamilton Island another time; of course, they never did.

'I tell him you came by?' Mr Zhang asks, straightening up.

'No, no. Please don't mention anything.'

He nods, his almost-black eyes full of knowing. He was her neighbour for eight years. He saw her at her worst, her most vulnerable. The old clothes and shoes, all the more noticeable compared to her well-dressed neighbours. Leaving for work on Thursdays and Saturdays, bleary-eyed and physically weak – Tilly barely a month old, Kane insisting they needed the money, delegating the babysitting to his mum and Joe. Mr Zhang would have seen Tilly in her baby sling until she was far too big and heavy, then graduating to the rickety second-hand stroller; no designer prams here.

Mr Zhang's dark eyes had borne witness to all her misery, but they were always kind.

She can trust him not to tell Kane that she dropped by.

~

Beth puts the car into gear, raises a hand to wave at Mr Zhang, and mutters to herself, 'Hamilton Island, of all places. Hope he crashes his golf buggy into a frigging palm tree!'

A small laugh as she imagines the scene. Kane cursing and kicking the wheel of the buggy. Georgia seeing a different side to him, his real self.

Whose idea was the holiday? Who paid for it?

Stop thinking about him. All that matters is that he isn't home. Yes, he could post bad Google reviews from Hamilton Island ... but he couldn't snip a flexi-hose in two! Unless he paid someone, and he is far too stingy to part with cash.

She is left with the same questions: *Are these things separate or connected? Am I the unluckiest person in the world or is there a target on my back?*

Beth changes gear again, and her mind changes gear, too. Backtracking to Friday last week, when the police supervisor phoned to discuss the footage from the café. The perpetrator had been careful. The hat, the angle of his head, the indistinctive clothing: extremely difficult to make a positive identification. Now, an idea that has been percolating since that conversation. If they can't identify the suspected thief, then what about the woman, 'Mary'? She was likely his accomplice, given the carefully orchestrated timing and the wrong phone number on the client information form. Who is she? A friend or partner in crime? Unfortunately, the footage of the woman is worse quality again; she didn't enter the café at any point, and the only images are from across the street. The difference is that Beth met her face to face. She would remember Mary if she were to see her again.

Beth stops at a set of lights. *Who is Mary? What's in it for her?* She glances at the row of houses on the far side of the road. In one of the houses, the front door is ajar; two women are having a conversation. The woman facing Beth is frowning at her visitor – from this distance, it doesn't appear to be a friendly exchange. Suddenly, Beth pictures herself standing on Mia Anderson's doorstep. Mia's cagey, mildly threatening manner. Then the small white car coming up the driveway and her rapid interception. It had felt odd at the time. How many strays open the gate and come all the way up the driveway? Did Mia know the driver? Was she afraid of the driver and Beth coming face to face?

The lights change to green and the car behind honks when Beth is slow to react. She works her way up the gears once again, each change posing a fresh question.

253

Who would come to visit on a Sunday morning? Is it possible the person in the white car was a relative? Can Beth rely on her gut instincts about Mia? Are all these bad things that have been happening to her connected?

Beth's turn-off is approaching. She has a decision to make. Indicate right, towards home and the instant headache of the dehumidifiers. Or keep straight, through Charlestown and all the other small lakeside towns until Morisset. The drive is almost two hours return, much of it meandering along the scenic foreshore of the lake.

Beth follows her instincts and goes straight, her foot pressing defiantly on the accelerator.

42
Ryan

Mia is buoyant on Saturday morning. The interview went well; she is expecting a second interview, maybe even a job offer, early next week.

'It's finally happening,' she says, beaming as she whisks eggs for a celebratory brunch. 'Our luck is changing.'

Ryan swallows the bile in his throat. How can she believe that everything that went wrong with Tara was down to bad luck? And how can she blithely dismiss the fact that their property was searched and warrants obtained?

Here's the thing: his wife has a tendency to lie to herself, to twist and turn the facts. She is intelligent and fast-thinking, but she is not always objective or truthful, at least not when it comes to her own culpability.

For a start, she often underestimates how much she has had to drink. In her university days, she would be sick the morning after a big night out, yet adamant that it was due to a stomach bug or something she ate. Throughout their married life, she would claim to be suffering from a stress migraine, never owning up to a hangover.

He remembers asking her outright on that awful night, Tara's lifeless body splayed on the gravel: 'How much did you have to drink?' He didn't try to temper the accusation in his voice.

'Just a couple,' she snapped.

He remembers the defensive set to her rain-slicked face, and he knew that her mind was already adjusting the facts, deleting however many glasses of wine that needed to be deleted to deliver her under the legal limit.

'We can say it was me driving,' he pleaded. 'Come on, we need to call an ambulance, the police ... We've already waited too long.'

Mia shook her head stubbornly, rivulets of rain trickling down her cheeks, dripping from her nose and chin. 'Kellie knows what time I left her house. All it would take is a few simple questions. And the police are trained to be on the alert for spouses covering for each other.'

One other thing Mia lied about was the speed she was travelling at. Ryan can imagine how it happened. Her relief at being off the main road, having avoided the risk of being breathalysed. How she always puts the foot down when she has got through a perceived challenge. Ryan can see her gripping the wheel, gravel spraying from under the tyres: the last stretch home, straight, long and empty – or so she thought. Poor Tara, forbidden to be dropped at the door, fending off the rain with her umbrella, only to get mowed down from behind.

Mia blamed Tara's impractical shoes. She blamed her drunkenness and slow reflexes. She blamed the fact that Tara wasn't a driver, therefore oblivious to the risks of inclement weather. She blamed the wireless earbuds she'd been wearing, listening to music instead of oncoming traffic (the second earbud had been found embedded in the driveway's gravel after an extensive search).

Mia barely attributed any blame to herself, other than 'I shouldn't have had that last glass of wine', and 'it was raining so hard, she came out of nowhere'.

The latest self-delusion is Mia's continued insistence that the police have 'nothing'. The police have footage of Mia in the hostel. Detective Goodwin obtained warrants on their property and assembled a team of forensic specialists. That's not 'nothing'.

Ryan just wants the lies to end, the terrible, toxic lies and the inexcusable excuses. He can't sleep, he can't concentrate at work, he can't look at Elliot without feeling they've failed him, horrendously failed him. *We didn't protect you at all. We've become monsters.*

'Ryan, are you listening to me?' Mia is frowning at him, one hand on her hip. 'Can you set the table, please?'

This he can do, the simple act of laying out plates and cutlery. But none of the other stuff she wants him to do. No more.

The scrambled eggs feel like slime in his mouth. He gulps some orange juice; it sloshes like acid in his stomach.

The doorbell rings, and he and Mia gawp at each other, forks poised. Another warrant? Perhaps an arrest this time?

'I'll get it,' he croaks. He stands up, walks slowly towards his fate.

It's his mum at the door, wild-eyed and flushed in the face. Any relief is short-lived.

'I saw her,' Dianne declares, cheeks puffed with indignation. 'I saw that obnoxious car, coming from *this direction*.'

'Who? What car?'

'Beth Jenkins, that's who.' She barges past him, into the house. 'She's been snooping around again ... Where's Mia? We need to talk.'

~

Involving Dianne was inevitable. She called around the morning after the accident, on one of her random visits, jabbing the doorbell impatiently.

'Goodness, what took you so long?' she said, when Ryan eventually – after a hissed consultation with Mia – answered the door. 'Any chance of a cuppa?'

Mia was pretending to be pottering in the kitchen and paused what she was doing to give Dianne a warm hug. Ryan recalled the first time they met, when Mia was invited to join his family for dinner. She was only seventeen at the time, but she held her own at the table, answering Dianne's rapid-fire questions confidently, articulately.

'That girl is something else,' Dianne said afterwards. 'You've landed on your feet there, Ryan.'

The implication was that Mia was too good for him.

'Stick with her. She'll take you places,' Dianne whispered on graduation night, when Mia received an award for all-round academic excellence.

Dianne's admiration intensified over the years, with Mia's success at university and in her early career. But it was the way Mia approached motherhood and Elliot's specific challenges that impressed her mother-in-law the most.

'If only I'd been as well informed when Ryan was young,' Dianne said. 'I just thought he was naughty!'

Delivered with a wry laugh but it was far from funny at the time. Ryan didn't have a parent batting for him when he got into trouble at school, or an action plan every time he had a meltdown. No special diet or routine, and no medication either. He spent a lot of time standing in hallways, outside classrooms: the preferred punishment for disruptive kids.

His inattentiveness and restlessness followed him out of school and into the workplace. It was mentioned in performance reviews, and, at Mia's urging, Ryan finally went to see a specialist. At twenty years old, he was diagnosed with ADHD and has been on medication ever since. He, of all people, can appreciate the extraordinary work that Mia does with Elliot. Her attention to detail in terms of his home activities and schooling. Her constant research into the best medications and their side-effects. The firm belief that he is as worthy as other kids and will reach his full potential. Dianne is right on the mark: Mia is an amazing mother.

But Mia, on the morning after Tara's death, was not her usual indomitable self. She was pale and jittery. Dianne, who had noticed nothing untoward about Ryan (who was just as jittery, if not more so), immediately registered her daughter-in-law's gritty eyes and lack of composure.

'Is something wrong?' Her eyes darted between Mia and Ryan. Elliot had been dispatched to Kellie's house shortly after breakfast and it was just the three of them in the kitchen.

Ryan and Mia had made a pact not to tell anyone, but Ryan faltered at the first hurdle: his mother. He desperately needed to hear a voice of reason. He desperately needed someone to take control and do what he'd been unable to do: convince Mia to call the appropriate authorities.

He broke down, sobbing like a child while his mother and wife looked on, horrified for vastly different reasons. 'There was an accident ... We've done something awful ...'

Dianne was aghast when she heard what had happened. 'Oh my goodness. This is terrible ... *terrible* ... I need to sit down ... Oh my goodness, the poor girl ...'

Surely this would signify the end of the love-affair between his mother and his wife? But all it took was fifteen minutes of Mia's persuasion, insistence and emotional manipulation before Dianne was nodding her agreement.

'You're right, the poor girl is already gone. No, you can't save her now ... Of course, you can't risk prosecution, Mia ... You have Elliot to think about ... *Nobody is as good with that child as you are!*'

Mia was livid with Ryan for blurting out the truth to his mother. But she later conceded that involving Dianne was inevitable. For a start, they needed her to babysit while they went to Sydney. Dianne was also a good sounding-board when it came to the minutiae of the plan. In fact, she was the one who came up with the idea of hiring a boat. 'Your great-grandfather was buried at sea, Ryan ...' Some family history thrown in for good measure.

More recently, Dianne was the obvious person to ask when they needed a decoy at the massage clinic. She became 'Mary' and carried out her role with aplomb. 'I was rather enjoying the massage ... Pity I had to faint ...'

The problem is, his mother is as threatened by Beth as his wife is.

Dianne is an accessory after the fact; she is implicated up to her eyeballs.

43
Beth

The insurance representative comes on Monday to remove the dehumidifying machines. The house is restored to exquisite silence; Beth can finally think. It's only a temporary respite. Someone is coming tomorrow to remove the carpet and floorboards. In addition, there are ceiling repairs that need to happen and – once everything else is done – a big paint job.

The disruption will go on for weeks; just thinking about it makes her feel weary. But everyone is being supportive, rallying around her, helping as much as they can.

Joe takes Tilly out for walks and bike rides, so Beth has time to get her thoughts in order.

Charlie sends links to online ads for second-hand sofas, a few of which are free. He also offers the use of a friend's ute to transport the sofa. She messages her thanks, at the same time letting him know that she is not ready to buy anything, not even if it's free: *Just need a few days to think things through.*

Caitlin phones and sympathises, before seeking reassurance that

Beth hasn't gone back to Morisset. Beth doesn't confess that she *did* go back there. On Saturday morning, she parked a hundred metres down the road from the Andersons' place and waited. She realised the futility of what she was doing when every second car that passed was a small white one. None of them turned into the gateway in the half-hour she waited.

Beth's mum sends money from London, $500 that lands unexpectedly in her bank account. Beth is both grateful and guilt-ridden. It's hard to accept handouts when you're an adult and should be standing on your own two feet, harder again when there's a step-parent involved and you're aware that the money is ultimately coming from them: Linda earns a pittance as a part-time receptionist. Tony is a nice man, but the fact is that Beth barely knows him and cringes at the thought of him financially propping her up.

She sends her mother a thank-you message: *You really shouldn't have, Mum. The landlord's insurance is paying for most of the damage. I feel guilty accepting this.*

She doesn't receive a response immediately: it's the middle of the night in London. The thought of her mum in bed with Tony leads to thoughts of Kane and Georgia on Hamilton Island, sunbathing and swimming together, sipping cocktails before romantic dinners, having sex in their turned-down king-size bed. Is Kane's new relationship flourishing or floundering? Will Georgia eventually see his true nature, or will she inspire a better person from the man Beth knew? Beth is satisfied with the deal they made – no family-support payments in return for no custodial rights – but the facts are indisputable. If Kane had been a decent man, she wouldn't be in this dire situation. If Kane had been a decent man, there would have been a fair split of assets and parenting duties. If Kane had been a decent man, the separation would have been amicable, if there had been a separation at all. Beth is ashamed that her radar was so off the mark with Kane. Is poor character-judgement a failing she will have for life?

This brings her full circle back to Charlie. How he is always on hand when there's an emergency in her life. The morning after the house break-in. The day her car was stolen. When she found out about the bad Google reviews. And even when the pipe burst; he was using old towels to soak up the water minutes later. What are the chances? Is she missing something obvious? How can she trust her instincts about Charlie when she has been so drastically wrong in the past?

These are some of the thoughts that swirl in her head once the dehumidifiers are removed and she can actually *think*. In summation: she can't commit to a new sofa, because she doesn't know if she can continue living here; she desperately needs the money Linda sent but is acutely embarrassed that Tony must think she's a failure, or a bludger, or both. Is Charlie's extraordinary timing and helpfulness a blessing or should it merit suspicion? Lastly – no, *firstly* – she is in this terrible situation because of Kane.

It is so difficult not to feel bitter and defeated when she thinks of him and Georgia on Hamilton Island, enjoying the honeymoon she planned so many years ago when she was full of optimism for the future.

44
Mia

Dianne is absolutely right: something needs to be done about Beth Jenkins. Her car being on their road is no coincidence. What was she doing in the area? Staking out their house? Gathering 'evidence'? She is obviously not going to let this go. She has no idea of the danger she's bringing upon herself. The impossible position she is putting them in.

Mia and Dianne have discussed options. Beth leads a simple life, commuting to work, school and her local shopping centre, with no obvious opportunities for an 'accident'. Presumably she has an ex, Tilly's father, but pinning something on him would take research, surveillance and time ... which Mia doesn't have.

Dianne favours a less final solution. Paying Beth money to buy her silence. Or sending a message, via Tilly, to back off. Perhaps a serious accident to readjust her priorities, but not a fatal one.

Mia was patient while she explained why none of those strategies would work. 'I've tried the less direct route. Her boss and landlord must be really pissed at her, and I reckon she's practically bankrupt. Yet she keeps coming back here.'

Mia still has some convincing to do with Dianne, but at least her mother-in-law is applying herself to the problem and willing to help.

Unlike Ryan. They have been arguing nonstop; she can't seem to get through to him.

'You're acting like I *want* to do this,' she spits angrily. 'This is the *last* thing I want to do.'

'Don't do it, then,' he retorts. 'Beth's suspicions aren't evidence. There's no real risk. Even if there was, it's still not reason to *kill* someone.'

'Why aren't you listening? If Beth walks into a police station and starts talking about us, then their focus is suddenly on the car. They may or may not find it, but what they *could* find is other evidence of the Corolla being in Sydney around the time of Tara's death. You made that stupid phone call to the boat company, remember? What if there's old CCTV from the jetty or car park? What I'm saying is Beth's suspicions could be the tipping point. Can't you see how dangerous she is?'

Detective Goodwin might decide – when all the circumstantial evidence is taken as a whole – to lay charges. There goes tens of thousands in legal fees. And there goes Mia's job prospects. Police use intimidation tactics all the time: laying charges even when the evidence is not strong enough for a reasonable chance of conviction.

Ryan is obstinate. 'I don't get it. Last week you were dismissive when we had a whole forensics team here. You kept insisting they had "nothing". How is the threat suddenly so big you're trying to justify murder?'

'Because Beth is *fixated* on us. She keeps coming back here. Nothing seems to distract or divert her. She's obviously not going to let it go.'

'Don't do it, Mia. She's a mum, like you. Think of that little girl.'

'Unlike you, I don't opt out when things get tough. I do what's necessary to protect my family.'

'You're not protecting me, and you're not protecting Elliot either. You're crazy if you think you are.'

Damn it. This is a *bad* time for Ryan to find his backbone. She needs him to execute the plan once she has finished developing it. The clock is ticking ... how long before Beth goes to the police? What has been stopping her from taking it further? Probably the fact that all she has are suspicions and instinct rather than actual evidence.

They need to hurry up and make a plan. All hands on deck. Damn it, Ryan *owes* her this. When she thinks of all the things she has done for him. He would have been fired from his job long ago had she not urged him to see a doctor and get a diagnosis. Their house and property would have been totally out of his reach without the boost of her salary in the early years.

He owes her this. He owes *everything* he has to her.

~

On Tuesday afternoon, Mia receives some welcome news. Jane from the agency phones to let her know that she is being offered the job.

'Congratulations. They were thrilled with you, felt there was no point in conducting a second interview. Now, just to confirm, you're okay to start next Monday? Just putting the final details into the contract. Should have it to you by this evening.'

Monday! Less than a week away! Now that it's actually happening, it feels far too soon.

Kellie has confirmed that she's happy to help with Elliot. A quick phone call was all it took to firm up the details; she is such a good friend. Mia will talk to Elliot this afternoon, explain what the changes mean, and how everything is relying on him being well-behaved and calm.

Less than a week to fine-tune the details with Kellie, to stock up the freezer with pre-made dinners, and to prepare Elliot for the upheaval to his routine.

Less than a week to sort out Beth Jenkins. Does Mia even have that much time? How long before Beth acts on her suspicions and walks into a police station? She is obviously someone who thinks things over carefully, weighing everything up before taking action. Rather like Mia in that respect.

Think of that little girl, Ryan said. Mia is doing everything she can *not* to think about the scraggly-haired girl who jumped and shrieked on the trampoline and made fast friends with Elliot. The girl who was dismayed when told it was time to stop playing, who shot Elliot an unmistakeable look of solidarity when he had a meltdown.

Oh, Beth. Why didn't you keep your nose out of it?

45
Ryan

He detours past Beth's house on his way home from work. It adds almost an hour to his commute; Mia will be irritated and suspicious when he eventually gets home. He'll have to invent an accident on the freeway or some other excuse. He can't admit that he feels compelled to check on Beth, to see with his own eyes that she is safe ... for now.

He parks across the road from her house; secrecy no longer feels so crucially important. Part of him wants her to glance out the window, to notice the strange car, to become wary of the driver who is sitting there for no obvious reason. Part of him wants her to rap on his driver's window, asking questions and demanding answers.

'You need to be careful, Beth,' he murmurs, the words absorbing into the interior of the car. 'You need to be extremely careful.'

Dianne has been coming to the house while Ryan is at work; traces of her lavender perfume choking him when he comes in the door, one of the dining seats left at a menacing angle, evidence that her larger frame was sitting there. His mother initially expressed doubts about the need for Beth's demise, dismayed at the thought of the little girl being left motherless.

'There must be another way, Mia.'

'I wish there was. But there really, *really* isn't. It's either that little girl or it's Elliot. And if I'm convicted, we *all* go down. Me, Ryan, *you*. Elliot would be practically an orphan.'

Mia's persuasion and manipulation tactics worked their same old magic; Dianne capitulated to her daughter-in-law again. *Elliot would be practically an orphan*; Ryan's resolve came dangerously close to cracking.

Since then, his wife and mother have been scheming and seeing each other every day. No doubt Mia has been employing her seven-step process. Define the problem. Gather facts and establish criteria. Develop and compare possible solutions.

Mia has tried to run their ideas past him: house fire, overdose, mugging, pedestrian accident. Ryan has desisted, fighting the urge to give in to her, terrified that it's only a matter of time before he does. He just wishes there was a way to communicate the danger to Beth without implicating his wife and his mother, without ruining his son's life.

You shouldn't let her boss you around so much, Tara says, her voice so clear it could be real.

'It's not so easy,' he answers aloud. 'You have no idea how hard it is not to give in.'

Mia is obsessively single-minded when she is set on a particular course of action. As for Dianne, being brutally honest, he still harbours an instinctual fear of his mother. How sad and pathetic is that?

As Ryan sits there, staring with growing desperation at Beth's house, a film reel plays in his mind of all the terrible things he has done. The *big* terrible things: storing the body in the freezer for two never-ending weeks, the horrific drive to Sydney and the burial at sea. The medium terrible things: breaking into Beth's house and workplace, stealing the car, incinerating it in the bush. The multitude of smaller sins: deep-cleaning the boot of the car when they got home from Sydney, Mia's instructions ringing in his ears, 'We're going to have to sell this one day ... don't damage the panelling'; waiting a few months before getting the dent on the bonnet repaired ('My son hit it with a cricket ball' was the story he told the panel-beater); using Paul's boat licence and credit card, abusing his trust; lying to Elliot about posting the earbud to Tara in Sydney, making him wash his hands straight afterwards, the horror of invisible particles of Tara's blood or brain matter being on his innocent hands; more recently, being petrified that Elliot would mention the earbud to Detective Goodwin when she questioned him. Because if one earbud had been found in the garage, where was the other? Ryan could have cried with relief when all that Elliot recalled about Tara was the fact that she didn't like vegetables.

The only thing that kept him sane throughout it all was the belief that the terrible things would end, and that life would return to normal. He consoled himself with the fact that they couldn't save Tara – there was nothing they could do to bring her back to life – but they could save Mia from prosecution and a prison sentence, and save Elliot from great distress.

But he realises now – too late! – that *there is no end*. The feeling reminds him of his school days, all those times when the rest of the class understood something before he did. The embarrassment of being so slow to 'get it'. The stab of self-loathing and the heat in his cheeks. The mocking voice in his head: *you're so fucking dumb*.

The burial at sea wasn't the end. Dousing Beth's car with petrol wasn't the end. Flooding her house wasn't the end. And Beth's death won't be the end either, because Mia is already making rumbles about her friend – the one in the park – and how much she knows.

There is no end. Curtains in one of the upstairs bedrooms are being drawn across the window, offering a glimpse of Beth's silhouette. Behind those curtains are a mum and a little girl, going through a bedtime routine, oblivious to the danger getting closer and closer. Beth has no idea that her Corolla hit and killed a young Irish girl on the cusp of adulthood. Beth has no idea that the boot where she put her grocery bags once held a defrosting corpse. Beth has no idea of the horror she has embroiled herself in.

Ryan starts the car, his hand trembling as he turns the key. He should text or call Mia, to let her know that he's been delayed. But he can't bear to speak to her, or even type a few words.

He drives through the suburban streets, without noticing the houses or the topography or anything at all. Back on the main road, his driving is slow and distracted, other cars overtaking with obvious impatience. All the old questions and speculations swarm in his head.

How fast was Mia going on the night she hit Tara?

Was she looking where she was going or driving on autopilot?

Maybe if she'd been going a bit slower, the night wouldn't have culminated with Tara's twisted body lying in the gravel, that deadly trickle of blood coming from her ear, her shoes whipped from her feet by the force of impact.

If Mia hadn't drunk however many glasses of wine. If he'd insisted on driving her to book club. If Tara hadn't been dropped at the gate. If he'd suggested that Mia stay at home ... or Tara ... *If ... If ... If ...*

He is driving through Warners Bay now, although he can barely remember how he got this far, the traffic lights he must have stopped at, the lanes he must have merged into. His body is rigid with dread and helplessness; it's all he can do to keep the car on the road. His thoughts have reached a roadblock: *there is no end, there is no end, there is no end.* The sun is edging closer to the horizon, blue leaching from the sky, leaving a paler, more translucent hue. Directly ahead, the lake, grey and secretive with ripples of yellow and orange from the setting sun. How deep is it here? Not deep enough.

He is required to turn right at this intersection; the lake will then be on his left for the rest of the journey home. Oh, but the urge to go straight ahead, the urge to put his foot to the pedal, to barrel through the grass and the bicycle track, to gather speed and air, and to feel the hard slap of water hitting the undercarriage of the car.

Not deep enough. No way near deep enough.

Ryan has always been saddened and perplexed by those tragic news articles. The ones where cars go careening off bridges into treacherous, fast-flowing rivers. The children are always young, the mum is always a combination of pretty and jaded, and it's nearly always the father behind the wheel. Ryan has never understood it. What could be so bad that the only solution is to trap and drown your entire family, the people you love more than anything in the world? He used to consider it an act of extreme control and cruelty, but what if it was due to extreme desperation?

The lights change and the cars in front of him move. One last straight-on view of the lake. The redemption of water. The image of a family sinking together. A last act of solidarity ... or evil ... or insanity ...

Ryan makes the turn, heart thumping with shame and the sick understanding of how some of those awful tragedies can happen.

There is no end. There is no way out. There is no fucking way to fix this.

46
Beth

The week marches on. Her family and friends continue to rally around her.

'Please accept the money,' Linda pleads, when she FaceTimes on Wednesday night. 'I just want to give you and Tilly a big fat hug, but I obviously can't so this is the only way I can help. For goodness' sake, it's not even that much money.'

Her mum is sitting at her dining table, wearing a fluffy white robe, her face vulnerable in the morning light. The balcony doors are directly behind her, lending Beth a view of a dreary morning in London, large blobs of condensation adding to the effect.

Beth sighs deeply. 'Tony must think I'm pathetic.'

Linda snorts. 'If only you knew! Tony is bailing his kids out every second week with one thing or another. He thinks you're amazing. We both do.'

Tilly appears, dressed in her pyjamas, and they put the conversation on hold.

'Ready for the story?' Linda asks, her eyes crinkling at the sides as she smiles into the camera. 'Let's get started.'

Linda came up with the idea. Every time she bought a children's book to send to Tilly, she would purchase two copies. One copy would remain with her in London, while the other was sent by Royal Mail to Australia. Thus, she could read to her granddaughter via FaceTime, both of them turning the pages of the same book. A bedtime story read from seventeen thousand kilometres away, technology and ingenuity conquering the distance.

Beth opens her arms and Tilly snuggles in, before flicking to the first page of the book. Beth closes her eyes and allows the warmth of her daughter's body and the rhythm of her mother's voice to ease the disquiet inside her.

~

'We're back up to an average rating of four,' Debbie declares, when Beth arrives at work the next morning. 'The bad reviews have been bumped down. At least they're not the first thing you see when you Google us!'

This is thanks to Charlie and Caitlin, who have both – independently – urged their huge circle of friends to leave positive reviews.

'None of these people have set foot inside the door,' Debbie reflects. 'I should offer them a discount, to thank them.'

Charlie and Caitlin have also taken it upon themselves to wait for Beth after work, to walk her to her car, intuiting that she doesn't feel safe.

Charlie did the honours Monday, which made sense because he was her last appointment. Beth analysed him as they walked, his thoughtful questions, his solicitous manner, the kindness in his eyes and voice. She couldn't be wrong about him, she just couldn't.

Caitlin happened to be passing by on Tuesday and waited in reception while Beth finished up work for the day. They hooked arms as they walked, gossiping about Kane and Georgia. Beth felt fifteen years' worth of friendship in the crook of Caitlin's arm.

On Wednesday, Beth was on her own. She walked so fast she was almost running, sensing eyes boring through her back. On the drive home she chided herself for being so jumpy; it was still possible that she was simply having a run of bad luck.

Nevertheless, she is inordinately relieved to see Charlie in reception when she emerges from her last client on Thursday.

'Your escort is here,' Debbie observes.

Charlie's phone rings just as they're about to leave. He checks the number and grimaces. 'Sorry, I've been waiting all day for this call. I'll just step outside. Won't be a minute. Sorry.'

'Are you absolutely sure he doesn't fancy you?' Debbie asks, studying him through the window as he listens to what the caller is saying, his expression serious and very consultant-like. 'Nobody is this nice. He must have an ulterior motive.'

Beth's smile is taut. 'He really *is* this nice, Deb. And I've already told you – he has a girlfriend.'

~

Beth has only just arrived home on Thursday evening when Pippa turns up with a pasta bake. Her neighbour has provided dinner twice this week: she seems to think that Beth has lost the ability to cook.

'Oh Pippa, thank you so much. Time for a cuppa? Sorry about the floors. And the awful smell.'

The builders have been and removed the flooring and skirting boards. Now the concrete slab needs a couple of weeks to dry out. The ceiling in the living room needs replacing, and there's a strong smell of damp. The house has the look and feel of a squat.

'Oh dear,' Pippa says, as she stops off in the living room on her way to the kitchen. 'Still a lot of work to do before this is back to normal.'

They proceed to the kitchen, where Beth fills the kettle and fishes out a packet of biscuits. Tilly comes bounding in from the garden, giving Pippa a quick hug before stuffing a biscuit into her mouth. Pippa and Beth watch her through the window as she returns to whatever game she was playing outside.

'It's lovely to see a child out in the fresh air,' Pippa smiles, as she sits on one of the dining chairs. 'Getting their hands and knees dirty in the garden instead of exercising their thumbs on a device.'

Beth swallows; a hard lump of guilt moves from her throat to the centre of her chest.

'I'm thinking of moving,' she says, her voice barely more than a whisper. 'Might stay with my dad for a while, till I get back on my feet.'

Joe's flat has miniscule proportions and the only outdoor space is a skimpy balcony. But living three or four months rent-free will help her build some savings, so the next time something goes wrong she doesn't have to dip into rent money or apply for another low-interest loan.

Pippa is crestfallen. 'Oh, Beth. I didn't know things were that bad.'

Beth blinks back tears, and busies herself fetching two mugs, placing tea bags in them. The truth is, she will miss Pippa terribly and so will Tilly. She really is the kindest, most wonderful neighbour and friend. But the last few weeks have forced Beth to face some truths. Putting it simply, she doesn't have enough money in her bank account. There is no buffer for when things go wrong, which seems to be happening a lot lately.

Pippa is looking at her closely, her watery blue eyes full of concern.

Beth shrugs and tries her best to be unemotional, as though this is purely a monetary decision. 'Every time something unexpected comes up, no matter how small, I end up being late with my rent. I'm constantly chasing my tail. I honestly don't know how the landlord puts up with me ...'

Silence. Pippa is obviously lost for words. The kettle switches itself off and Beth pours the boiling water into the mugs. Milk and one sugar for Pippa. How many cups of tea has she made for her neighbour over the last two years, and vice versa?

Beth places Pippa's drink in front of her and sits down at the small table with its scratched veneer top: more proof of their hand-me-down existence.

Pippa leans closer and clasps Beth's hand in her own, squeezing hard. 'Ian and I never intended to tell you this, because we didn't want you to feel awkward, or that we were watching your every move ... The house is ours, Beth. We built the two houses, one to live in, and one to rent out. We're the landlords, me and Ian, not some faceless person overseas. And everything will be okay, do you hear me? Everything will be okay.'

47
Mia

Ryan is late getting home from work for the second night in a row. Another accident on the freeway, allegedly, but he is a terrible liar – the telltale flush on his neck, the fact that he cannot look her in the eye.

She calls him out on it. 'Come on, you and I both know there was no accident, no traffic jam. You're hiding from me. Shirking your responsibilities. Your mum and I need your help ... You can't just leave us to do this alone.'

He seems stricken at being caught out, but then musters some bravado. 'You need to stop this crazy plan.'

Mia grabs him by the wrist, her fingers tightening until she can see the discomfort and fear on his face. 'You're unravelling, Ryan. Losing concentration, losing sight of what really matters here. You're not helping the situation *one little bit.*'

She glares at her husband, mentally itemising his flaws, all the things she does not want Elliot to be when he gets older: blundering, emotional, useless in a crisis.

When Mia got pregnant, she envisaged the child being like her:

focused, diligent, successful. Instead, Elliot was like Ryan. Her son's flaws haven't diminished her love for him, far from it. She has made untold sacrifices, invested infinite time, patience and love, and Elliot has responded superbly. But it's been a battle. Every single day, hammering home the routine and the rules, fighting the school and the prejudices, pushing her own professional fulfilment to one side. Her son's flaws haven't diminished her love for him, but they have, she is realising now, diminished her love for Ryan. It's *his* genes that were passed on to poor Elliot, his disorder in addition to the hair colour and eyes. Therefore, it's ultimately Ryan's fault that they're in this *impossible* situation. If Elliot had more of Mia's genes, they could have used the school's after-hours care program, instead of hiring Tara. And if Elliot had his mother's self-sufficiency and resilience, she needn't have been so damned worried about throwing herself at the mercy of the courts.

'Don't do this,' Ryan mumbles, nursing his wrist with his other hand. 'I can't let you do this.'

'Try and stop me,' she snarls, at the end of her tether with him.

~

As plans go, Mia is the first to admit that it's not her best. Dianne agreed there weren't many options, but her mother-in-law was adamant that the child not be a witness. This whittled them down to Beth's commute. Ryan had already done some of the groundwork, when stealing the car was all they had to worry about. The specifics of Beth's route to work, where she usually parks at the Sportsground, and the ten-minute walk to the clinic: up Union Street, crossing at the King Street intersection, finally the trams and bustle of Hunter Street.

Mia has followed Beth on two occasions, once when she was with her friend – the one from the park – and the next day, when Beth was on her own. She noted Beth's position on the footpath, her fast pace, her level of preoccupation, how her eyes were trained downwards. Mia watched Beth, and she also watched the traffic, cataloguing the points where it was travelling fast, where the lane next to the footpath was particularly narrow, affording little room for error, for drivers and pedestrians alike. Mia concluded it was a good thing that Beth was a fast walker and always in a rush. All the overtaking and weaving in and out meant that she was often right next to the kerb.

The annoying thing is that Ryan is obviously the best person for this. He is less recognisable than Mia: a hat and some bland clothes and he would fade into the rush-hour crowds. He is also taller and more muscular. A well-timed shoulder to send Beth stumbling from the pavement, into the path of one of the buses or trucks or trams that rumble along the busy streets.

Damn it, Ryan *owes* her this. She has sacrificed so much for him. His poor career prospects and limited earning capacity would have deterred many women. Others would be irritated by his short attention span and restlessness. And how many women would risk those defective genes being passed on to children?

He *owes* her this and there is still a small chance that he'll step up, although they are running out of time. It needs to happen tomorrow, Friday. Mia's new job commences next week: she wants to start without this hanging over her, without the gnawing worry of what Beth Jenkins might do next.

The other problem is Beth's friend. The incredibly pretty one. The one with the big mouth. The one who suggested that the Corolla might have been involved in a crime.

What's her name? How much does she know? Does she need to have an 'accident' too?

48
Ryan

The lake is not deep enough. It would have to be a river, a *big* river, like the Hunter. And a bridge that's the right height, with a barrier that's poorly fortified. Fuck, he can't believe he is actually considering this!

How did he get here? To the point where he can't stop thinking about driving off a bridge, the car launching into the air, his family strapped helplessly into their seats? Has he really become one of those deluded, insane, evil, murderous men?

Fuck, fuck, fuck! From their early days – the disbelief and joy that Mia said yes when he asked her out, the all-consuming pride that she was his girlfriend – to this! He couldn't believe his luck the first time she smiled at him, the first time they held hands, the first time they kissed, when she allowed him to touch her, to have sex with her, to accompany her to Sydney while she studied at university. What followed were more firsts: their first flat (a cockroach-infested dump!); the first furniture they bought together; their first overseas holiday in Bali. At every milestone, and in fact every single day, he couldn't believe his luck: that this beautiful, smart woman had chosen him, a dumbo who worked in a dead-end job. When she hinted that it was time for a ring, he ran out and bought one (exactly as she specified: white gold, solitaire, princess cut). When she decided it was time to get married, he could not get down the aisle fast enough (she looked breathtaking that day, like a model from a glossy magazine ... and she was his *wife*). Then Elliot, who was a joy but also a dramatic change to the dynamics. Here was someone, a tiny baby, whom Mia could not entirely control. She couldn't control when he fed, or slept, or cried ... or, as he got older, how he behaved. Thank God, she didn't take her frustrations out on their son, but what followed was another series of firsts, where Mia showed the other side of her. The first time she pinched Ryan's arm, to bring him around to her way of thinking. The first time she slapped him across the face, berating him for his pathetic salary and their financial worries. The first time she bulldozed him into a major life decision: the selling of their apartment in Sydney, and the purchase of the property in Morisset. Ryan wasn't particularly good at maths but he figured out that the new mortgage would be a significant stretch. Her unkind laugh when he suggested that maybe he should be the one to stay at home with Elliot, given that her earning potential was so much better. *Don't be ridiculous. You can't play 'mummy'. You don't have the skills to negotiate with doctors and schools.*

Ryan must give praise where it's due: Mia has been an extraordinary mother. His son has all the support and resources that he himself failed to receive at school or at home. Dianne used to call him lazy and stupid, and his dad was of the generation that believed a whip of his belt could solve everything, even learning difficulties. Maybe if Ryan had different parents, he'd have the confidence and self-worth not to be railroaded into things today.

You shouldn't let her boss you around so much, Tara's voice pipes up, adding to the noise in his head.

She's the strategist, he argues back. *I'm operations. That's why I'm here.*

He needs to move. It's 7.30am; Beth will be leaving soon. It's imperative that he gets out of the car, confronts her. This is the only thing he can do in the circumstances. Otherwise, there is no end to this, no way out. Other than the river. *Fuck! Stop thinking that the river is a real option.*

His face is wet; he didn't realise he was crying. No time for sobbing, or regrets, or trying to understand how it has come to this.

Do it for Elliot, Mia has pleaded, over and over and over.

He *is* doing this for Elliot. He *is* doing this for Elliot. And he is doing it for Mia too, although she doesn't know it yet.

He opens the car door with sweat-slicked hands and hauls himself out.

He walks down the paved driveway, knees knocking so hard that he's swaying from side to side, like someone who's drunk.

Is he really going to do this?

Do it for Elliot. Do it for Elliot.

He presses Beth's doorbell. This is the first time he will enter the house in the traditional manner. Memories of being on his hands and knees on the garage roof, his whole body shuddering. A few days later, forcing the lock on the sliding doors, hands shaking so violently he nicked himself with the screwdriver. No more sneaking around or breaking locks.

He presses the doorbell again, and gulps back some air, some courage, while he waits for Beth to come to the door.

49
Beth

There is a man at the front door wearing jeans, work boots and a navy polo shirt. He has a dark-grey cap on his head, and he looks similar to all the other workmen who have called to the house this week.

'Are you here about the ceiling?' she asks, flashing him a quick smile. The property manager said someone would be around this morning. Weird that she is still dealing with the agent rather than Pippa and Ian. Even though she was gobsmacked to learn the truth, it made immediate sense. The suspiciously low rent, the lack of drama when she was late with a payment, all the times the landlord unexpectedly chipped in for improvements. As soon as Pippa left, Beth immediately checked her tenancy agreement. The landlord was listed as PIC Family Trust; there was no way she could have known it was Pippa and Ian. The couple wanted the property rented to someone in need, someone who needed a leg-up in the world, someone with a child who could enjoy the garden.

Now, as this strange man stands in her hallway, Beth is conscious of the time and the fact that traffic on Friday mornings can be unpredictable. Tilly is brushing her teeth upstairs, and has her schoolbag packed and ready, although she is renowned for realising that she has forgotten something just as they are getting in the car.

'I need to leave in the next fifteen minutes,' she says with another smile. 'Is that enough time for you to measure up for your quote?'

He doesn't answer, and she looks at him more closely, noticing the beads of sweat above his lip, the movement of his Adam's apple as he swallows.

'Beth,' he begins, and takes off his hat.

Her heart lurches painfully.

It's *him*. The husband. Ryan Anderson.

She inadvertently takes a step backwards, conscious that her daughter will come bounding down the stairs any moment now. She opened the door and invited this man in. Oh God. Stupid. Stupid. *Stupid!*

'You don't need to be frightened,' he says. 'I won't hurt you.'

She has never been more frightened in her life.

'Stay there! Don't come any closer,' she squeaks. 'What do you want?'

'You were right about the car, Beth. Something did happen. A girl died.'

Oh God. What girl? What actually happened? Strictly speaking, it was Caitlin who was right. Her friend will feel vindicated ... if Beth lives to tell her the truth.

Beth hears a sound from above, the familiar tread of Tilly's feet on the carpet.

'Mummy? I'm ready. I—'

'Don't come down,' she calls out frantically. 'I'm talking to a man about something important. Don't. Come. Down.'

Ryan's eyes veer to the top of the stairs, where Tilly is standing, deliberating on whether to follow her mother's instructions.

'I'm not going to hurt her, or you,' he murmurs.

'Move it, pumpkin,' Beth shouts, not prepared to believe him. *A girl died.* 'Go to your room.'

Tilly resists. 'What about school?'

'We're going to be a little late.'

'I've got two things to tell you,' Ryan interjects, sotto voce. 'It won't take a minute. But I strongly recommend that your daughter doesn't go to school today.'

Beth is caught in a nightmare. Any moment now she will wake up and marvel about the level of detail: the piercing blue of his eyes, the sinewy muscles on his arms, the apparent sincerity in his voice.

'I don't want to be late,' Tilly whines from above. 'Who is the man, Mummy?'

'Just go to your room. And lock the door.'

'Is he a burglar?'

'Yes!' Beth screams, because she needs Tilly to do as she is told.

It works. The quick patter of feet, the click of Tilly's door. The poor thing is terrified of burglars.

Beth reminds herself to breathe. She visualises the lock on Tilly's doorhandle. Will that flimsy mechanism offer any real protection if Ryan is lying about not hurting them?

'What do you need to tell me?' she asks him, hearing the terror underscoring every word.

50
Mia

There is one thing she has kept from Ryan, one monumental thing that she never confessed. She didn't discover it until a few days after the accident, when Tara was frozen solid and it was impossible to change course. Mia assumed that she'd be charged with driving under the influence and dangerous driving, and sentenced harshly as an example to others. On deeper investigation, using the computer facilities of a library in Newcastle West, she learned that she couldn't be charged with DUI because she was technically at home when the accident occurred and not on a public road. Of course, dangerous driving causing death was still applicable, but the police would need to prove, beyond reasonable doubt, that she'd been reckless or speeding. Difficult to prove without any witnesses to the accident. She found a case where the defence successfully argued that a man's blood alcohol concentration was not admissible. Another case where a young mother was given an Intensive Corrections Order at home, avoiding prison altogether. Mia's situation wasn't as desperate as she'd thought; a top lawyer could have achieved a palatable outcome, albeit costing a fortune. Had she known this crucial information, she would have called an ambulance, the police and the whole shebang within minutes of the thud of Tara's body striking the car. But it was too late to wind back the clock. Too late to dial those three zeros. Too late to trust that there wasn't enough culpability for an actual prison sentence. Too late, too late, too late.

Many times this week, Mia has fought the impulse to tell Ryan the truth. *All those terrible things you did? Well, maybe they weren't necessary after all.* She can imagine his reaction. His initial confusion (he always takes so long to *get* things). His horror. His guilt ballooning to even greater proportions.

Her desire to turn his world upside down is strong. Revenge for his resistance. Revenge for his refusal to recognise the danger that Beth poses. Revenge for the fact that she is the one who will have to push Beth, the one who risks being caught or getting it wrong. She is trying to summon her inner strength, the steeliness and grit that got her through two years ago. But that plan was more substantial than this one. Today, she gets two chances. Beth's morning route and her evening route. If the right opportunity fails to present – a heavy vehicle passing at the appropriate time – the accident will have to be at Beth's home. A fire or gas leak. Tilly becoming involved. Damn it, no wonder she's nervous.

'Elliot, have you got everything? Grandma will be here soon.'

Dianne is doing the school run today. She has been instructed to leave Elliot at the gate, not to go in (even if he acts out) or start a discussion with any parents. Mia is worried that Kellie will spot Dianne, and find the change in routine odd enough to commit to memory.

Elliot does not have everything ready to go. His hair isn't combed, and his school shoes are on the Missing List.

'Oh, Elliot. Where did you leave them? Come on, buddy. Grandma will be cross if you aren't ready.'

The shoes are outside, next to the trampoline. Lucky it didn't rain overnight. As Mia re-enters the house, she hears her phone ringing.

Dianne. Is her mother-in-law delayed? Damn it. Mia needs to leave in the next few minutes in order to be in situ for Beth.

'Hi. What's up?'

'I can't get in.' Dianne sounds flustered. 'There's a lock on the gate.'

'What?'

'A lock. It looks new. What's going on?'

Ryan wouldn't have. Passive resistance is one thing. This is another level. He wouldn't dare.

'I'll drive down. I'll just be a minute.'

Mia grabs her handbag and Elliot's schoolbag. A quick check that the appliances are turned off and the back door is locked. A rummage in her handbag for her keys. The rummage becomes a more thorough search. Where are her keys? She checks some other likely places. The kitchen bench. The hall table. Her bedside table. The pockets of yesterday's jeans. Then she checks the drawer where they keep the spare set. No spare keys either.

Realisation dawns.

He dared.

51
Ryan

His phone starts ringing in his pocket. Mia. He knows this without having to check. Each ring resonates with his wife's fury and incredulousness. He can see the scene at home playing out. Dianne huffing and puffing and rattling the gate. Mia's frantic search for her car keys. She didn't take long to call him: fast on her feet as always.

'What do you need to tell me?' Beth asks, her voice shaking in terror.

Hearing her fear makes him even more ashamed and determined to carry through with this.

'Don't go to work today. Go somewhere safe. My wife is planning something ... You're in grave danger.'

He can see Mia clearly in his mind. She is jogging down the driveway, formulating a revised plan as she goes. *Kellie to bring Elliot to school. Dianne to drive Mia. How to make up for time lost.*

Beth goes a shade paler on learning that the danger she feared is real. Her eyes glance upwards, obviously thinking about Tilly and what this means for her. The little girl's voice can be heard in the distance. Muffled. Scared. Calling out for her mum.

'Oh my God. This is a nightmare. Who was the poor girl? How did she die?'

Suddenly Tara is there in the hallway with them. Ryan can feel her skinny arms around him, her warm mouth open under his, her strong perfume overtaking the smell of damp. One kiss, lasting no more than a few seconds, replayed a thousand times over. She launched herself into his arms one night on arriving home from the pub. The temptation was real and unexpected. The lure of not having to impress her, of not falling short all the time. Before the realisation that she was little more than a kid, and that he steadfastly loved his wife. His beautiful, meticulous, manipulative wife.

He swallows. 'Her name was Tara. She had an accident. Mia ran her over, then tried to cover it up.'

'Why would she do that?' Beth shakes her head and repeats, 'This is a nightmare ... I can't believe it's real.'

She is verbalising exactly how he has felt these last two years.

'It's real.' He reaches for his shirt pocket, extracts the card he put there this morning. 'One other thing. There's a reward. If you contact the police, you might be entitled to some of it.' He holds out the card, offering it to Beth. 'This is the number: Detective Goodwin. Just tell her you suspect that your car had something to do with the death of Tara McAllen.'

Beth's eyes are wide and incredulous. 'I don't understand ... Is this some kind of trick?'

'It's true. Tara's family and the New South Wales Police posted a million-dollar reward, to encourage people to come forward with information.'

'A million dollars?' she gasps.

He can read her thoughts. Criminals don't call to your house to personally deliver the business card of the detective in charge, or to helpfully let you know there is an enormous reward at stake. None of this happens in real life.

He smiles faintly. 'They never pay out the full amount, Beth. Well, not according to my wife's research. But you might get something if you connect your car to the crime.'

'Why are you doing this?' she whispers. 'Why are you telling me about *money*?'

'Because we stole from you, we wrecked your home, and now my wife wants to kill you.'

She still hasn't taken the card, obviously too scared to come closer. He bends down, places it on the bare concrete.

'Remember what I said: get out of here, go somewhere safe, call the detective in charge.'

When Mia figures out that Beth isn't at work, she'll come here. Mia will be in disaster-recovery mode, manic.

He takes a few steps backwards, towards the door.

'And what about you?' she cries. 'What are *you* going to do?'

He winces, the question wounding him, inflicting a blow somewhere around his middle. *He is doing this for Elliot.* No matter how painful, this is the best thing for his son.

'I'm going to hand myself in, make a full confession—'

He is cut off by the sound of furious pummelling on the front door. He and Beth look at each other in a moment of mutual fear. Mia? It couldn't be. Not this fast.

A male voice calls out. 'Beth, Beth, are you okay in there?'

'It's Ian,' she croaks, relief flooding her face. 'My neighbour.'

Ryan cautiously opens the door.

Ian is an elderly man, and next to him is an equally elderly woman. The two are standing straight, shoulders back, in an endearing attempt to appear more daunting.

'Is everything all right?' Ian asks gruffly. 'We heard Tilly calling for help.'

The old woman corrects him. '*I* heard Tilly calling for help, dear, not you. As per usual, you didn't hear a thing.'

There is something reassuring and grounding about the woman's affectionate chiding and the old man's bravado.

Until this week, Ryan thought he and Mia would grow old together, making right some of their wrongs, becoming mellow in their old age.

His phone starts ringing again. He ignores it.

It's over, Mia. This is where it ends.

'I'm done,' he informs the neighbours and Beth, before walking out the door.

52
Beth

Six months later

She received $48,600 for the information she provided; God knows what kind of complicated algorithm they applied to calculate the final amount. She was fully transparent, told the police everything she knew, including the fact that Ryan had prompted her to contact them. She honestly didn't expect anything to come of it. Ryan had made a full confession; her contribution seemed irrelevant in the scheme of things. But the detective in charge was insistent that she had played an important role, her doggedness bringing the case to a head, and at great personal risk. Detective Goodwin submitted a report to the Rewards Evaluation Advisory Committee, who then made a recommendation to the Police Minister.

Beth used the money to move to another suburb, another house. She also used the money to buy insurance: car, health and house contents.

'I'm insured up to my eyeballs,' she informed Charlie. 'You should be proud of me.'

She changed jobs shortly after she moved house. Better to make a clean break. She didn't want Ryan, Mia or Dianne to know where she could be found; Kane either, for that matter.

Beth's rent is more expensive now, but she has a buffer, so she can afford the extra. Her new boss is not as accommodating as Debbie but the pay is marginally better. A huge positive is Tilly's new school, which has a dedicated Learning and Support team. The improvement has been astonishing: Tilly has been reading books to her grandmother in London rather than the other way around.

Beth misses Pippa being right next door but still sees her regularly. Her old neighbour comes for lunch every other weekend, and sometimes drives all the way – fifteen kilometres! – just for a cup of tea. Beth values her friendship, her kindness and her calm 'seen it all before' approach to life. She will be forever grateful for the leg-up Pippa and Ian provided to her: there is no way she would have been able to afford the house if it had been rented at market rate. Another single mum lives there now, another woman getting back on her feet while her five-year-old twins infuse the garden with their noise and games.

Caitlin is also a regular visitor to Beth's new house. She swishes in with her trademark glamour and feel-good buzz, lavishing Tilly with attention, and imbuing Beth with the wisdom that comes from years of social work.

'I still don't understand why it took Ryan so long to go to the police,' Beth mused one night, as she and Caitlin shared a bottle of cheap wine.

Caitlin stared at her glass thoughtfully. 'All the usual reasons, I imagine. Gaslighting, coercive control, financial and emotional abuse. Mia made him think that he wasn't as smart as her, that her plan was the only option, and if he loved her – and the kid – he wouldn't question it.'

Beth has readjusted her thinking, her assumption that women are the only ones on the receiving end of abuse and manipulation tactics. The man who rang her bell that morning had obviously been to hell and back. It had taken him a long time to see things for what they really were, to find the courage and strength to resist and break away. Beth knows what that feels like.

Charlie is still going out with his girlfriend, whom Beth has met on several occasions now, and who is just as nice as he is. He was disappointed when Beth had to sell the rainbow car – it was far too conspicuous – but stoked when she got $500 more than she paid for it. 'What a car! What a legend bloody car!'

Charlie has restored Beth's faith in the goodness of men. Now she can see that Charlie is at one end of the spectrum and Kane is at the other. Charlie with his generosity, innate kindness, work ethic and enormous circle of friends from all walks of life. And he is convinced that one of those friends could be her future boyfriend, convinced that he can find her a partner as easily as sourcing a new car or couch!

Thanks to Charlie, Beth knows what she is looking for in a man, what the minimum standard is.

For now, she is happy to enjoy this phase of her life, to delight in her little girl, and to celebrate her friendships and hard-fought independence.

Not a day goes by when she doesn't think about Tara McAllen. The girl whose adult life stretched in front of her, brimming with possibility and personal growth. The cherished daughter, sister and friend who would never return home. The anguish of her family and everyone who loved her.

Especially her mother.

53
Siobhan

One year later

'I love your bones': I love every little thing that makes you who you are, good and bad. Siobhan, more than anyone, knew that Tara wasn't perfect. She saw her daughter's nature at its most pure, long before she learned how to act or develop a private self. The baby who snuggled in her arms and slept through the night from five weeks of age. The small toddler who scooted around on her bum, and screamed blue murder when presented with vegetables of any form. The little girl who loved dress-ups, dancing and animals, and hated pencilwork, cleaning her room and – there was absolutely no changing her mind about it! – vegetables. As she got older her flaws became less endearing. Tara was easily bored, atrociously untidy and at times downright lazy. Yet she was always a bright presence in their lives. Extensive preparations on Friday and Saturday nights, the hair dryer droning, the smell of fake tan and perfume permeating the house. Stumbling into the kitchen never before noon the following day, seeking caffeine and Panadol, recounting in detail what had 'gone down' the night before. Beneath the social butterfly was a straightforward girl who didn't expect much beyond having some fun; a girl with firm ideas

on what she liked and didn't like; a girl who truly cared about her family and friends. She was exasperating, authentic, full of contradictions, full of potential.

Siobhan believed that going overseas would help Tara grow up a bit, force her to become better at taking care of herself (basics like cleaning, cooking, living to a budget), and open her eyes to the world and other ways of life. Siobhan had even suggested Australia – somewhere she'd always wanted to visit herself – and went as far as trawling the internet for positions that she could apply for. She encouraged her daughter to leave, and now has to accept the tragic reality that she is never coming back. Tara's remains are approximately three kilometres off Bondi Beach, on the bottom of the Pacific Ocean. Her darling, vibrant, quirky daughter has been absorbed into nature and never again will there be the chance to hug her scrawny body or despair at the state of her room or hear wry stories about what went down last night.

Beth Jenkins phoned a few months ago, from Sydney. She introduced herself at length, unnecessarily, because Siobhan knew exactly who she was.

'I just want to say how sorry I am.' Her voice sounded young and breathless and Australian. 'I had no idea about the car's history. I feel awkward about accepting the money. I thought I should speak to you ...'

In Siobhan's view, Beth deserved every cent she was paid from the reward pool. The information about the car had limited use – any remaining DNA had been destroyed in the fire – but there was no doubt that Beth's involvement had brought things to a head, spurring Ryan Anderson to make a full confession. The fact that he cooperated with the police, prevented harm to Beth, and was proven to be acting under duress saw him receive an extremely lenient two-year sentence. Mia got fifteen years: conspiracy to murder Beth, among a raft of other charges. Her mother-in-law, Dianne, got ten years. The boy will be fostered by a neighbouring family until his father has served his sentence. Mia's precious child will be a grown man in his twenties by the time she gets out. Her heart must be aching almost as badly as Siobhan's.

Siobhan watched the trial and the sentencing via video-link.

'Everything I did was in Elliot's best interests,' Mia testified, her expression beseeching as she sought out sympathetic members of the jury. 'He depends so heavily on me ... I was scared what the fallout would mean for *him* ... Even though I felt sober and perfectly in control driving that night, I was worried that my blood alcohol concentration could be as high as mid-range. I was convinced I was going to jail, convinced we'd lose the house, convinced that Elliot would suffer and permanently regress ... Survival instincts kicked in and once I'd set out on that path – not reporting the accident or Tara's death – I just couldn't find my way back.'

Crazy, crazy, crazy. And the terrible, excruciating irony? Mia was found *not guilty* of the charge of dangerous driving occasioning death. There was the lack of evidence due to the passage of time, with no medical assessment of the victim's injuries, no details of the vehicle damage from impact and no official blood alcohol reading to tender to the court. But there were also other significant mitigating factors: the accident had occurred on her own driveway, in a rural area where pedestrians were not the norm, and the weather and visibility were extremely poor that night. Concealing the death indicated a consciousness of guilt, but that wasn't enough to secure a guilty verdict more than two years later.

Billy couldn't bear to watch the trial, finding it too upsetting. Siobhan summed it up for her husband as follows: at the end of the day, concealing the death led to a worse outcome for everyone. Especially Mia. In her attempts to cover up what had happened to Tara, she'd instigated a series of even more serious crimes.

It was kind of Beth to phone; she could have taken the money and not cared about the people affected.

'Thank you for reaching out,' Siobhan said, closing her eyes and imagining the endless Australian sky that Tara used to rave about. 'Please don't feel awkward about the money. I hope it's made a positive difference to your life.'

'It has.' A pause. Then Beth continued, her voice quiet yet strong, 'My marriage ended a couple of years ago – badly – and I was barely making ends meet. The money made a world of difference.'

'That's good,' Siobhan murmured. 'I'm happy to hear it.'

'How did you know?' Beth asked tentatively. 'The distance must have made it hard, yet you persevered ... How could you tell something was wrong?'

A number of things gave it away. The first was the fact that Tara didn't phone her sister on her twenty-first birthday. Tara could be accused of laziness and self-absorption, but not when it came to family or friends. She adored Ciara, looked up to her, and was sad to be missing out on the celebrations. Failing to call was out of character and the first alert that something was amiss. Communication continued after the birthday, brief updates via Messenger: no voice calls. Photos of train stations, stunning beaches and the Sydney Opera House, but none of Tara's trademark selfies. Siobhan missed hearing her daughter's voice, missed seeing her face tilted upwards, lips pouting for the camera. The initial excuse was that she was run off her feet with Elliot. In Bondi, she was apparently having too much fun to remember to call home. *Sorry, Mam. Brilliant place. Loving it.*

It took two years of back and forth with NSW Police before Siobhan's concerns were given the appropriate weight. Two long years, with a revolving door of different lead detectives – the first one had a health scare, the second was transferred to a new command centre and the third took ages to come up to speed. Siobhan decided there was nothing to be gained by regaling every little detail to Beth. She offered the summarised version instead.

'I knew Tara wouldn't have gone out of her depth at the beach.

300

Whether it was patrolled or unpatrolled was irrelevant – she was wary of the ocean, of wet sand in particular.'

When Tara was four years old, Siobhan had taken the kids to Portmarnock on a sweltering – by Irish standards! – summer's day. It was midweek, Billy was at work, so it was just her and the kids – and a plethora of buckets, spades and floating devices. The water line was a long way out, as was customary at low tide, and the younger two played in the wet sand with their buckets while the older two splashed in the shallows. Siobhan had brought a book with her, and perceiving the children as safe, she became immersed in the story, remembering the kids intermittently and glancing up to do a quick headcount. A shout dragged her attention away from the book. Another quick headcount. One, two, three, four. The shouting was coming from Ciara and Tara. Ciara was waving her arms and Tara appeared to be kneeling. What on earth was the matter? In the time it took Siobhan to stand up and put the book down, Tara was waist-deep in the sand. Siobhan ran at full pelt, screaming at Ciara to stand back – the last thing she needed was two children in need of rescue – and at Tara to stay calm, and at other beachgoers to 'help, help, help'.

A man got to Tara before she did. The poor child was up to her armpits at that stage, hysterical. The man sank to his thighs while rescuing her, and Siobhan had to help *him* lever himself out. They moved to a safe distance away and Siobhan held Tara's screaming, wriggling body against her own, kissing her tear-streaked, indignant face.

'It swallowed me. The sand *swallowed* me.'

'It's alright, you're safe. Oh, I love your bones, you little scallywag. Oh my God, what a scare! Wait till Daddy hears about this.'

Tara never quite got over the day the sand 'swallowed' her. Years of swimming lessons followed, and she became a confident swimmer in the pool, reassured by the guarantee that her feet would eventually hit solid ground. But her distrust of the ocean, and particularly the sand, never went away.

'Well, that's one thing you won't have to worry about,' Tara commented, as she and Siobhan watched an episode of *Bondi Rescue* the week before her flight to Sydney. 'Still can't find it in me to go deeper than knee-height. Just think of all the money you wasted on bleedin' swimming lessons!'

The backpacker who had been rescued from the surf was sitting on the golden sand, head between his knees, vomiting saltwater.

'Might vomit for other reasons, though,' Tara said drily. 'Can't be perfect.'

Siobhan remembered their laughter: Tara's full of nervous excitement, the undercurrent of sadness in her own. Her baby was leaving home. Please God, she would be safe.

'I see,' Beth said, on the other end of the phone. 'Mothers know their children better than anyone.'

Exactly! Because Beth seemed to understand what she was talking about, Siobhan told her about the final thing. A small thing, really, but just as telling.

It was to do with the pile of clothes left on the beach. Yes, they were Tara's clothes; Siobhan recognised them as soon as the police sent the photos, for identification purposes. The leopard-print sweater, the yellow H&M shorts, the bright gold flip-flops. Here was the thing she couldn't get her head around: the fact that the clothes and towel were folded so neatly.

Never in her life had Tara folded anything in such a careful, fastidious manner.

Siobhan looked at the photos and immediately knew that someone else had left those clothes on the beach; not the darling girl she loved to her very bones.

ACKNOWLEDGEMENTS

I can't quite believe that *The Other Side of Her* is my eleventh novel. I started off intending to write just one book (to get the writing bug out of my system) and never thought beyond that. I feel privileged and grateful to be here eleven books later (a little battle-weary, too, but let's gloss over the hard-work part!).

Thank you, as always, to my early readers ... I couldn't do this without you: Conor Carroll, Rob Carroll, Erin Downey and Brian Cook. Thanks also to Merran Harte, Ashling Carroll and Christina Chipman, my last-minute speed readers, who stepped in just as I was about to lose the plot. A very special thank you to Petronella McGovern for reading more than one draft and for fielding thousands of questions, rants and crises.

Thank you Martin Hughes and everyone at Affirm Press for believing in this book and working so hard on every aspect of its publication. And thank you to my agent, Sarah McKenzie, for being so enthusiastic from first draft to last.

This is the first time I've written a book with a rural setting, and I loved the potential it offered for an undetected crime. I used a little artistic licence in terms of geography, and a lot of artistic licence to create a sense of menace. My family has holidayed in Caves Beach and around Newcastle for many years; it is a beautiful, safe place that I highly recommend to everyone.

Huge thanks to Seth Gibbard, Michelle Ivins, Donna Heagney,

Steve Heagney, Kellie Green and Helen Watson for your technical expertise and for putting up with all my weird questions.

A big thank you to Dianne Blacklock and Liane Moriarty, who have been steadfast and wise over the years, and who celebrated last year's award nominations as though I had actually won. Thank you Sally Hepworth and Nicola Moriarty for reading early copies and saying nice things. Many thanks to all the other writers, bloggers, reviewers and readers who have supported me along the way. And a heartfelt thank you to my family in Ireland and Australia: your love and cheerleading mean the world.

Go raibh míle maith ugat,
Ber

AUTHOR'S NOTE

The Other Side of Her was partly inspired by my experience of arriving in Australia from Ireland twenty-odd years ago, how thrilling and daunting it was. There was so much I didn't know about life in this country, so many close scrapes in those early years. It was also inspired by the fact that my children are now of an age where they are wanting to travel. As a parent, the idea is terrifying!

Every backpacker sets off on their adventure with hope and excitement packed tightly alongside their clothes. Every parent waves them off with trepidation and the plea to come home safe. Travelling is a rite of passage for the young; parents know they must let them go, to grow and see how other people live. They'll come home older, wiser and better for the experience ... Won't they?

The three mothers in this novel are close to me – I relate with their fear, desperation and even their ruthlessness. Children, and our love for them, push us to do things we thought we would never do. And children propel us into situations we cannot control. I can especially identify with Siobhan, Tara's mum in Ireland. Siobhan's shock, grief and suspicion radiate from thousands of miles away. I felt that she deserved to find out what really happened to her daughter and to have the last word in the novel.

I hope you enjoyed *The Other Side of Her*. The characters are everyday people, just like you and me. I can imagine myself going to extraordinary lengths, just like these mothers ... and I can also, all too easily, imagine myself as a naïve, party-loving, nineteen-year-old backpacker.

READING GROUP QUESTIONS

1. For all her faults, Mia's commitment to Elliot never wavers. Ryan says she is an amazing mother – do you agree?

2. Siobhan hoped that Tara's overseas experience would help her grow up a bit. Do you think Siobhan should have better prepared Tara for living away from home?

3. To what extent did Ryan's poor self-worth play a part in the events of the novel?

4. Do you think Kane, Beth's ex-husband, was capable of becoming a better person with his new partner, Georgia?

5. Mia has lost even more than Siobhan by the end. Do you feel any sympathy for her?

6. Dianne and Mia have a special bond. Discuss the mother-in-law/daughter-in-law dynamic in the novel.

7. Charlie is presented as a possible love interest for Beth. Were you disappointed that their relationship turned out to be one of friendship?

8. Discuss the similarities between Beth's marriage and Ryan's.

9. Mia, Beth and Siobhan have one thing in common: they are mothers who would do *anything* for their children. Discuss how this commonality presents in different ways for each woman.

10. The novel's title, *The Other Side of Her*, could be applied to Mia, Tara, or even Beth, who found a strength she didn't know she had. Which character do you think the title best applies to?